Tall, Duke, and Dangerous

"I do want you to show me things," she continued, sounding both hesitant and alluring. An intoxicating combination. She took a deep breath. "I've been thinking about what I want you to show me. And now, for example, I want you to show me how to kiss."

And before he could react, she was leaning up on her toes, putting her hands on his biceps to steady herself, and placing her mouth—her luscious, soft, sweet mouth—on his.

His hands went automatically to her waist, curling his fingers around her body. He felt her shudder, and he froze again, but then she slid her hands down his arms all the way to his fingers and placed her hands on top of his, squeezing them in reassurance.

Their bodies were nearly—nearly—touching.

And still, her mouth stayed pressed on his. Just there. Not moving, not doing anything.

She wanted to know how to kiss? She was asking for his help? For his instruction?

He'd give it to her.

By Megan Frampton

The Hazards of Dukes

TALL, DUKE, AND DANGEROUS
NEVER KISS A DUKE

The Duke's Daughters

THE EARL'S CHRISTMAS PEARL (novella)
NEVER A BRIDE
THE LADY IS DARING
LADY BE RECKLESS
LADY BE BAD

Dukes Behaving Badly

MY FAIR DUCHESS
WHY DO DUKES FALL IN LOVE?
ONE-EYED DUKES ARE WILD
NO GROOM AT THE INN (novella)
PUT UP YOUR DUKE
WHEN GOOD EARLS GO BAD (novella)
THE DUKE'S GUIDE TO CORRECT BEHAVIOR

Megan Frampton

Tall, Duke, and Dangerous

A HAZARDS OF DUKES NOVEL

AVONBOOKS

An Imprint of HarperCollins*Publishers*

First Avon Books mass market printing: November 2020

Print Edition ISBN: 978-0-06-286744-5
Digital Edition ISBN: 978-0-06-286745-2

Cover design by Patricia Barrow
Cover illustration by Victor Gadino
Cover photographs © Konstanttin/Dreamstime.com; © Jay Beiler/Dreamstime .com; © Johnson175/Dreamstime.com; © Johnson175/Dreamstime.com; © Fingers234/Dreamstime.com; © Sergey Volkov/Dreamstime.com
Author photograph by Ben Zhuk

FIRST EDITION

20 21 22 23 24 QGM 10 9 8 7 6 5 4 3 2 1

To Scott. Thank you for everything.

Chapter One

If Nash, Duke of Malvern, had envisioned at all the scenario in which his life was to be irrevocably changed—which he had not, by the way—he would most certainly have thought he would have been wearing trousers.

He was not.

He was not, in fact, wearing anything at all. Excellent attire if one were planning on posing for a statue of some ancient Greek god or taking a refreshing dip on a hot summer day in the privacy of one's personal estate. But not for life-changing events.

Unconventional though he was, Nash would have imagined trousers in that scenario.

And yet here he was.

"Get up."

Nash reluctantly opened one eye, wondering who could possibly have the effrontery to disturb him so early in the morning.

He definitely did not recognize the voice, and it was definitely not friendly. Even if he didn't know the person, weren't they aware of his reputation of hitting first and asking questions later?

"Get. Up." This time, the irascible words were accompanied with a poke to his lower limbs, making him snarl in response.

"Your Grace, this is the dowager duchess of Malvern." That voice he recognized as belonging to Finan, but he'd never heard his valet sound so apprehensive.

Nash rolled over onto his back, opening the other eye. He stared up at the ceiling, blinking in an attempt to clear his head.

"Disgraceful." The dowager duchess's words were no less harsh than words Nash had spoken to himself, but he did not appreciate someone else pointing out his faults. Besides Finan, that is.

He sat up abruptly, the covers falling to his waist as he saw the lady, who immediately made some sort of yelping sound and turned to scurry out of his bedroom, her cane thumping on the floor.

"Told you you should wear a nightshirt," Finan grumbled.

"If going to bed naked means I frighten elderly aristocrats from my bedroom then why would I ever bother with a nightshirt?"

Finan just shook his head.

Nash shrugged. It was a reasonable question.

"I will wait for you in the blue salon," the dowager duchess's voice came from down the hallway. "Come as soon as you are properly dressed."

Finan marched to the wardrobe and flung it

open, yanking clothing out and dumping it at the end of Nash's bed.

"You heard her. Get up."

Nash glared at Finan, who glared back. One of the reasons he was able to tolerate the man's company as well as he did—Finan never kowtowed to him, nor did he let Nash get away with anything both of them knew was privileged nonsense.

"Just how terrifying is she?"

Finan folded his arms over his chest. "Somewhere between a loaded cannon and a barrel full of live eels."

Nash winced. "That bad." He threw the covers aside and walked to the washbasin, dipping his hands into the water and flinging it onto his face. The water was cold, and he shuddered at the shock of it on his skin. But he'd need to be as alert as possible to confront his grandmother—a woman he barely remembered.

"What do you think she wants?"

Finan snorted. "I have no idea. I wouldn't dare to ask her either."

Nash felt an unsettling feeling of dread in his stomach. Not something he was accustomed to feeling; he was Nash, Duke of Malvern, naked sleeper determined to do what he wanted when he wanted. Always.

That he was also determined to do right by his responsibilities, no matter how much he chafed at them, was likely why he had that dread. It was clear the dowager duchess was here on a matter of some importance, since he hadn't seen her in at least ten years. His father had cut off visits from all respectable members of his family, effectively isolating Nash from anyone who might not be a complete reprobate.

Had she heard about his work assisting his father's bastards? It was the least he could do, given how many lives his father had ruined. Hopefully she didn't know his butler was also his half brother.

Actually, he didn't care if she knew. It was the right thing to do, along with only inflicting his temper on bullies.

Why else would she be here, though? He couldn't imagine anything that would bring any of his family members into willing contact with him—his father had burned all the family bridges, and Nash saw no need to rebuild them. If they wanted to know him, they would have to take him as he was.

Well, he wouldn't find out the answers to any of his questions by staying here.

Fifteen minutes later, Nash was dressed nearly appropriately, though he'd refused to put on a cravat, despite Finan's pleading looks.

"Your Grace," he said as he walked into the blue salon. He rarely used this room, much preferring his library, which had a sofa made especially for his long frame. The sofa here was more of a love seat, which would be fine for two people of average height to sit on, but not for someone of Nash's size.

The dowager duchess was seated primly on the love seat, her equally prim maid standing behind her. The poking cane leaned against the leg of the sofa, inches away from the dowager duchess's hand.

Both ladies managed to look down their noses at him, despite their height differential.

Remarkable feat.

He hadn't gotten a good look at her when she'd been in his bedroom, what with her running away at the sight of his naked chest and all. But now he could see the resemblance to his father; both of them had strong cheekbones, dark brown eyes, and a general look of hauteur.

A resemblance he knew he shared, unfortunately.

Unlike his father, however, his grandmother was slight, with gray hair pulled away from her face and fastened on the top of her head with an enormous bow. Her eyes looked keenly intelligent, and held a cordial warmth he had certainly never seen from his father.

He found himself regretting, for just a moment, not wrapping a hellcloth around his neck.

"Your Grace," the dowager duchess said, inclining her head a fraction. "I have been remiss in not coming to see you—"

"Perhaps because I haven't extended an invitation?" Nash cut in.

It was best to let her know who he was as soon as possible. That way she wouldn't be disappointed later on.

She sniffed. Apparently made of strong stuff, his grandmother. A tiny part of him had to respect that.

"But I am here now, and I have some urgent business to discuss."

Well, he knew that already. Else why would she have come? He crossed his arms over his chest and waited. Bracing himself for her disapproval.

"Sit down." She spoke as though there was no possibility of his not doing as she commanded.

So he sat, holding his breath as he lowered himself onto the chair that matched the love seat. It only creaked a little, and he gripped the armrests in a futile attempt at controlling whether or not it collapsed.

Perhaps he should redecorate. He had taken possession of the town house after his father died three years ago, but hadn't bothered to change anything, even though he disliked most of it. It felt like another ducal duty, which he loathed.

Of course he discharged his responsibilities—he wasn't like his father, ignoring everything except that which brought him pleasure—but he didn't do the superficial things, like attend parties or be seen in the most fashionable parts of town engaging in frivolous activities.

Could that be why she was here?

And if that was so, why hadn't she come

when her son had died? Why was he just seeing her now?

His last memory of her must've been from when he was about ten years old, not long after his mother left. He'd been too confused, too distraught, and too terrified of his father to pay attention to visitors.

"Well?" he said impatiently.

She looked unsettled, and he wondered just what the hell kind of business she had to discuss.

"Is this about an allowance? I don't know anything about those things. I let my man of affairs handle that." His man of affairs who was another half brother.

"No. My allowance is adequate, thank you."

"Good."

The silence stretched, and Nash began to shift in his chair, the creaking noise audible in the room. His grandmother arched a patrician eyebrow.

"I did not like your father. My son," she said.

That would explain why he hadn't seen her in all these years.

"We have that in common, then."

"I regret his behavior toward your mother. When I realized what was happening, I did as much as I could, which wasn't very much, unfortunately." She spoke in a tight tone.

The familiar tension—the anger that simmered within at all times—rose up in his chest, and he clamped down so he wouldn't reveal his emotions.

So he wouldn't lash out. As he always did. Or at least tried to—hence his reputation.

"I gave her money to escape. Your father found out, and forbade me to come in contact with you. I should have come earlier. That is my fault."

He couldn't speak. "Escape. Do you know where she is?"

She shook her head. "I do not. I just hope she is safe."

Letters had come sporadically, smuggled to him from sympathetic servants, so he knew she was alive, and that she cared deeply about him and worried about him. It had been a relief to know she was doing well, even if she was helpless to save him.

His father's death had been the only thing that could rescue him.

"So you're not here about my mother, then."

His grandmother's expression grew somber. "No. But I need to interfere where I wasn't able to before." She took a deep breath. "It seems that your heir, Mr. John Davies, has some of your father's more . . . unpleasant habits." She paused. "You hadn't heard?"

Nash shook his head no as he bit back a snarl, his grip on the armrests tightening. "I don't speak to many members of the family." At least not the legitimate ones.

"I have it on good authority that you are not at all like my son." He could hear the pain and regret in her voice. She took a deep breath and gave him an intent, purposeful look. "The dukes of Malvern stretch back to Henry VIII's reign, and it is an honorable title."

"Honorable until my father." Memories flooded his brain, memories he usually expunged by getting into a brawl, or drowning with brandy. His mother, pleading with his father not to hit her. A young Nash grabbing his father's arm so he wouldn't strike again.

A young Nash splayed out on the floor, his nose broken.

She spoke again. "I have heard rumors that you intend never to marry."

Because he would not subject any woman to the possibility of his father's behavior. He'd lost count of how many times his father had reminded him that they were alike—that it was inevitable that Nash would eventually unleash his temper on an innocent.

She continued in an urgent tone of voice. "But you must. The sooner your cousin has no possibility of inheriting, the better. He has heard the same rumors about you, and is borrowing heavily against his future, and his behavior is growing bolder. It is therefore imperative that you marry and produce an heir. Immediately."

Nash's throat closed over.

"I will stay here to assist you in your search for a bride," she announced. "It must be a lady of the highest birth, one who will do her duty as your duchess and provide children."

"What? No!" Nash said, leaping to his feet. He didn't know if he was saying no to her staying with him or a bride.

He just knew he didn't want any of it. He eased himself back into his chair, forcing himself to breathe evenly.

"Stand up."

He rose before he'd realized he'd obeyed her orders.

"You are quite handsome." It didn't necessarily sound like a compliment. "Excellent height, and your shoulders are quite broad. More suitable for a blacksmith than a duke, wouldn't you say?" she said, turning to look at her lady's maid. She turned back around without waiting for a reply. "We'll have to ensure you are dressed properly, and that your hair is neat, although I understand some ladies like that disheveled look." Her tone was disapproving.

"I've never had complaints before," Nash said, folding his arms over his chest.

His grandmother made another one of those disdainful sniffs. He did like her, in spite of what she was asking him to do.

What she was asking him to do—he'd almost forgotten. He sat down abruptly, the chair moaning its displeasure. "I will not get married."

She narrowed her gaze at him. "Do you want another duke like your father? Do you want to allow someone like that to oversee the tenants and the household staff?" She raised her chin. "I have heard of your kindness toward Richard's . . . mistakes," she said. As though a child was a mistake. "Do you want your cousin to have power over them?"

"Fuck."

Her horrified expression told him he'd said the word aloud.

"My carriage is arriving soon with my luggage. If you will ring for your butler I will retire to my chambers." She rose as she spoke, and Nash saw her wobble for a moment before her maid clasped her arm to steady her.

Nash gritted his teeth. "Yes, Your Grace."

Because what else was he to say? The lady was determined to stay, and he couldn't very well throw her out, even though she had woken him up to demand he marry, the one thing he did not want to do. Ever.

Not to mention she poked him with a cane.

But she was his family, and she had already admitted she loathed his father. And he did already like her, despite himself. And despite that blasted cane.

"Meanwhile," she said as she made her way slowly to the door, "please review your invitations so we can discuss what social events you should be attending. I will see you at dinner. Five o'clock, I presume."

Nash's mouth opened in protest, but no words emerged.

As soon as the door shut behind her, he did the only thing that he could—he picked up the chair he'd been sitting on and smashed it against the bookshelf, the pieces scattering over the plush carpet. But because of the damned carpet, the pieces didn't make a satisfying cacophony, but instead thumped softly on the ground.

He stared down at the now broken chair, that previous dread turning to panic as he realized what he'd just done—reacted in a violent way to unpleasant news.

You take after me. In every way.

He had to take control. He couldn't allow himself to lash out without cause. He never used violence unless it was justified—that was how he justified using his fists to exorcise his demons. There were plenty of reprehensible people he could pick fights with to assuage his constant anger, if only for a short time. And it was all for a greater good.

But the broken chair had done nothing to him. A ridiculous thought, of course, but what if he erupted around a person who had done nothing to him?

Could he trust himself?

Goddamn it, but he knew the answer to that question.

"ACHOO!"

Ana Maria blinked to clear her damp eyes.

"My lady?" Jane, her lady's maid, held out a handkerchief.

"Stop calling me that," Ana Maria said in a

grouchy tone, taking the handkerchief and wiping her nose.

Ana Maria and Jane were seated in the main salon of the Duke of Hasford's house, which was where Ana Maria also resided, newly redecorated by Ana Maria in colors that made her spirits soar, nothing like the room's previously staid blues and browns. Bright reds and purples and pinks created a fantastical setting that made Ana Maria grin every time she walked in, only now the room was also filled with flowers that were just as bright, but they made Ana Maria sneeze as well as smile.

She had to figure out which one was the culprit and forbid them entrance to the house. She hoped it wasn't the tulips. She loved tulips. Though she loved all flowers, so a tiny part of her hoped it was just dust. She did not like dust.

"You've been my lady for as long as I've known you," Jane replied tartly. "It's just the dragon wouldn't let us call you that."

"The late duchess," Ana Maria corrected.

"The dragon duchess," Jane said, accompanying her words with a rolling of her eyes.

It had been six months since the carriage accident that had claimed the lives of Ana Maria's father—the duke—and his wife, Ana Maria's stepmother. Six months since Ana Maria had been released from her life of servitude, treated as an unwanted, unpaid servant by the duchess. She still lived in the London town house she'd always lived in, except now her room wasn't the tiniest one in the attic, but the most sumptuous room on the upstairs floor.

"But can't we just be Ana Maria and Jane here, as we used to?" Ana Maria couldn't help her plaintive tone.

The words weren't even out of her mouth before Jane had folded her arms over her chest and was shaking her head. "You have to accept it, my lady. You're a lady, daughter of a duke, cousin to another duke. Like it or not, you are entitled to being treated as though you are a special person." Her voice softened. "And you *are* special, it is just that the dragon—that is, the late duchess," she said, at Ana Maria's stern look, "was determined to keep you in a particular place. And now she's gone, you should take your rightful place among all those other ladies."

My rightful place. What place was that? Ana Maria wondered. For more than twenty years, she'd been the late duchess's unpaid and unappreciated drudge, doing anything that required doing, if the duchess ordered her to.

And now? Now she was supposed to become a lady overnight, a person who didn't know how to polish silver, who would order a bath without considering just how long it would take to boil water, and who treated the help as though they were just that—*help,* not people or even friends. Who did not have an opinion about dust, because she wasn't aware it existed.

But even if her status was suddenly elevated, she was not.

If only her half brother, Sebastian, had remained as the duke she would have been far more comfortable. But Sebastian was not the rightful duke, not since it was discovered that the late duchess—in this particular case, the dastardly duchess—had lied about her relationship to Ana Maria's mother. When it was revealed that the two duchesses were sisters, not cousins, it had invalidated the second marriage because English law forbade marrying the sister of one's dead wife, making Sebastian a bastard, so the title went instead to their cousin Thaddeus.

Thaddeus was kind, in his way, but he wasn't Sebastian. Ana Maria had only wanted to become a lady because Sebastian had seemed to want it for her so desperately. And now that he was established in his new life with his new lovely wife, it all seemed so pointless.

But it wasn't as though she could toss off her elegant clothing and grab an apron and pretend things hadn't changed.

They had. This room, redecorated to her taste and overflowing in flowers from potential suitors, proved it.

She liked the flowers—even if some of them made her sneeze—but she did not appreciate the attention. The gentlemen who sent them would never have noticed her when she'd been wearing her apron, and she knew full well why they were noticing her now. Thaddeus, continuing what Sebastian had promised, had bestowed a generous dowry on her, one that was drawing all of Society's eligible bachelors like—like ants to sugar.

"What are you thinking about then, my lady?" Jane's voice said, interrupting her thoughts.

"Flowers, ants, and sugar," Ana Maria replied, snorting at her own words.

"It'd be better if you were thinking about your suitors and which one of them you'll decide on. I like the looks of that earl's son, Lord Brunley. He's quite handsome and has nearly all of his teeth."

"High recommendation," Ana Maria replied drily. "So I can look at him while he chews." Is that what marriage was? *Dearest, let me pop that toast in your mouth as I gaze upon you.*

"What else is there to require in a husband?"

It was unfortunate Jane asked so many questions. So many questions Ana Maria could answer, but not to anyone's satisfaction but her own.

What else is there to require? A kind soul, someone who would listen and care for her? Someone who would want *her,* not the daughter and cousin to a duke with a fortune?

How would she be able to tell if a suitor truly cared for her? Someone who would ask her why she was thinking about flowers, ants, and sugar instead of regarding her with a horrified look because she wasn't thinking about proper ladylike things?

Someone tall and protective and solid.

Someone very like—no. She could not finish that sentence, not even in her own mind.

She'd rather die by sneezing than admit to her own interest. If Sebastian, or Thaddeus, or worst of all *him*, at all suspected she harbored a secret fascination for a certain tall, grunting gentleman with a penchant for frequent pacing she would be completely mortified, and it wouldn't do any good anyway.

He treated her as a sister, and not even as a much beloved sister. More like a forgotten sister who was only noticed when she was a nuisance. And since Ana Maria was so well behaved, she was never noticed. Not by him, anyway.

No. Better to consider the gentlemen who were now noticing her. Or even better, figure out something that didn't involve gentlemen or marriage so she could at least be satisfied in her own life, even if she ended up alone.

There was a knock at the door, and then it opened, revealing the butler, who always seemed as though he were disapproving of Ana Maria.

Or that could be her imagination.

"My lady?"

"What is it, Fletchfield?" Jane answered.

The butler gave a slight frown, indicating what he thought of Jane's presumption.

"Miss Octavia Holton is here to see Lady Ana Maria."

Ana Maria smiled. "Please see her in, Fletchfield. We will take tea as well." Miss Octavia was Sebastian's young sister-in-law, and a welcome addition to Ana Maria's acquaintance, though their ten-year age difference made it seem as though Ana Maria was Octavia's older sister. Until Octavia, Ana Maria hadn't had any friends in her new world, and the friends from when she was a drudge all treated her differently now.

Even Jane.

That was one of the reasons she'd refused to hire a companion—it was shocking, Ana Maria knew, not to have someone to chaperone her, but the last thing she wanted was yet another person treating her differently. Thankfully, Thaddeus was too engrossed in his new duties to see the impropriety of it.

Fletchfield bowed, and Ana Maria turned to Jane. "I'll be up later this afternoon to discuss what gown to wear this evening."

"I thought the blue—" Jane began.

"Later this afternoon," Ana Maria interrupted. One of the few good things about being a lady—besides not having to scour kitchen grates and sweep dirt—was getting to choose which of her new gorgeous gowns she'd wear. And Jane had an opinion, as she always did, but Ana Maria was beginning to trust her own taste better than her lady's maid's.

That felt wonderful, at least. To know she

was looking her absolute best thanks to her own decision.

She'd never had that kind of confidence. Not least because she always wore whatever castoff her stepmother allowed her to. But also because nobody had entrusted her with making any kind of decision her entire life—and even now that she was supposedly a lady in the highest echelon of Society she was denied the same choice.

Well, she'd have to say no, thank you, to that. She was going to make her own choices and live her own life, which meant going where she wanted to when she wanted to, by herself if she wished, even if Society would raise its eyebrows. Or not marrying someone merely because he sent her some posies and could chew on his own.

It wasn't much as standards went, but it would do for now.

Fletchfield held the door open for Miss Octavia, who stepped inside, her customary lively expression on her face. "Good afternoon, my lady." Her eyes widened as she scanned the room. "Look at all those glorious colors!"

Ana Maria felt the unfamiliar warmth of a welcome compliment. "Thank you." She patted the cushion of the seat next to her. "Do sit down. Tea is on its way."

"Please tell me you decided on everything entirely on your own."

That warmth furled throughout Ana Maria's whole body. "I did." She tilted her head to regard the bright silk of the curtains. "I've never done anything like this. I wasn't certain I'd like it."

"You have to tell me where you got all this. Or better yet, take me yourself." Miss Octavia squinted in concentration. "You have a real talent."

"Thank y—achoo!"

"You're achoo—welcome," Miss Octavia replied with a cheeky grin.

Her friend's exuberant delight infected Ana Maria, making her want to cast off all the doubts and hesitations that had claimed her imagination since she'd first been elevated to her current social status.

And why shouldn't she cast them off? Shouldn't the whole point of being independent be . . . to *be independent*? To stride forward in life without worry?

"What in heaven's name are you thinking about? You have the most intense expression on your face." Miss Octavia wrinkled her nose. "You look like my sister Ivy when she's puzzling out a particularly difficult bookkeeping problem."

Ana Maria shook her head. "Nothing nearly that complicated." *Only the rest of my life.* She smothered a secret smile as Fletchfield arrived bearing the tea things, including some of Cook's most excellent lemon scones.

She would decide on her future after she had some tea and possibly a few scones. A person had to have their priorities straight, after all.

Chapter Two

"The silver one," Ana Maria said in a firm tone.

Jane humphed and shook her head as she withdrew the silver evening gown from the wardrobe.

They were in Ana Maria's new bedroom, a grand step up from her previous living quarters in the attic. The bedroom had been a guest bedroom, used very rarely since the late duchess did not like visitors. Or, honestly, she did not like anybody but her son, Sebastian, Ana Maria's half brother.

Ana Maria hadn't gotten to redecorate this room yet; she'd wanted to live with what she'd chosen in the salon for a bit before taking on a bigger project. But now that she was pleased with the results there, her fingers were itching to change everything in here to reflect her taste.

Bright, vibrant colors instead of demure beiges and browns; plenty of pillows for lounging rather than the standard two per person; a small scattering of rugs rather than the enormous carpet.

But redecorating here would mean finally accepting that this was her life, and she was close to that, but not nearly there yet. *What else would you want to do?* a tiny voice murmured in her head.

I don't know, but I want it to be my choice, Ana Maria replied.

But for now she was choosing her own gown for the evening. She sighed in satisfaction as she regarded it. It was the most outrageously opulent gown she had ever owned, but that wasn't saying much, since until six months ago her gowns had been the duchess's lady's maid's castoffs.

But even when measured with opulent gowns in general, this one was *opulent*. It was made of a silver fabric, but that wasn't its entirety; it had tiny puffed sleeves made of sheer netting, while the body of the gown had small clear gems sewn on, only a few at first, then cascading to gather in a momentum of brilliance at the bottom.

"It's the kind of gown," Jane said in a worried tone, "that wears you more than you wear it. You have no experience wearing this kind of thing. I don't even know how we're going to do your hair either."

Jane's words, spoken with love, nonetheless shot straight to the heart of Ana Maria's insecurities. Worry that she wouldn't be accepted in her world paired with an equal worry that she *would* be, thus making her precisely like every other lady prancing about on dance floors and sipping tea.

It was an oxymoron, but it was *her* oxymoron, so it made sense to her.

"But that's precisely why I should be wearing it," Ana Maria reasoned. She couldn't resist reaching out to stroke the gown, its thin fabric a silky whisper under her fingers. "I want to begin as I mean to go on, and I won't hide at the corner of ballrooms, embarrassed about my past." *Even though that would be my preference.* "If I am to make my way in this world as it seems you and everyone else who knows me wants me to, I will do it my way—wearing beautiful gowns, unashamed of my past and my heritage, and if someone does not like that, then I do not want them in my life."

Bold words from a woman who had only recently begun to be bold. *Begin as you mean to go on.*

"You're going to look absolutely spectacular in this," Jane warned. "I just hope you're up to the challenge."

"I am," Ana Maria promised, vowing to herself as much as to her maid.

SHE WAS NOT, as she soon discovered, up to the challenge.

Ana Maria stood at the entrance to the ballroom, her cousin Thaddeus at her side, holding her breath as she surveyed the crowd.

So many people, none of whom she knew. Of course not, how would she have met them? Unless they accidentally stumbled into the duchess's kitchen when she was sweeping the ashes from the stove. And even then they would have looked over her head, or anywhere but at her, since she was clearly a lowly servant and they were—well, they were the cream of Society. People who wouldn't have the first idea of what to do with a stove, much less how to clean it.

First you had to assemble your tools: a brush, a dustpan, a piece of cloth destined for the garbage. Then you had to clean from the back forward, using patience to collect all the ashes and scrape the stuck-on bits.

Thoughts that would no longer be of use to her. Now she needed to know how to sweep into a room, not sweep out a stove.

It was just far more intimidating than a pile of ashes. Though far less dirty.

The room was enormous, cleared of all furniture except for the chairs that lined the walls and a large table that held a sparkling bright punch bowl, filled with some sort of enticing pinkish-red beverage.

The musicians sat on a raised dais diagonally to the right of where Ana Maria and Thaddeus stood while footmen weaved in and around the crowd bearing massive silver salvers holding champagne glasses. The music had just stopped, and Ana Maria could hear the low chatter of people exchanging pleasantries. Or gossip that would shred someone's reputation in a single whispered word.

"Breathe," Thaddeus commanded.

"Perhaps I can give a short lecture on stove management," Ana Maria muttered. The thought made her chuckle, which then had the effect of forcing her to breathe.

"Pardon?" Thaddeus said.

She shook her head. "Nothing. Just working on breathing." *As you ordered.*

Thaddeus had, until recently, been in command of an army regiment, and still spoke as though everyone was serving under him. Of course, now that he was a duke, that behavior was entirely warranted, so perhaps there was no need for him to change.

"Good," Thaddeus said.

"The Duke of Hasford, Lady Ana Maria Dutton," the butler announced.

And then all the breath whooshed right out of her again as everyone in the ballroom turned, as if on command, to look at them.

To look at *her.*

She tightened her grip on Thaddeus's arm and stepped into the ballroom, an imperious expression she'd stolen from the late duchess on her face.

NASH STOOD WITHIN arm's length of the punch bowl, even though the punch was barely drinkable. What with not being brandy and all. His grandmother was seated just behind him, and he was annoyingly aware of her every movement.

After a nap, she'd descended into his office and badgered Robert Carstairs, his secretary, and one of his numerous half siblings, into handing over all of the invitations that Nash normally declined.

She'd insisted they attend a ball that very evening, even though he'd had plans to—well, do what he usually did. Eat dinner, then go out for hours to stride about London, steadfastly avoiding anyone who might recognize him. If he was lucky, he'd stumble into a situation requiring he use his fists to right a wrong and then return home in the wee hours of the morning, exhausted and bloody.

It kept his demons at bay.

But he couldn't very well tell his grandmother any of that. For one thing, it would reveal that he shared some of his father's . . . *tendencies,* though Nash worked like the devil to control them. And now he had a purpose so he could prevent someone who apparently did not control them from inheriting the title when he was gone.

Which was why he looked like a gentleman who would far rather drink punch than throw one.

"That one looks tolerable," she said, poking him with her infernal cane, then raising it to point toward a lady who was nodding and smiling at some sod who looked as though he actually liked getting dressed like this.

She was medium height, medium build, and

wearing a gown in pristine white, her blond hair drawn up with a few curls spiraling to her ears.

As he perused her, she happened to glance over at him, her eyes widening as their gazes met. And then she arched one perfect eyebrow and her lips curled into a faint smile, and he could practically see the wheels churning—*I've caught the eye of a duke.* Because there was no possibility she would offer him that look based just on his appearance. He knew he was too tall, too broad, and too scowling. Not to mention his hands kept moving up to tug on his far-too-tight neckcloth.

"No."

"And why not?" His grandmother's tone made it sound as though he was refusing a sweet, not the person he might possibly spend the rest of his life with.

Though he didn't want to care about his potential life companion nearly as much as he would a sweet. And if the option was a glass of fine brandy?

Well, he'd take the alcohol every time.

"I could reconsider." He hadn't entirely thought this all through yet, had he? His grandmother wanted him to marry, to produce children, so that Mr. John Davies of the Violent Tendencies wouldn't inflict the family's particular affliction onto the title. He hadn't thought much—or at all—about marriage before, except to know he didn't want it, because the only example he'd ever seen was fraught with tears and angry blows, ending with a mother who'd deserted her only child because the alternative was likely death at the hands of her husband.

But since it seemed he had to marry, he should marry someone he didn't feel any emotion toward. Someone he could tolerate. Someone, he thought, he could live apart from, once they'd ensured the succession. That would be the ideal situation—a wife who lived her own life while he lived his, neither of them bothering about the other. Neither of them caring enough about the other to incite violence.

The blonde in the distance? The one with the raised eyebrow and the faint smile? The one whose appearance was pleasant enough?

She could be tolerable.

He was opening his mouth to speak again when he spotted *her*. Standing at the front of the ballroom, a vision in silver, looking as though she'd been plucked from the night sky and sent to honor Society with her presence.

Her hair was the black of night also, caught up in a luxurious swirl of curls, bound only by a simple silver ribbon. Her figure was lush, and curved, and he would have sworn his hands knew how she felt. Or more accurately, his fingers itched to touch her.

Her skin wasn't the moonlight pale of most of the ladies in the ballroom; it was touched by gold, as though the sun had claimed a bit of her loveliness as well.

"Who is that?" he heard his grandmother say, distinct disapproval in her tone.

"I have no—" And then he froze, because he recognized the gentleman next to her, and he swallowed as he realized who she was.

"That is Lady Ana Maria Dutton," he said.

"Oh!" his grandmother replied, sounding surprised. "She is the cousin to the Duke of Hasford, she is quite respectable."

Her meaning was implicit in her words.

"Out of the question."

"Why—?"

"No." He tore his gaze away from her to face his grandmother. "Absolutely not."

Because it was Ana Maria, and that meant he *knew* her, had known her for most of his life. Had cared for her, in his way. He would not subject her to his passions.

Not when he was terrified of losing control, and how could he not lose control when confronted with such a delicious package encasing a person he knew to be kind, warm, and intelligent?

And he nearly snarled when he met Thaddeus's gaze, and saw Thad speak to her, and then both of them began to walk toward him, each step an increasingly agonizing reminder of who he was, and who he could be—if he didn't keep himself tightly contained.

"Over there, it's Nash," Thaddeus said, no doubt trying to sound soothing.

He didn't, of course, because she doubted Thaddeus had ever tried to soothe anyone in his life, but she appreciated the effort nonetheless. He took her arm again. "Let's go speak with him."

She nodded, simply because she couldn't speak. She hadn't expected to see him here. He seldom, if ever, attended these kinds of entertainments. For all she knew, he had a seraglio of women at home who enjoyed his brute-like manners and inarticulate noises that passed for conversation.

And that idea should not have caused a frisson of sensual awareness coursing through her, but then again, she was a walking oxymoron, so it did.

But he was here. And what was more, he was wearing apparel perfectly suited to the evening—not just a worn jacket that showed the strain at his broad shoulders. For goodness' sake, he was even wearing a cravat. She didn't think she'd ever seen him wearing a cravat.

Someone had managed to slick his hair back, and he'd gotten a shave more recently than a few days ago as well. He looked every inch, every foot, a gentleman, and she felt her breath hitch.

He should not be that handsome.

He should not be that commanding, as though his presence obliterated every other person's appearance in the room.

He should not be the focus of so many of her thoughts, especially late at night.

Damn it.

She swallowed, attempting to regain her icy late-duchess demeanor. Difficult to do when one's heart was pounding, and one was entirely, keenly aware of another person's presence.

"Your Grace," Thaddeus said, making both Nash and Ana Maria stare at him. "What?" he added, glancing between them both. "We are not who we were, we have different obligations now, and different obligations require different courtesies."

Different obligations require different courtesies.

So perhaps she could just pretend she'd never met the Duke of Malvern before, and that this handsome behemoth in front of her was merely a new acquaintance.

That might work to take her mind off the absolute Nash-ness of him. If she could just think of him as another aristocrat who shared the same beliefs as all the others, beliefs that insisted that women like Ana Maria were only noticed because of their lineage and their wealth, not because of who they were. An aristocrat who would be horrified to learn that until six months ago, Lady Ana Maria had peeled potatoes and scrubbed pots and been treated as less than even the lowliest servant. Because the lowliest servant at least received a salary, whereas Ana Maria had gotten exhortations to do more because she was less.

"Ana Maria?" Thaddeus's sharp tone pulled her out of her thoughts.

"Yes, Your Grace? Your Grace," she added, nodding to Nash, whose handsome face twisted into a frown.

"My lady," he replied, before scowling even more, turning his back to them. "Stop poking me," he said, and Ana Maria peered around him to see an older woman sitting regally on a chair, her cane stretched toward Nash's leg.

He held his hand out to the lady, who glared at him but took it, allowing him to draw her to her feet.

Who could possibly make Nash put on reasonable clothing, poke him as though he weren't an angry bear, and get him to be somewhat polite?

"I'd like to introduce my grandmother, the dowager duchess of Malvern."

Ah. Ana Maria held her hand out to the other woman as Nash continued speaking. "This is Lady Ana Maria Dutton, and this is the Duke of Hasford."

The lady peered at Ana Maria, who felt suddenly self-conscious, as though she had a crumb stuck on her lip or something. Then again, she usually felt self-conscious, so perhaps it was just a reminder of her self-consciousness.

She licked her lip just in case.

"It is a pleasure," the dowager duchess said, even though her tone held no indication that it was. "I have just come to town, and my grandson here has been accommodating enough to allow me to stay with him for a time."

Ana Maria glanced at Nash, whose expression was set, though she saw his jaw was clenched.

So it was his grandmother who had succeeded in getting him garbed up and here, but she hadn't been able to do the impossible—make him anyone other than Nash, irritated and taciturn.

And so much for trying to think he was just another aristocrat. She was already keenly aware of every flicker in his expression, every shift in his stance that seemed to scream out, *I despise being here, and I might go punch something if I don't get to leave soon.*

But he didn't. Instead, he did the thing she'd least expect, not in all her years of knowing him.

"Lady Ana Maria, would you care to dance?"

Chapter Three

"Lady Ana Maria, would you care to dance?"

Nash knew it was the correct thing to do, since she didn't know many people in Society yet, and he imagined she might feel awkward about being seen not dancing.

But it also made him wildly uncomfortable because just a few minutes earlier he had been looking at her as though she was an attractive female, not his best friend's sister.

Dancing would mean touching her. And touching her would mean—well, *touching* her. This was Ana Maria. Someone he'd known from when he was ten years old, reeling from the shock of his mother's departure, searching for someone to take refuge with. He'd found Sebastian and Thaddeus, and by extension, her. Though he hadn't paid much attention to her, neither then nor even more recently, except to think of her as a sister.

What he was thinking now was not remotely fraternal. Which made it feel like it was wrong, especially when he thought about how Seb and Thad would react if they knew.

They could never know. *She* could never know.

He still felt as though he couldn't breathe from the impact of seeing her. And he couldn't blame it entirely on the neckcloth. It was her. Up close, her gown was even more flimsily beautiful, not that he'd ever thought such a thing about an item of clothing before. But the threads in the fabric shimmered in the candlelight, and now he could see the soft, golden swells of her breasts, which were on gorgeous display thanks to the gown's structure.

Her gown dipped in at her waist, then flared out at her hips. Wide, curvy hips that were a woman's hips. Hips made to be held while—damn, he should not be thinking that. Not any of that.

"I would love to dance, thank you."

Her voice reached him through a distant fog of confusion, discomfort, and a fierce longing.

"Excellent," he heard his grandmother say.

"Excellent," Thaddeus echoed, only he didn't sound nearly as convinced as the dowager duchess. Because he knew full well what Nash's opinion of parties and dancing and such were, and that Nash was usually spoiling for a fight.

Although he only spoiled for a justified fight. And he doubted there would be any cases of systemic oppression here.

He reached for her hand, and she raised it, placing her fingers in his palm. Was it his imagination, or did they tremble?

He wished she weren't wearing gloves so he could feel her skin. No, he was relieved she was wearing gloves so he couldn't feel her skin. That was it.

They walked to the dance floor as the musicians began to play again.

A waltz. Of course.

He placed his hand at her waist. Keenly aware of that hip just below. That breast just above. She slid her hand onto his shoulder with a faint smile.

"What?" he blurted.

"It's just you're so tall it's a bit of a stretch."

He grunted in reply.

The music began, and he moved, trying to recall the steps of the dance while also trying not to step on her feet. He had far more experience with dodging blows than twirling steps.

They danced in silence, him keeping his gaze steadfastly on her face—not allowing his eyes to slide lower, toward where all that golden skin gleamed in the candlelight.

"We were supposed to dance before."

"What?" He bumped into another couple and glared at the gentleman, who quickly ensured he and his partner were out of Nash's range.

"We were supposed to dance at my party. Not precisely my debut, since I'm far too old"—she accompanied those words with a rueful chuckle—"but the party Thaddeus gave after when—after . . ." she trailed off.

"When everything happened," he supplied. As though those words weren't the vaguest description and therefore actually helpful.

"Yes." She smiled as she spoke. Perhaps the words were actually helpful. He wished words were as easy to master as punches.

If they were, he might never stop talking. Or he might even start talking. Of his own volition, not because someone spoke to him.

"But then Sebastian went and . . ." she said, shrugging.

"Mm," he said in agreement.

Her half brother, Sebastian, had punched a gentleman in a ballroom. Something all of them would have predicted Nash doing, not Seb or Thad.

"So this is our first dance," she finished with a bright smile. He nearly staggered at the impact, which would definitely have resulted in some squashed toes.

"Mm," he said again.

Her smile faltered, and he wanted to growl at himself for doing whatever it was that had made that happen. He was supposed to protect her from disappointment, not cause it.

But it didn't matter. It *shouldn't* matter. She was his best friend's sister, which meant not only that he already cared too much about her—because he cared fiercely about the few people in his world—but also that he would not allow himself to be anything but her protector.

"Did you like your party?"

It wasn't much of a conversation starter. First of all, it was a yes or no question. And what kind of person would possibly say no?

It was the same kind of inanity he scorned in other people: "How are you?" "Fine."

Meaningless. What was the point of speaking if you weren't going to say anything? Far better to *do* something.

"Yes."

Right. Exactly what he had anticipated.

"I wished that it had been Sebastian hosting. Nothing against Thaddeus," she said, nodding toward where Thaddeus stood in his usual rigid stance, "but Sebastian is why I was persuaded to do it in the first place."

"You—you didn't want a party?"

He thought all ladies liked parties.

She shook her head. "Not particularly. I don't like the attention."

They had that in common, then.

"And yes, it was a relief when"—she raised her fingers off his shoulder and waggled them vaguely—"but it wasn't that I was longing to join Society." She glanced down, her cheeks turning pink. "Although I do like the clothing."

So did he. He liked her clothing a lot. The contrast of the shimmering silver fabric encasing all of that luscious golden skin.

Damn it, he needed to forget all that. His mind

searched frantically for something that wouldn't indicate where his thoughts had gone.

"What *were* you longing to do?"

Her gaze snapped back to his, her eyes wide in clear surprise. They had that in common as well—he was shocked he'd managed to ask a reasonable question despite being entirely distracted by her.

And then her lips curled into a faint smile and he discovered he really, really wanted to hear the answer to the question.

WHAT WERE YOU *longing to do?*

So many thoughts flooded into her mind at his words—thoughts that spiraled out from one another like a fantastic pinwheel adventure. Things that were directly in contradiction to one another, as suited a walking oxymoron.

Things like study, and travel, and stay at home and redecorate everything. Things like wear all the gowns and dance all night and go to the country and tromp about in the fields and converse with cows. Things like find a purpose and be aimless.

"Uh—" she began after a moment.

"Never mind, it was a foolish question." He sounded—wait, was he actually regretting something? Nash, of the Grunts? Who stalked through life as though he were determined to imprint his very large presence everywhere?

How could someone like him possibly regret anything? And what hope did the rest of humanity—the non-grunting, not massive part—have?

Well. She should be able to answer that. She was going to forge ahead in her determination to find her purpose. What she longed for.

"It wasn't fool—" she began, then stopped because the music stopped. Her voice floated out into the sea of people, thankfully not too loud, but loud enough that she winced to hear it herself.

Stop that, too. Stop embarrassment, and the potential for wincing, and anything that might indicate that you are not all you could be. That you are going *to be.*

"Hold on a minute." His words, his command, made her freeze. His hand was still on her waist, and his touch there made it feel as though she were burning.

Ice and fire.

Making her turn into a lukewarm puddle.

"What is it?" she asked.

"I don't want you to get trampled." He nodded toward the flow of people leaving the dance floor, others walking eagerly to take their places. A gentleman jostled her, and he snarled.

She suppressed a giggle at the gentleman's startled expression.

"Thank you for my dance, finally," she said. She met his gaze, and she felt her breath hitch.

His eyes were dark brown, she knew that, she'd known that since the first time she'd met him, for goodness' sake, and yet the deep mahogany depths of them, the intensity, made it feel as though she were looking into them for the first time.

First time dancing together. First time feeling the impact of his gaze.

Even though that was not true. She'd felt the impact of it earlier, when his eyes had traveled over her face, down her neck, lower down to her chest and lower still, ending up, eventually, at her feet.

Each of his looks had sent off a skittering of sparks through her whole body, as though his look was igniting her.

Fire.

She licked her suddenly dry lips, and he made another noise, a growl deep in his throat. A noise she'd heard many times from him, and yet this was the first time it had caused such a reaction, low and deep in her belly.

The first time for that, too.

The dancers—both arriving and departing—had found their spots, so they were standing on their own. There was no longer a need for him to hesitate, and yet he hadn't moved.

Why hadn't he moved yet?

"I'll take you back to Thad."

Why had she even thought about his moving? When she would have been perfectly happy to just stand there, burning and freezing all at the same time.

But he was walking. Even though it was so much more than that.

If there was a word for "confident, predatory walk" she wished it would pop into her brain right now. Because that was what he was doing, keeping her beside him, his arm holding hers, his every movement one of purpose and intent.

I'll take you back to Thad.

And that was precisely, exactly, and efficiently what he was doing.

She shouldn't wish he would want to spend more time with her. Unfortunately for her, she was an oxymoron, and so she very much wished he wanted to spend more time with her. Even though there were myriad reasons why she shouldn't wish that.

All that this told her was that she needed to figure out her purpose, and quickly. She couldn't very wall walk around wishing and not wishing, wanting and not wanting, when none of that—or all of that—would get her nowhere. Or somewhere.

Tomorrow. She'd get up tomorrow and go find something she longed for. Not a person, or a status. Some sort of goal that would carry her through this purgatory she'd found herself in, albeit a purgatory where she got to wear beautiful gowns.

She grinned at the thought.

Chapter Four

"I hope you received my flowers, Lady Ana Maria."

Lord Brunley was pleasant enough, she supposed. Teeth and a general appearance of handsomeness. If that was what one wanted.

She was fairly certain she did not want that.

Perhaps she could take a poll in the ladies' withdrawing room and find out what, precisely, other ladies were looking for. No, *longing* for. What—or who—were their goals?

Perhaps then she would discover her own.

"Ah, yes, thank you, my lord," she said quickly when she realized she'd been hesitating too long.

He gave a satisfied smile. "My father, the earl, keeps a hothouse stocked all year. The temperature ensures that there are always flowers in bloom for when we require them. Which is all year," he added.

Well, yes, because that is what a hothouse is for. The ability to procure flowers all year.

So she could add pleasantly intelligent, but not too much so, to the list of his attributes.

"That is lovely," she murmured. The music was likely too loud for him to hear her, but he could see her lips moving, and she hoped that that would suffice.

This was all pleasant enough. It was just that she was tired from smiling, and making polite conversation, and reassuring Thaddeus that she was having a splendid time.

Lord Brunley was fine. He was absolutely fine.

She just wanted something more than this. She knew, for a certainty, that whatever goal she settled on would definitely be more than this.

"Would you mind, my lady, if we stop dancing?" Lord Brunley said, his mouth curled into a warm smile. A smile that ignited neither ice nor fire.

Just more lukewarmness.

She suddenly felt prickly, which made her feel awful, because it wasn't this gentleman's fault that this wasn't what she wanted.

"Of course, my lord," she replied.

He escorted her off the dance floor, walking not nearly as quickly as Nash, which conversely made her more irritated. Because she could keep up, damn it, and she wanted to be *challenged,* not kept up with.

He guided her to the table with refreshments, directing that friendly smile toward her again. "Something to drink?"

She nodded. "Please."

Instead of getting her a glass himself, he gestured toward one of the passing footmen, then indicated the punch bowl.

Since he couldn't possibly deign to dip a glass of punch for her himself?

She truly was irritated. But then again, if he was so snobbish that he wanted a servant to do something for him that he was perfectly capable of doing himself—well, that would seem to indicate all manner of things about him, none of which Ana Maria found appealing. Never mind the easy things like assist someone out of a carriage, or pluck an errant feather from a hat from an unsuspecting cheek; what about the things that Ana Maria knew perfectly well about, having spent most of her life in and amongst servants, who were far more blunt-spoken than their aristocratic counterparts?

Things like what happened between a husband and wife.

Not that she'd suspect he'd palm *that* duty off onto a footman, but she doubted he would be enthusiastic about it. And she knew, even though she had no idea what it would feel like, or if she would enjoy it at all, that she would require enthusiasm in that arena from any potential partner.

"Thank you," she said as the footman handed her the glass. Whether she was speaking to Lord Brunley or the footman, she didn't know.

"We should sit down somewhere. You look flushed."

She wrinkled her brow. She didn't feel flushed,

certainly not as hot and also cold as she had been when waltzing with Nash; furthermore, it wasn't precisely polite to comment on a lady's appearance in any way that could be taken as disparaging.

But she wasn't accustomed to arguing, so she allowed him to take her arm, place her barely touched glass of punch back on the footman's tray, and escort her to one of the small salons at the edge of the ballroom.

The salon was tastefully decorated, and Ana Maria spent a moment taking in the clever use of hanging silk on the walls, swags of which were fastened together to spotlight some of the paintings. The paintings were of varying images, but they shared a color palette, and Ana Maria was nodding in approval before noticing the thing that most ladies would have picked up on immediately when entering a salon with a gentleman who was neither her husband nor her betrothed.

"The room is empty, my lord, we should return. My cousin is no doubt looking for me."

Lord Brunley smiled again, that same easy smile, as he closed the door behind them.

If Ana Maria had been one of those "most ladies," she might have felt a sense of trepidation at what was about to occur. About what he had planned in escorting her to an empty room.

But since she was Ana Maria the former drudge, she only felt annoyed. Or actually *more* annoyed, and prickly, and irritated, because this time she had actual cause rather than her own peevishness.

"I'd like to return to my cousin, the Duke of Hasford," she repeated, this time in a stronger voice.

"And I would like to plead my case to you, my lady." He twisted the lock on the door, making his intentions clear.

She folded her arms over her chest, tapping her foot at the same time. "What case? I cannot imagine what you wish to say to me." That last bit said in a sarcastic tone as she rolled her eyes. Because of course she knew what he was going to say to her—he'd sent her flowers, for goodness' sake, he'd danced with her, surely he deserved to have her hand in marriage—not to mention her enormous dowry—for those kindnesses.

Men. She shook her head.

"Don't say no straightaway, my lady," Lord Brunley began, misunderstanding her gesture. He took her arm and led her to the sofa, where he indicated she should sit.

She did. She might as well be comfortable as she planned her response.

There was a small fireplace to the left of where she was seated, and the fire tools—brush, shovel, tong, and most importantly a fireplace poker—were within stretching distance of her hand.

Excellent.

There was a decanter of something on the small table to her left as well. She couldn't see what liquid was inside, but she could see it was half full, and the decanter itself appeared to be made of a sturdy glass, not at all delicate.

"You know I have long admired you, my lady," Lord Brunley said, getting down on one knee on the carpet.

"I know no such thing."

He blinked. Likely not expecting that response.

"And my dearest wish is that you will accept my hand in marriage. That you will agree to be my wife."

"Thank you, and I appreciate your kind offer," she said, "but I am not convinced we would suit."

He clutched her skirt, still kneeling. "You must allow me to persuade you otherwise, my lady. My dearest Ana Maria."

He tugged on her skirts then, making her tilt forward a bit before she steadied herself.

"No, my lord. No."

"Surely you cannot mean that 'no,'" he replied, giving her what he likely thought was an irresistible smile.

"I assure you, I do," she said, twitching her skirts out of his grasp as she rose from the sofa, leaning to snag the poker from the set as she stood. His eyes widened, and he scrambled up from his kneeling position.

"You would not—"

A childhood learning from female servants about what to do in case a gentleman got overly familiar would not be in vain, it appeared, though Ana Maria had yet to test her education in a real-life setting.

"You would not," he repeated. "Because if you do, it will come out that you and I were alone together, and the scandal will require that you marry me." He held his hands out in supplication. "Why not just skip the violence and agree to terms now? I promise I will be a tolerably pleasant husband."

She wrinkled her nose at his words. She did not want tolerably pleasant. If anything, she wanted the opposite—intolerably agonizing, so much passion and emotion that one could not bear to live with it, even as one could not bear to live without it.

A walking oxymoron, indeed.

"I will not be blackmailed," she replied. She used the poker to gesture toward the door they'd entered from. "Unlock that, exit quietly, and I will follow. Nobody need know what happened here. But I will not marry you."

Instead of retreating, however, he stepped toward her. She'd have to take more desperate measures, since she would not be bullied into marriage, for goodness' sake. She brandished the poker up over her head, making his mouth drop open in surprise. *I have more surprises for you if you continue,* she thought. He reached for her weapon, but lost his footing, instead hurtling over the sofa and onto the small table with the decanter of liquid, which crashed onto the ground with a deafening sound, spilling brandy—because she could see and smell it now, it was most definitely brandy—over both of them, staining the skirts of her beautiful silver gown and splashing up onto her face.

He was on the floor staring up at her, his pleasantly handsome face also now covered in brandy, and she couldn't help but burst into laughter at the sight.

At which he scowled, scrambling up to his feet, starting to approach her with what he probably thought was a threatening manner.

She still held the poker, however, so she lowered the tip of it enough to hook it into the top of his waistcoat, then pushed him toward the door. "No."

He opened his mouth as though to argue again, but she shook her head. "No," she said more loudly.

He snapped his mouth shut, then turned and began to walk to the door. Only to reel back as the door snapped open, revealing Nash in all of his elegantly dressed fury, his fists clenched, a menacing expression on his face.

"Nash, it's fine," she said, holding her hand out in a vain attempt to stop him. "I have it handled."

And then Nash did what Nash always did.

THE BALLROOM WAS filled with what Nash supposed were beautiful women, many of whom seemed intrigued by the Dangerous Duke, but

Nash couldn't seem to stop watching her. He kept his eye on her as he danced with the smiling blond woman—a Lady Felicity, as it happened—and rebuffed the lady's attempt to lure him onto the terrace.

He was well aware of terrace shenanigans, even though he'd never partaken himself.

He watched her as she danced with a variety of partners, noting her smile, seeing how much she seemed to enjoy herself. He was surprised to find he was mildly irked that she had so many partners—he had only asked her because he'd assumed she didn't know anybody, and yet here she was, dancing and smiling with people he didn't think he had ever seen before.

Humph.

Had she enjoyed herself as much when she was dancing with him?

Was it the music, the rhythm of the dance, or the partner that made her so happy?

And why didn't he know? Why didn't he know more about her? Of course he knew her, it felt as though he'd always known her, but what did he know *about* her?

He scowled as he thought about it. He knew she loved Sebastian. They had that in common, even though neither Nash nor Sebastian would ever say things like *love* to one another.

He knew she was always cheery, even when she was being berated by her stepmother, Sebastian's mother. He'd been at the house several times when the late duchess—*good riddance to bad rubbish,* he thought sourly—had summoned Ana Maria to be dressed down in front of everybody.

And Ana Maria had taken it, keeping that same slight, accommodating smile on her face as her stepmother told her just what she thought about her stepdaughter.

If it had been Nash, he would have resorted to violence long ago.

Then again, that was who Nash was. It was not who Ana Maria was.

Other than that? He knew nothing about her.

Except that she apparently liked dancing and music and gentleman partners.

It was frustrating that he didn't know.

It was even more frustrating when he saw her being guided to the refreshment table by some cur who seemed far more pleased with himself than Nash would have liked. And the most frustrating when he saw that same cur, probably some lord's son who had no ideas of his own, lead her through a door into a room where he couldn't see her any longer.

He narrowed his gaze, searching the crowd to find Thaddeus. Her chaperone should have been watching her as well. Not leaving it up to Nash, who didn't know her at all.

But Thaddeus was at the far side of the room, his hand clamped on some military man's shoulder, speaking intently to the man, his gaze unwavering from the other man's face.

Damn it, Thad.

Nash took a deep breath and began to walk toward the room she'd gone into, ignoring his grandmother's sharp call to him, ignoring the people who seemed to want to address him, then wisely backed away when he snarled in reply.

He heard a crash inside, and his pace quickened, reaching the door in just a few more moments. He hesitated for a second—what if she didn't welcome the intrusion? After all, he didn't truly know her, he didn't know what she might want in this situation—but decided it was better to ask for forgiveness than beg for permission, particularly where this lady was concerned.

He turned the knob, only—nothing. It was locked.

And he heard her voice, commanding and dismissive, and he leaned his shoulder against the wooden door and pushed, hearing something splinter and break as it opened.

It took seconds for him to assess the situation—her, advancing on the man with a poker, the man's expression belligerent as he grasped the pointy end of the poker and tried to remove it from his chest.

She glanced up to meet his gaze. She didn't look terrified, as he would have expected; she looked annoyed. As though the man had stepped on her foot, or disparaged her choice of gown. Not as though she were trapped alone in a room with him where her only choice was to resort to fireplace tools, of all things.

He advanced, the anger feeling righteous, one of those moments where he reveled in his temper. He would flatten this gentleman, who was clearly no gentleman, and he would save the day. Save her.

"Nash, it's fine," she said, sounding exasperated. "I have it handled."

But he ignored her, unable to stop moving forward, his clenched fists itching to make contact with the lord's face. Nearly as much as his fingers had itched to touch her skin while they were dancing.

And where had that thought come from? His righteous anger seldom allowed for any other thoughts.

Thwack! His fist connected with the man's jaw, sending him flying, sprawling onto the carpet. Landing with a soft, unsatisfying thud. Just like the broken chair, though this miscreant deserved it.

"Now look what you've done." She dropped the poker, scurrying over to the now-unconscious man. She began to actually *touch* the blackguard, loosening his wretched hellcloth.

"What? I took care of things."

Wasn't that what his temper was for? The swift dispersal of justice? God knew it wasn't for unleashing on loved ones. If it wasn't useful for anything, then there was just no point to being him.

"You punched him."

He frowned in confusion. "Yes. As I said. I took care of things."

She yanked off the cur's neckcloth, snapping it out and dabbing at the man's face.

He did not want her dabbing at anybody's face.

The man moaned, moving his head from side to side, his eyes fluttering open. "He hit me." He said it as though it were a complete surprise, which was baffling to Nash; after all, he'd been the one to be seen pinioned by a poker, so it stood to reason there would be retribution.

"He did, my lord." She leaned over the man, assessing his situation. "You will be fine in a moment or two."

"I need some brandy."

"I think that is the last thing you need," she replied tartly, rising to her feet. "I will send someone to assist you, my lord." She advanced toward Nash, grabbing his lapel between her thumb and forefinger. "You should come with me."

Nash allowed himself to be removed from the room, wondering why she seemed so piqued when all he had done was help her.

That was what he always did—help people. And most of the time, his helping people meant that other people got sprawled onto carpets, or flattened on the street, or brought unwillingly to the authorities.

But it seemed she didn't want that, which made him wonder just what she did want.

Chapter Five

She wished she weren't so conflicted.

But wasn't that the story of her life now? *Lady Ana Maria Dutton, Conflicted Oxymoron.*

Yes, it was redundant. No, she didn't care.

She pulled Nash by his jacket out the door and into the ballroom, moving swiftly to the edge of the room and heading straight for the doors that led out onto the terrace.

"Ah, terrace shenanigans," she heard him murmur.

"What?" she said, startled. "No, on second thought, never mind."

There were a few people out on the terrace already, and she turned so she couldn't make eye contact with any of them, taking Nash to a bowed-out nook that was home to an enormous potted tree.

They wouldn't be seen, but more importantly, they wouldn't be heard.

She let go of his lapel, unable to keep herself from smoothing it down. She would never rid herself of the need to tidy things up, would she? Another reason she and that flattened lord would be a terrible match—he'd be appalled whenever she tried to do something for herself, whereas she was appalled he couldn't.

But she didn't want to spend any more time thinking about him. She needed to make this right, to see if Nash could understand.

She spotted a footman, making eye contact with him as she gestured with the hand not holding on to Nash. "Could you go in there and see to the gentleman?" she asked.

Nash snorted.

"He is in need of assistance," she added. The footman nodded, moving toward the room where Lord Brunley was likely still moaning.

And now she had discharged her duty, she had to get him to hear her.

"Don't do that," she said at last.

His eyes were dark and intense in the moonlight. She couldn't look away.

"Do what? Rescue a damsel in distress?"

She shook her head. "I am neither a damsel, nor was I in distress. Didn't you hear me say I had it handled?"

"But I can handle it so much more quickly. I always can." He spoke as if it were a hard fact, which it was, she supposed. He was renowned for his ability to handle things quickly, which mostly meant with his fists.

"I don't want to be rescued." She spoke in a soft voice, but she hoped he heard the truth of her words.

He didn't say anything. She could hear him breathing, see the rise and fall of his broad chest under that crisp white shirt. But he didn't speak. Instead, he reached out and took her hand in his.

He bent his head over her glove, undoing it quickly and then clasping her fingers. His hand was so warm. And so big. She felt the impact of his touch through her entire body.

"I wanted to take this off when we were dancing," he said in a low tone that made her shiver.

She started to speak, to rush past the importance of this moment. She couldn't let him know what she felt about it—he was merely comforting her, even though she didn't need comfort. "I got brandy all over my gown. Some of it even splattered onto my face." She knew she was saying whatever popped into her head to avoid saying what was in her heart—*thank you for caring. Thank you for not judging me. For being as imperfect as I feel.*

"Where?"

She brushed at her face, feeling the stickiness of the brandy. "I think mostly on my cheeks and my nose."

And then he was touching her face, sliding his finger over her skin, pausing as he found a sticky spot, then trying to wipe it away.

Her chest tightened. "It's fine, I will take care of it in a moment."

"I will do it," he began in his naturally assertive tone.

"Hush," she replied, putting her index finger to his lips. They were surprisingly soft. She emitted a gasp, dropping her finger as though it had been burned. Scorched.

"I won't apologize," he said in a much stronger tone. "He deserved it. Whether it was from you or me."

She drew back in surprise. "I wouldn't have punched him."

"Maybe you should have." He made it sound as though it was a reasonable suggestion. And to him it was.

"Ana Maria!"

She turned at the sound of Thaddeus's stentorian tone, pulling her fingers from his hand. Feeling guilty, even though nothing had happened.

He touched me. My skin. My cheek, my nose, my fingers.

I touched him. His skin. His palm, his mouth.

So don't pretend nothing happened. Even though he likely thinks it was nothing.

She stepped out from under the tree, unconsciously straightening her shoulders.

"There you are." Thaddeus's gaze narrowed as he saw Nash emerge also. "And you." His tone was accusatory.

Ana Maria felt her cheeks start to heat—*please don't make this into anything,* she begged inside her head. *He is my friend, we are all friends.*

"Nash."

Nash nodded in reply. Of course, taciturn Nash spoke with his fists, and his nods, and his expressions.

"The carriage is waiting."

Thaddeus held his arm out and Ana Maria took it, wishing it was Nash's arm. She glanced back behind her, where he still stood, all the broad massiveness of him. His expression set, his gaze shuttered, and she nearly went back, to see if she could break him open, to understand him, but Thaddeus must have sensed it, since he put his other hand on hers to hold her more firmly to him. "The carriage, Ana Maria," he said in a low tone. "We need to go."

THE DOOR TO the carriage had just shut when Thaddeus spoke. "What happened?"

We held hands, he wiped brandy off my face.

"With that lout Brunley."

Oh. Right.

"It's nothing, I don't want either you or Nash to bother about it."

"Was that what Nash was doing? Bothering about it?" He sounded disapproving, and she felt herself get defensive on his behalf.

"He only meant to help."

Thaddeus sighed. "Which means there was violence involved."

She couldn't refute that, so she said nothing.

He leaned forward, resting his elbows on his

knees and clasping his hands. A very uncharacteristically casual Thaddeus pose. This must be serious.

"Nash isn't—you know, never mind about that."

Drat. She generally disliked Thaddeus's reticence, but never more so than now.

"The important part is that Lord Brunley informed me the two of you are engaged." A pause. "Is that true?"

Ana Maria's mouth dropped open.

"Absolutely not! He did make a proposal"—*of sorts, by cornering me in an empty room and then threatening me*—"but I declined." And then Nash declined even more forcefully.

The thought should not make her warm inside—after all, she'd rebuked him for treating her as a damsel in distress—but she had to admit there was something thrilling about all that strength focused on protecting her.

No wonder early cavemen were able to find mates. And the idea of Nash clad only in a scanty fur was rather appealing.

"Good," Thaddeus replied in satisfaction. "I know you are a sensible woman, Ana Maria, but I also know that you are newly arrived to Society, and you might not be able to see through some of these more charming gentlemen's subterfuges."

Ana Maria felt her hackles—and her eyebrow—rise.

"Are you saying I am too naive to realize when

someone is being sincere and when someone is trying to use me?"

"Uh—" Thaddeus said. He sounded uncertain. Good.

"Because you should not worry, cousin. I am perfectly capable of taking care of myself. I am not—nor will ever be—a damsel in distress." The vehemence of her tone matched the vehemence of her emotions.

Men.

"I see that, of course I see that, but I just wanted to let you know that I—that we—that Sebastian made us promise to take care of you."

She was not mollified. Because who had taken care of Sebastian for the first eighteen or so years of his life? Had she been incapable then?

"Ana Maria?" He sounded anxious, and she suppressed a smile. That was precisely what she wanted, even as she wanted someone to protect her—she wanted both protection and the assurance that nobody would vault in to do something she was perfectly capable of.

Oxymoron.

"I know you have my best interests at heart. As does Nash. I assure you, I can take care of myself."

"Good. Because if I had to call that Brunley my cousin I'd probably swallow my tongue."

She laughed at how forceful he sounded. Thaddeus, the most honest and forthright man of her acquaintance. The one she knew would leap to her defense, even though he didn't seem to understand her. The one who'd insisted his home would remain hers, who had been generous with his money, who'd given her the freedom to do what she wished.

"Thank you."

"Well, so that's that, then," he said, sounding awkward. She smothered another smile and watched him turn away from her gaze, as though embarrassed at his emotion.

NASH STEPPED BACK into the cover of the tree after Thad and Ana Maria left the terrace. He far preferred being in the shadows to being in the spotlight during normal times, and this wasn't a normal time. It was far, far worse.

His palm tingled where he'd held her fingers. He raised his hand to his mouth, smelling the slight scent of brandy on his fingers from where he'd touched her skin. He licked his finger, licked the sticky sweetness off.

Goddamn it. He shouldn't be thinking about her that way, shouldn't be wondering where else he could lick brandy off her. He was supposed to be searching for a woman who wouldn't make him feel anything, not discover one who could make him feel everything.

If he let her.

He wouldn't let her.

He couldn't. He'd promised himself not to hurt

anybody he was determined to protect, and he'd hurt her if he let her into his heart. *You take after me. In every way.*

"Duke!"

The command came from his grandmother, who was peering out of the doorway. The lights of the ballroom shone behind her, outlining her slight form, making him realize just how frail she was in body, if not in spirit.

Her damned cane was there, too, and she stuck it out of the door onto the terrace, her expression hesitant.

"Over here," he said, walking out from under the tree to the door. "Don't come out, it's dark, I don't want you to risk falling."

"Don't you worry about me," she snapped back. Sounding much like another lady of his acquaintance. "I came out here because you are not inside meeting anybody. What are you doing skulking about?"

He took her arm, turning her so she was facing back into the ballroom. "You said it yourself. Skulking."

"Humph," she muttered. "We won't get anywhere with this if you refuse to engage with any young lady."

But I have. Of course he couldn't say that to her; she would leap to the next logical conclusion and wish him to make an offer for her. She definitely wouldn't understand if he told her he couldn't marry her because he actually *liked* her.

The sooner he found a lady he didn't care for the sooner she would be out of his house. He should be focusing on that, not on the taste of brandy from Ana Maria's skin.

His grandmother was still talking.

"What?" he said, interrupting her.

She planted her cane down on his foot. "Not 'what,' it's 'pardon.' 'What' makes you sound like a commoner."

I wish I were. The thought wasn't a new one—he had it any time someone said, "Your Grace," but now he had to temper that—*ha!*—with the thought that if he weren't the duke that would mean someone else was. Someone who was even less capable than he of managing a temper.

"Pardon, then. What did you say?"

She huffed an exasperated breath. "I was saying that there don't seem to be many suitable candidates here. I would expect the Duchess of Malvern to be impeccable in breeding, education, manners, and appearance."

And how do you expect that paragon of perfection to agree to marry me? I might be a duke, but I am also a sullen, scowling man who doesn't care for Society's trappings. Never mind that if she was that excellent a specimen he would run the risk of falling in love with her, and that he could not do.

Perhaps he could find a lady who abhorred brandy, enjoyed making polite conversation, and insisted that gentlemen be garbed as gentlemen at all times. His ideal match.

"I will review *Debrett's*, and compile a list."

The promise felt like a threat. His future was being as tightly squeezed as his neck in the hell-cloth.

He swallowed all that anger, as he always did. Unless it was a justified reprisal. Or he'd lost control. *That innocent chair.* "Good," he replied in a tight voice.

"We will have you married off and with children in no time," she said determinedly.

He grunted.

He needed to go punch something else right now. Something or someone that deserved it.

Or Finan.

"INSTEAD OF TAKING pokes at me with your slow fist, why don't you just tell your grandmother you refuse to marry?"

Nash shook his head in regret.

The two men were in Nash's sparring room, a room that had once been purposed as a guest bedroom, but since Nash never invited anybody but Sebastian and Thaddeus over, he had decided to make the room useful. He'd had the furniture removed, the rugs stored, and all the paintings taken down from the walls. He'd put in special flooring to muffle the sound of feet, and put extra padding on the walls to muffle the sound of the blows.

The room held only a few pieces of furniture now: a chest of drawers where the linens for wrapping fists were stored, a small sturdy table that held a pitcher of water and a few glasses, and two mismatched chairs for when the opponents needed a rest.

Nash hadn't even needed to tell Finan what he wanted; as soon as his valet saw his face, he'd risen from his chair and gone to his room to change. Nash went to his own bedroom and quickly stripped off his evening wear, giving an especially disdainful look as he tore off the hellcloth, dropping it onto the ground and deliberately stepping on it.

He knew he'd have to go out again wearing the same blasted outfit, but at least this particular hellcloth would never serve its hellish purpose again.

"I can't tell her I won't marry because I have to marry." Nash punctuated his words with quick feints toward Finan, who dodged them easily. There was a reason that sparring with Finan was so satisfying. Nash had yet to meet an opponent who could best him, but Finan was the closest he had come.

That was how they had met, actually—Nash had come upon Finan in an unequal battle, there having apparently been a dispute about politics, and Nash didn't think three against one was a fair fight. Three against two, however, when one of the two was Nash and the other one was Finan, meant that the two would win immediately.

"And that is because—?" Finan asked, twisting to avoid a direct hit.

Nash grunted.

"That's not an answer," Finan replied, not sounding out of breath at all. Disappointing.

Nash had shared some of his past with his friend, but Finan didn't know the whole of it. Nor did he know about Nash's heir. So he'd have to get over his usual reticence and actually talk.

He'd much rather punch.

He didn't speak, but kept sparring, the thoughts building up inside his brain until he felt as though he were going to burst—those were the only times he found he actually wanted to talk, when not talking would be more painful than the alternative.

"We're done," he said at last, backing away from Finan's upraised fists. "Sit down, and I'll tell you."

"Took you long enough," Finan grumbled, his hair wet with sweat, his shirt sticking to his skin.

Nash quickly unwrapped the linen from his hands, dropping it into a basket specifically for that purpose. Then he yanked his sodden shirt over his head, tossing it on top of the linen.

He grabbed the pitcher of water and poured two glasses, handing one to Finan, then sitting in one of the chairs. Finan followed suit, taking a swig from his glass and dragging his chair so it was closer to Nash. "Well?" he said.

"Well."

Finan shook his head and made noises indicating his irritation during Nash's recital.

"So you're going to marry, after all," he said

at last. He tipped his head back in thought. "But why not marry someone you know?"

Nash's chest tightened at Finan's words, because of course Nash only knew one unmarried young lady. Mostly because he'd spent the three years of his dukedom specifically avoiding young ladies so as to prevent this whole marital occurrence.

"That Ana Maria is pleasant enough," Finan said at last. As though Nash couldn't have thought of the only unmarried young lady himself.

"No." The word shot out of Nash's mouth like cannon fire.

Finan's eyebrows drew up into his hairline. "It sounds like you have a reason. She's not hideous to look at, so it's not that." A pause. Nash thought frantically of what he could possibly say that wouldn't be the truth—not because Finan wouldn't understand, but because Nash didn't want to admit to him, admit to *anyone*, that he was deathly afraid of exhibiting the same weakness his father had.

He didn't want pity, and he didn't want people in his life protecting him from potential upset. He would most certainly unleash his fury at *that*. Which would be the opposite of what anyone wanted.

"Lady Ana Maria is more like a sister to me." Hopefully that would satisfy Finan.

"A sister who isn't related to you, who is beautiful and intelligent and seems to like your sullen self," Finan pointed out. "That's a rarity, and you might actually be happy at the end of it."

The words struck more terror into Nash's heart. Because if he could be happy, he could also be sad. And angry and furious and explosive. It was far better not to care about anything than to risk that possibility.

He'd rather spend the rest of his life keeping everyone—including and especially a wife—at a distance.

"Out of the question," he said, getting up out of his chair.

"You're an idiot," Finan called out after him as he left the room. "And I won the match."

Nash didn't bother replying. There was only so much talking a man could do in an evening, after all.

Chapter Six

"I want the peach-colored gown today," Ana Maria said. She sat at her dressing table, brushing her hair, although Jane kept reminding her that ladies did not brush their own hair.

But Ana Maria did. Another reminder that she might be a lady in name, but she was not a lady in action.

Thank goodness, she thought wryly.

"That one looks more orange to me," Jane replied. It did not sound as though she liked the orange gown.

"It doesn't matter what color it is. You know which one I mean, so can you bring it out? Or I can," Ana Maria said, beginning to rise from her chair.

Jane held her hand out. "No, no, don't get up. You're not supposed to be doing any of this."

"Apparently I'm not supposed to be deciding what gown I wear either," Ana Maria remarked in a dry tone.

Jane went to the wardrobe and searched through the gowns, Ana Maria watching her in the looking glass. The wardrobe was full to bursting with gowns, nearly all of them new. And brightly colored, not the white it seemed Jane thought was proper.

Though, to be honest, everyone else thought white was proper for a young unmarried lady as well. Except for Ana Maria. She wanted color, riotous color that would make her smile every time she saw herself.

Once she'd succumbed to Sebastian's constant nagging, she'd let herself be subsumed in the pure delight of it all, visiting modistes and hatmakers and cobblers. He'd footed the bill, and then when he had left, Thaddeus had done the same, insisting on providing her with her own money so she could feel more independent.

Ana Maria thought it also might be so that he didn't have to bother with it. Thaddeus seemed to dislike bother.

"Where are you going in your orange gown?"

"Peach," Ana Maria said, rolling her eyes.

Jane brought the gown over, holding it up so it wouldn't wrinkle.

And, just as she'd hoped, Ana Maria smiled when she saw it.

It had two flounces, one going halfway down on top of the other as though she were a cake come to life. The peach-colored fabric was warm and vibrant—"Definitely not orange," she muttered—and sported several whimsical additions that made it thoroughly and absolutely a lady of leisure's gown. Suitable only for standing or walking slowly while appearing gloriously beautiful.

The sleeves had multiple layers also, and the modiste had designed the gown so it could be quickly swapped out to transition from a day dress to a ball gown.

Ana Maria was extravagant, but at least she wasn't foolishly so. Although being a Practical Lady seemed contradictory. Suitable for her walking oxymoron self, she supposed.

"Going? Oh yes. I am taking Miss Octavia to the fabric house. She wished to see for herself the fabrics that inspired my salon."

"That Miss Octavia seems like a wild one," Jane said in a warning tone.

"Excellent! Since I am mild myself, perhaps we can meet in the middle and be wildly mild. Or mildly wild."

Jane rolled her eyes.

Once dressed, Jane worked on Ana Maria's hair, persuading it to curl where it never had before. Another benefit of being a lady—not having to stand with arms akimbo over your head as you attempted to smooth your tresses into place.

There was something to be said for being a lady. It was just that it felt as though a piece of her was missing.

She'd have to make it part of her Practical Lady mission to find it.

"GOOD MORNING," OCTAVIA said with a bright smile as Ana Maria descended from the coach. Octavia lived in a small apartment in the back of Miss Ivy's, the club owned and named after her sister. Ivy had just married Ana Maria's brother, Sebastian, so Octavia was living on her own, something that would have been scandalous if it weren't already scandalous that Octavia was also working at Miss Ivy's as a host and occasional dealer.

"Good morning."

Octavia pushed the door to the club open, gesturing for Ana Maria to walk through. It was empty, of course, but with just a little imagination Ana Maria could envision it in the evening, filled with chattering people from all strata of Society, the clink of coins, the sounds of chips being stacked on top of one another, or scraped away to end up in the house's bank.

She'd only been here when the club was closed, and she resolved—because this was what she wanted—to come some evening when it was open, to see if she liked gambling. She'd never had the opportunity before, of course, but now Thaddeus was giving her a more than adequate allowance, and she had friends here.

"Come along to my rooms, Carter is already making tea."

Ana Maria jolted herself out of her reverie of high stakes play, following Octavia as her friend walked briskly to the far corner of the room, opening another set of doors and walking through.

They settled themselves in the small room that was the catchall for anything that wasn't sleeping or dressing, the maid Carter coming in to deposit a tray of tea things onto the table that was nestled between the two comfortable chairs.

"You should come some evening," Octavia said as she poured the tea.

Had she read Ana Maria's mind?

"I should. I will," Ana Maria replied. "I know Sebastian and Ivy are here most evenings, but is there—is there anyone else I have met?"

Octavia raised one knowing eyebrow. "Sebastian's friend, that glowering duke, comes a few nights a week. Never gambles, only drinks. Tips well." The last bit was spoken as recitative facts, and Ana Maria chuckled.

The description likely fit Nash more generally as well—never gambles, because gambling was a risk, and she didn't get the feeling he did risks, and she knew full well he liked to drink, though she'd yet to see him drunk. The tipping well bit also sounded like him, because even though he worked on his gruff facade, she suspected that he was softhearted, and despised his wealth when it meant others went without.

"When—that is, is there an evening the Duke of Malvern comes more frequently?"

Octavia folded her arms over her chest and leaned back in her chair with a frank look of appraisal. "Are you interested in that lummox?" She paused. "I can see him having a certain brutish charm," she said, emphasizing the last two words as though she were saying something far more salacious, "but I would have thought you might have preferred a more social person. Someone who, perhaps, will exchange pleasantries rather than grunting."

"I like the grunting."

The words were out before she realized she'd spoken, and then she felt her cheeks heat, far hotter than the tea she'd yet to taste.

She picked the cup up off the table and brought it to her lips, lowering her head in a vain attempt to hide her face.

"You do, do you?" Octavia sounded amused. And, more frighteningly, she sounded as though she were pondering something.

"He is a family friend," Ana Maria hastened to explain. "We've known him since he was about ten years old, of course I am accustomed to his . . . noises." She could have compiled a dictionary of what his various sounds meant—some grunts were clearly approval, while others were just as clearly annoyance.

"And he is attractive, in a brooding, villainous way. Rather as if one of those fearsome lords from the novels came to life. He doesn't have a castle, does he?"

"Not to my knowledge." Ana Maria didn't necessarily want her friend to take an interest in who Ana Maria was interested in, but she did enjoy the circularities of Octavia's mind. No wonder Sebastian now counted her amongst his closest friends.

"Pity." She tapped her lip in thought. "Still, it's not enough for him to stomp around and mutter inarticulately. At least not for you. What is it that you like about him?"

This was dangerous territory, not the least of which was the very distinct possibility that Octavia would find some indiscreet way to throw the two of them together, and she already knew what Nash would have to say about that.

He regarded her as his friend's older sister, nothing more.

"Shall I tell you where we'll be going today?" Ana Maria said brightly.

Octavia rolled her eyes, but didn't comment on the blatant change of topic. "Certainly. I am considering redecorating some of the chairs in the club, and I'd like to look at fabric."

Ana Maria forgot all about how prickly and uncomfortable she felt, launching into a detailed description of the places she'd been to already, and the places she wished to go. Finally, Octavia held her hand up.

"Shouldn't we just go there? Much as I'd love to hear how this one store displays their fabrics from India more charmingly than the other does their fabrics from China."

Ana Maria winced. "Right. I am sorry, I just—"

"You're just enthusiastic," Octavia cut in. "I appreciate that very much. It is wonderful to see a lady in your position enthused about something that isn't male and with a title."

At which point both ladies burst into laughter, Ana Maria laughing at her friend's obvious sarcasm, and Octavia grinning at having been so obviously sarcastic.

At least they weren't talking *directly* about Nash anymore.

"WHAT ABOUT THIS one?"

Octavia held a bit of fabric up to show Ana Maria, who was internally debating between cloth that was a vibrant fuchsia in a paisley pattern or a more demure seafoam green with bizarre approximations of sea life.

Ana Maria frowned in Octavia's direction. "What would you use it for?"

Octavia wrinkled her face up in thought. "I was considering covering the bar at the far end of the room. Although I don't think liquids and this fabric will mix."

"Likely not. That one doesn't look sturdy enough for upholstery. Perhaps only for a wall hanging."

Octavia made a disappointed noise as she dropped the fabric.

"You seem to know a lot about my wares, my lady."

The shop owner stepped out from behind his long counter, an appraising expression on his face. He was Chinese, which made Ana Maria think that was why his fabrics were so much more extensive than British merchants. She presumed he could negotiate directly with the fabric makers in his home country, at least, and the Chinese silks were her favorite. "You were here a few months ago? You purchased the bolts of silk that had just arrived from China." He shook his head in fond remembrance. "I had many customers for that fabric, but you purchased the most of it. A truly remarkable color."

"Yes," Ana Maria replied.

"And you're back with your friend to buy more?"

"Yes. That is, I am considering redecorating. This is just a preliminary visit, my friend wished to see where I found the fabrics I used."

"Ah." His gaze traveled from Ana Maria to Octavia and back again. "And this young lady, your friend? Is she as knowledgeable as you?"

Octavia snorted as Ana Maria shrugged.

"You are here to assist, then," the merchant said.

"Look at this one!" Octavia enthused, waving another piece of fabric in the air.

It was nearly iridescent, shimmering in the mid-morning light.

"Let me see that," Ana Maria replied, striding forward. She ran her fingers over the fabric, marveling at how the colors seemed to shift under her hand.

"That is nacre velvet," the shopkeeper said. "Just arrived from Italy. You have a very fine eye, my lady."

"Well, actually, I am the one who spotted it first," Octavia said, grinning at Ana Maria.

"Yes, but—"

"My friend is teasing. It is lovely. I can't see it on a wall, though. How would you get the full impact of it?" Ana Maria moved the fabric as she spoke, and the colors changed from a greenish blue to a blueish purple.

"That would be spectacular as a gown," Octavia said.

"Not too bold?"

Octavia grinned. "Not at all. Perhaps you might even make someone grunt in approval."

Ana Maria chose to ignore that comment.

"I'll take all of it," she said to the shopkeeper. His eyes widened, and then he sprang into action, gathering the bolts and laying them all on his long table. He gestured to the far corner of the room. "If you like that one, there are others I think might pique your interest."

An hour later, Ana Maria felt as if she'd been transported into fabric heaven, while it seemed Octavia viewed it more as fabric hell.

"I have to get back to the club," Octavia said, glancing at the watch pinned to her bodice.

"It's not even lunchtime. You can say it—we are good enough friends. You are absolutely and completely bored here, and you might scream if you have to stay a moment longer."

Octavia's face was relieved. "Yes. Exactly." And

then she knitted her brow. "Will you be all right here? On your own?"

"I spent the first twenty-eight years of my life doing things on my own. I promise I know how to take care of myself."

"You do, but do you know how to take care of yourself now that you are a 'my lady'? I doubt you went around town dressed like that when you were doing errands for the duchess."

It was a good point, but Ana Maria did not want to have to leave, not now when she was just getting into the depths of Mr. Lee's collection. Nor did she want her friend to expire from boredom.

"Just go ahead. Mr. Lee will see me safely into a cab."

Mr. Lee nodded, then held up his index finger to make a point. "I will ask Mrs. Lee to come out, she is doing the bookkeeping, but she should be finished by now."

Ana Maria turned to Octavia. "See? I will have a chaperone, after all. Go on, don't worry."

Octavia gave her friend a kiss, then swept off with her usual confident stride. Ana Maria watched her go, envying the younger girl's self-assured poise.

Perhaps one day Ana Maria would master the art of walking without worrying.

Mr. Lee returned in a few minutes, an Englishwoman by his side. She was dressed in a plain gown of dark blue, but the quality of the fabric was impeccable.

"This is my wife, Mrs. Lee. She is technically the owner of the shop, though she prefers to work behind the scenes. I explained about your friend leaving."

Ana Maria held her hand out to the other woman, who took it after a moment of hesitation. "Thank you for taking time out of your work."

"You are welcome, my lady." Mrs. Lee spoke softly, as though she wasn't accustomed to conversing with strangers.

By the time Ana Maria had finished, she had purchased not only all the bolts of the shimmering fabric from Italy, but also a selection of silks, satins, taffetas, muslins, and some serviceable cottons that would be a vast improvement over the clothing the current duke's female staff was wearing.

"That won't all fit into a hansom," Ana Maria said as she surveyed her items. She picked up one of the bolts of the shimmering fabric and tucked it under her arm. "I'll take this one, and send a carriage for the rest later. Perhaps tomorrow?"

"Excellent," Mr. Lee said. "Let me find a cab for you." He stepped out of the shop onto the street.

"It was a pleasure to meet you, Mrs. Lee," Ana Maria said when the ladies were alone.

"Thank you for your patronage. Not everyone wishes to do business with us, and I appreciate your courtesy."

"Not do business—oh!" Ana Maria exclaimed as she realized why. "Well, the products are excellent. Those people are missing out."

Mrs. Lee's mouth curled into a shy smile. "Thank you so much."

Mr. Lee poked his head into the shop. "I have a cab, my lady."

"Yes, thank you, but don't you want a deposit?"

He offered a reassuring gesture. "That is fine, we don't—"

"A deposit would be wonderful," Mrs. Lee interrupted.

Right. Mrs. Lee did the books, so she would know.

Ana Maria tugged off her gloves and reached into her reticule for the notes she'd tucked in there. Thaddeus was more than generous with her allowance, which meant she had a sizable amount to put down. She knew, from having been sent to merchants when she was working, that the nobility usually decided to pay tomorrow, or the next day, when given a chance. And if they weren't given that chance, they'd take it. So she knew full well the delicate balance Mrs. Lee was probably navigating.

"Here," she said, placing all but one of the notes on the counter. "You can tote that up, and send me a note as to what I owe. I am—"

"Of course we remember you, my lady. Lady Ana Maria Dutton living with the Duke of Hasford in Hanover Square."

"Yes."

Mr. Lee popped his head back out, then ducked back inside with a frown. "The cab was purloined by somebody else."

"It's fine," Ana Maria said. "It will do me good to walk, it's not that far."

"But—"

"I know it's not done." She repressed her irritation. The Lees didn't know she hadn't been treated as a lady six months ago. "But I have been traveling around London on my own for some time now, and I would prefer not to be cooped up in a cab."

Mr. and Mrs. Lee's faces were matching expressions of horror, and Ana Maria tried not to laugh.

"I'll send the carriage tomorrow for the rest, remember. And please do tell me how much I owe. Thank you so much." She kept speaking until she was at the front door, then slipped out before they could argue some more.

"DRAT," ANA MARIA muttered to herself. "I am thoroughly and entirely lost."

She'd begun the walk home half an hour ago in such joyful spirits; she had found fabrics that made her heart sing, and she felt as though she was actually being useful, even if it was only to help her friend decorate the way she wanted to.

But she'd been lost in her thoughts, pondering if there was something more she could do, something more official, and she must've missed a turn, and now she was in a less reputable part of town and it was starting to get dark.

And she didn't have a poker on her. Perhaps she should not have been so quick to insist on going home alone.

Though she did have her new bolt of fabric—perhaps if someone accosted her, she could point out how remarkable the shifting colors were.

Or thump them on the head. With soft fabric.

Not the best plan.

She glanced around, trying not to look as though she were lost. She knew a well-dressed lady looking confused in a rougher part of town was a sure invitation to trouble.

She heard the distinctive squawk of seagulls, and knew she must be close to the docks. Where she definitely did not want to be. Drat.

When she'd been a maid of all work, she'd gone into far worse neighborhoods than this, but she'd been wearing the clothing the duchess allowed her, which were drab rags, and had a knife strapped to her shin. She'd never had occasion to use it, but she suspected it gave her an air of confidence to act as a deterrent.

"Miss?"

She turned at the sound of the man's voice, relieved to see he had a kind smile. Not that a kind smile was an indication of being a reasonable person, but it was a promising beginning.

"Yes?"

"I think you might need assistance." He gestured across the street, a sign proclaiming it was the King's Arms. "Perhaps we might go in and have a pint?"

Because assistance equaled an ale. Of course it did. Thank goodness she wasn't a naive young lady, though even naive young ladies would have to look askance at his kind of help.

"No, thank you," she said, beginning to step away.

He grabbed her arm, swinging her back around to face him. "But you're clearly lost, and if it's not me, it'll be somebody worse."

Was it wrong she wished this man had given Lord Brunley lessons on how to propose? "Somebody worse" was not precisely a good recommendation of character.

"I'll take that chance," she replied, twisting out of his grip. She slid the bolt of fabric out from under her arm and held it in front of her as a barrier.

Which he chuckled at, but at least he couldn't get his hands on her.

He lunged toward her, and she swung the bolt up over her head, slamming it down on top of him, making him stumble.

And then she heard a growl from behind her, and a long arm shot past her and into the man's face, sending him straight down onto the cobblestones.

That must have hurt.

She spun around, finding herself nose-to-chest with Nash. Of course.

"I had it handled."

One dark eyebrow rose. "Didn't look like it."

"That's because you interfered."

He peered over her shoulder at the man lying on the ground, then his gaze darted to the bolt of fabric. "Your plan was to smother him?"

"I'll have you arrested!" the man moaned, his hand cradling his chin.

Nash strode past Ana Maria to stare down at the man, his hands curled into fists at his side. "You won't." His words settled, the threat in them nearly palpable. "In fact, you'll beg pardon of the lady."

"I will not!" the man replied.

Nash bent down to stare into the man's face, not moving, just staring. The man responded by glaring at Nash's feet. Ana Maria suppressed a giggle.

"Beg pardon," the man said at last.

"Apology accepted," Ana Maria replied, tucking the bolt of fabric back under her arm. Nash was still towering over the would-be assailant, and she tugged on his sleeve. "Why don't you escort me home, Your Grace?"

He snarled. Whether it was because he wanted an opportunity to get into more altercations or because she'd reminded him of his title, she didn't know.

"Your Grace?" the man echoed.

Ana Maria raised her voice to address him.

"Yes, you've just been punched by the Duke of Malvern."

"Ohh."

"Let's go," Nash said in his usual abrupt way. He took the bolt of fabric from her, tucked it under his arm, and held his other arm out for her.

She opened her mouth to inform him she was perfectly capable of carrying her own things, thank you very much, but it wasn't as though he didn't know that. He was just being Nash—assuming all the physical duties around him, taking charge without asking, being proprietary about the things and people he cared about.

Oh. That was an unsettling thought. He did care about her, of course. He cared about her because she was Sebastian's sister, and Thaddeus's cousin.

But did he care for her as Ana Maria? A person in her own right?

Because she had always been so keenly aware of him, but she'd known he hadn't paid much attention to her. Ever. Until the night of the ball.

And now it seemed he was turning up everywhere—not so much like a bad penny as a brutal force of nature.

There was something rather primitively exciting about it all. Though she should not be having those kinds of thoughts about her brother's best friend.

She gave herself a mental shake, then realized he was guiding her toward a pub. Not the King's Arms, but another one. What was it about men wanting to buy her ale?

"I thought you were escorting me home?" Unless he was so determined to get into a physical altercation he couldn't wait until he saw her to her door.

"We need to talk."

She snorted. "You? Talk?"

He pushed the door to the pub open, leading her inside, and heading toward a table where one lone man sat. "Off," he said, and the man scurried away.

Nash grunted, and settled her in the man's seat. "I can talk," he said at last.

Ana Maria rolled her eyes. "Yes, and I can sing. But neither of us can do those things very well."

A barmaid appeared at the table. "What'll ye have?"

Nash looked at Ana Maria. "Well, I don't know what to order," she said.

"Two ales."

"Right away."

"What do we have to talk about?" She didn't mean to speak in an aggressive tone, and yet here she was. "Because I don't think we have anything to talk about. Except for you agreeing to let me handle things on my own."

"Not going to do that." His eyes held an intensity that made her tingle. "I'm going to handle things for you."

Oh.

Chapter Seven

Even in the relative dark of the pub, Nash could see the angry spark in Ana Maria's eyes. "You're not going to do that? And who are you to decide how I am to comport myself?"

I'm your protector.

And her brother's best friend. That was all.

But he couldn't rid himself of the memory of walking into that room where that oafish lord had her cornered, feeling the fierce urge to pummel anything and anyone that might hurt her. And then coming across her in a dockside street, for God's sake, as another man accosted her. Feeling the righteous anger surge within him, glad to put it to good use.

"Can we agree on a compromise?"

Not that he was going to actually compromise, but she didn't have to know that.

"Compromise?" She sounded skeptical. He didn't blame her; he couldn't think of any time in the past he'd compromised. Mostly because people didn't usually even try to compromise with him—they just left him alone. And if they didn't? He hit them.

The barmaid returned with the ales, placing them on the table. He took the glass, gesturing for Ana Maria to do the same.

"Are we toasting to something? To you staying out of my business?"

She was far more irascible than he'd remembered. Not that he'd thought that much about her before; it was only now, now that Sebastian wasn't there taking care of her that he'd started to pay attention. Not to mention seeing her in that gown.

The protector. Stepping in when required, even if not desired.

"No."

Her mouth twisted into an adorable pucker.

"But I will if you learn to protect yourself." He took a sip of the ale. She did the same, sputtering as she drank.

The look on her face made him almost laugh. Except he never laughed.

"It's unusual!" she muttered. "I'll get used to it." She took another sip, this time mastering her expression. "How do you propose I learn to protect myself?"

"I'll teach you."

Her eyes widened. "Oh." A moment of silence. "So—you'll teach me how to punch people? Like you do?"

She sounded intrigued, not horrified, thank God.

"Yes."

"But—but I am nothing close to your size. How will that work?"

How will that work?

The question brought all sorts of unwanted images to his mind—images that were most definitely not suitable when thinking about Ana Maria.

But still.

Him sliding his hand down her arm, showing her the correct way to hold her fist. Feeling the movement of her body as she thrust her hand into an imaginary opponent.

Helping her become stronger.

They were intoxicating thoughts.

"Well," he said at last, realizing she was giving him an impatient look. "I'll train you. I have a room for boxing—"

"Of course you do," she murmured.

"And we can work together until I feel as though you can handle yourself. Until then, you'll need to let me know when you're likely to be in the kind of neighborhood I just found you in."

Both eyebrows rose incredulously. "And why would I do that?"

He leaned forward. "Because if you don't, I'll tell Thaddeus, and you know how he'll react."

That adorable pucker again. He should probably tell her she shouldn't look so cute when she was mad, but he knew that would likely make her madder.

"That's blackmail."

He shrugged. "I just want you safe. Sebastian would expect no less of me."

"Humph." She downed the rest of her ale in a defiant gesture. Then ruined the effect by wrinkling her nose.

"Fine. When do you propose we start these lessons?"

Another shrug. "You can tell me. You won't need them if you can promise me you won't venture into any dangerous areas by yourself."

"We'll start tomorrow, then."

He smothered a grin at her irritable tone.

ANA MARIA HAD never felt so many disparate emotions in her prior twenty-eight years. Contradictory emotions, as suited her new role as the walking oxymoron.

Gratitude, because she wasn't entirely certain she could have handled that man on her own. Annoyance, because he'd had to rescue her. Something else that surged when she thought about the power of his body, and how he'd rushed in to protect her.

And something on top of that when she imagined what it would be like to train with him.

Alone. In a room where he presumably wore less and sweat more.

Oh dear.

She needed to get her mind off all of that. "Can we order another?" she asked. He'd finished his ale as well.

"Mmph." He lifted his hand to beckon to the barmaid, then raised two fingers.

"I didn't realize your grandmother was in town." That was an excellent change of topic—if she was thinking about older judging relatives she wouldn't be thinking of him in his shirtsleeves, thrusting his fists toward an invisible opponent.

"I didn't either."

The barmaid returned with their drinks, taking their empty glasses and setting the full ones down. "Pay now, if you please," she said.

He withdrew some coins from his waistcoat pocket and handed them to her. She looked down in surprise. "Thank you, sir," she said in an effusive tone.

Generous on top of everything. As she'd anticipated.

"So why is she here?"

He took a long swallow instead of answering. "My heir."

That wasn't helpful. "What about your heir?"

Another drink instead of a reply. "Like my father."

"Oh." She knew about his father, of course. Not all of it—Nash was even more taciturn when it came to his own private matters—but she knew there was a reason a young Nash was suddenly at their house all the time, sometimes sporting unexplained bruising.

Sebastian had pleaded with Nash to let him help, but Nash had refused. They were both so young at the time, and how could they possibly go up against a grown man? A duke?

"And how does your grandmother come into it?"

"Says I have to get my own heir."

Which meant— "Oh! So you're planning on getting married?"

Goodness, why did her voice have to squeak at the end like that?

"Have to do it eventually."

"Ah." She took a sip of her ale instead of responding, which was probably for the best, since her first emotions were disappointment, jealousy, and envy. None of which she precisely understood, or would allow herself to understand, but were there nonetheless.

"And your grandmother is here to . . . assist you in finding a bride?"

He grimaced. Which answered her question.

"So that is why you were at the ball the other evening." Dressed like every other gentleman, looking impossibly handsome and dangerous all at the same time.

A grunt of agreement.

"If I can help—" But he was already shaking his head before she could finish her sentence.

"No help."

She drew back in her chair. "So you can demand that I take lessons in fighting from you, but you won't let me help in finding someone to marry?"

"Not your concern."

This time, there was only one emotion. Anger.

"I know that you are entirely self-sufficient," she said in a low, furious tone, "but can't you see how unbalanced it is to help me without allowing me to help you?"

"And what will you do?" His fierce tone startled her. "You'll tell me which young lady seems to be the least terrified of me? Or which one is the most desperate for a husband?" He snorted. "I can figure that out by myself, and if I can't, my grandmother will apparently be doing it for me. I don't need your help."

Her chest tightened in response. That he thought so little of himself, that he was refusing a genuine offer of help, that he was so obviously reluctant to embark on marriage, but was determined to do it to stave off a potential reprisal of his father's behavior.

All things that made her concerned for him, angry at him, and proud of him all at the same time.

"I should be getting home." She couldn't speak all the words in her heart, she wouldn't dare to, so she should get herself out of his vicinity until she had composed herself.

Which might mean she would next see him when she was eighty years old.

By which point he would have gotten married, so that would be taken care of.

So there was a bright side to being conflicted.

"I'll take you home." He rose, holding his hand out to her in assistance. She glanced at his hand, the strength of it, marveling that he was so willing to help others but not take any help himself.

What would it look like if he did?

What kind of help could she offer?

And why did that question raise so many fascinating thoughts?

THEY WALKED IN nearly companionable silence back to Thaddeus's house. It was a long walk, and at first he'd wondered if her delicate lady feet could handle so much walking, but then he recalled that prior to a few months ago, she'd been doing all the duchess's most unpleasant work.

Albeit not in her delicate lady slippers.

"Are your feet comfortable?" He sounded so awkward. No wonder he never spoke.

"My feet?" she replied, sounding surprised.

"Yes. The walking. We could hail a cab, if you'd like." Or he could just carry her.

"I am fine," she replied, sounding vaguely offended. So he wouldn't offer to pick her up. Likely a good thing, what with all those soft curves in his arms.

"Why would you worry about my feet?" she asked after a moment.

He shrugged.

"That's not an answer. I appreciate the concern, but I can walk all by myself, Your Grace. I can dance and speak and defend myself."

"No you can't." He tilted his head back toward where they had come from. "Your idea of defense is to whack someone with fabric. Here, give that back to me," he said, tugging the bolt of fabric from under her arm. He'd attempted to carry it out of the pub, but she'd been too quick for him.

She yelped in surprise, and then glared at him.

It felt good, in an odd way, to have her glare at him. It meant that he could provoke a reaction, not just a tolerance. That she treated him as a person with opinions, albeit opinions with which she did not always agree.

Such as that she should be taught self-defense.

But the thought of her wandering about London, her delicate lady feet taking her to disreputable neighborhoods in search of something pretty—that was enough to make his chest tighten and his fists clench.

"I do appreciate your concern," she said, this time in a softer tone. "I know Sebastian has likely asked you to watch out for me. I will tell him you are doing a splendid job, if you like."

"He did not—" Nash began, then clamped his jaw shut. It would be far better for her to believe that he was doing this out of some best friend appeal rather than out of his own worry. If she thought that he was acting out of anything other than honoring a friend's request—then she would think he cared for her.

He did not want her to know he cared for her.

Because he didn't, of course. That is, other than the usual care one would have for a friend's sibling. A person to be tolerated by virtue of that person's relationship to the person you truly cared about.

And not that he'd ever tell Sebastian he truly cared about him. For one thing, he assumed Sebastian knew.

For the other, that wasn't anything Nash had ever done—express, out loud, his true feelings toward somebody.

"We're here. You can leave me now." She spoke abruptly. Had he been silent too long?

Well, he could answer that question: always.

He hadn't realized they were as close to the house as they apparently were. They approached it, the waning afternoon light making the many windows sparkle, as though touched by fire.

It was truly impressive, even though Nash knew Sebastian had taken it for granted and Thaddeus sincerely wished it wasn't his.

Nash could sympathize with both points of view.

The door swung open, as though someone was waiting for them, and the butler stepped out. "My lady, Your Grace," he called.

Nash and Ana Maria ascended the stairs to the front door, him holding his hand out toward her in case she stumbled.

Something he wasn't aware of doing. Just that he always did that sort of thing around her.

Why hadn't he noticed that before? He drew his hand back as though he'd touched a flame.

Goddamn it. She was the flame. And he would

not allow himself to get burned by the fire that was sparking within.

He waited until she was safely inside, then turned to go, but paused as he heard Thaddeus call his name.

He hoped to God Thad wasn't about to warn him away from Ana Maria. Because he was warning himself away well enough, he sure as hell didn't need his friend to add to it as well.

"Thank you for escorting her home," Thad said in a gruff voice. "I am not accustomed to worrying about her being out. I will ensure she has adequate protection when she leaves the house." He shook his head. "I could use a drink, how about you?"

Nash grinned. "Of course," he replied.

So this was to be a social visit, one where Thad groused about his new pampered life and Nash agreed and drank Thad's excellent whiskey.

He followed Thad to the study, noting how it had changed since Sebastian had left—the surface of the desk was spotless, no random stacks of paper on it. The letter opener was at a perfect perpendicular angle to the edge of the desk, and the chair was pushed carefully under the desk, not as though someone had just popped up out of it.

"Have a seat."

Nash sat in the chair opposite the desk, crossing his legs.

Thad busied himself pouring the drinks, squinting at the glasses as though making certain there were precisely equal amounts in each.

Nash took his, raised it to Thad, and downed it all in one gulp.

Thad lifted his eyebrow, then took a sip. He sat in the chair, placing the glass carefully on top of a leather coaster.

The two sat in silence. Nash always appreciated that about Thad—he didn't make conversations when there was no conversation to make.

And now, oddly, he felt like talking.

"You met my grandmother the other evening."

Thad nodded. "I hadn't realized you and she were friendly."

"We're not," Nash said, getting up to pour another drink. "She's here because of my father."

Thad hesitated, as though unsure of what to say. "Your father."

"Yes," Nash said, returning to his seat. "It seems she disliked my father as much as I did, and for the same reasons. She's here because she believes my heir is like him in some important respects."

Thad grimaced. "Oh. I see."

"Yes, you do." Nash sighed. "She insists the only way to prevent my cousin from inheriting is for me to marry and produce an heir."

A pause. "She's correct."

Nash scowled. "I know."

"So—you're going to get married?" Thad sounded skeptical. Likely because Nash had told him and Sebastian he would never marry, and Nash suspected they knew why.

Nash grunted.

"And your grandmother is here to assist?"

Another grunt.

"Ah."

Thad swallowed the rest of his whiskey in one gulp. "How will that happen?"

Nash frowned. Wasn't it obvious? "I'll meet some lady, we'll dance a few times, and I'll speak to her father."

"You'll dance. And speak?"

Why did Thaddeus have to sound so skeptical? Nash scowled even more. "I can dance and speak, you know. I just prefer not to."

Nash leaned over to the bar cart and poured another serving of whiskey into his glass.

"You say that." Thaddeus did not sound convinced. "And you'll spend the rest of your life with this person you danced with and spoke with a few times."

Nash nodded. It was precisely what he planned to do—the less he cared for his future bride, the better it would be. For everyone. They'd marry, have an heir or two, and then go their separate ways.

Thaddeus shook his head. "I wish you luck."

Nash tried not to take it personally that Thad sounded as though he would need a lot more than luck.

"YOU'VE—WHAT?" FINAN asked, dodging a blow.

Nash growled. "I'm going to train her."

Finan rocked back on his heels, an exaggeratedly shocked expression on his face. "You. The one who you insisted is just like a sister to you. That you won't marry, but you'll train in the art of self-defense?" Finan shook his head in woeful regret. Nash wished he had already managed to land a punch, that way Finan couldn't keep making those rueful expressions.

"I can't have her unprotected."

"What about *your* protection?"

"That's what I have you for." Nash bounced on his heels, his fists up in position.

Finan sighed, raising his own fists. "You're still an idiot. And she'd still be the perfect wife for you."

"Not going to happen," Nash said, before launching a blow that narrowly missed Finan's jaw.

Finan danced back, his eyes gleaming. "I suppose you have some ridiculous reason that makes sense in your brain why you won't even consider her."

Nash landed a hit to Finan's side. He staggered, then popped back up, still bouncing on his toes. "Good one."

Nash shifted to avoid Finan's fist, which landed in the air instead of in his stomach.

"And what will any of your prospective brides think about you spending time alone with Lady

Ana Maria, the lady you've known since childhood who is not at all related to you?"

"They won't know."

Finan's eyebrows rose. "Ah! So this self-defense training will all be conducted in secret. Even better."

"Shut up."

Finan held his hands out in a smugly satisfied gesture. "You're making my point even better than I could. And all without saying a thing."

Nash advanced on Finan, who held his hands up in surrender, his eyes laughing as he stared Nash down.

HE WISHED HE'D exhausted himself into oblivion in his boxing salon. Because if he had, he would have been passed out in his bedroom by himself instead of taking tea—*tea!*—with his grandmother in the largest of the receiving rooms.

"I've made a list."

The paper wavered in her hand, as though she were trembling. He knew she wasn't frightened of him. Perhaps it was old age? Was she ill? Was that why she was so determined to see him settled? So she could die in peace, knowing that the dukedom wouldn't be passed on to someone like his father?

Not that he could ask her any of that. She would likely refuse to answer, and then he'd be left having revealed how he did not want her to die, not when he'd just found her. Or her him.

And who would have thought he'd have wanted

even more family? Given he was employing all the ones he'd found in his house already.

She held it up to her lady's maid, who stood behind her chair. The woman brought it to him, giving him a look that seemed to warn him: *don't disappoint my lady, or you will be sorry.*

He admired that loyalty.

He took the paper, his thoughts churning as he read the names, none of which were familiar to him.

"Well?" the dowager duchess said in an impatient tone.

"I don't know any of them." He tossed the paper on the table between them, narrowly missing the sugar bowl.

Her mouth curled into a supercilious smile. "And that is why you are so fortunate as to have me here."

"You forced your way in." He hadn't realized he'd spoken until he saw her look of surprise. And the lady's maid narrowed gaze.

"I did so for the good of the family."

He felt that impotent anger rise in his throat. "The good of the family would have been doing something about my father in the first place. The good of the family would have been twenty years ago, when my mother left me alone with that monster. You knew who he was, you said so yourself."

The dowager duchess's face crumpled. "It is my profoundest regret I didn't do more at the time. I wish I could have ensured your mother was able to take you. But your father would absolutely not have allowed that. For that I am sorry."

She sounded sincere.

"But I can't change the past," she continued in a stronger tone of voice. "I can only help you to correct the future. And the future lies with that list," she said, pointing to the paper on the table.

He picked it up again, scanning the names. Lady Mary Arbuthnot. Miss Grace Collins. Lady Felicity Townshend.

"Lady Felicity—the one I met the other evening?" When he'd danced with Ana Maria in her silver gown, and punched that oaf, and wiped brandy from Ana Maria's face.

"Yes. Which reminds me, we should add Lady Ana Maria to the list as well. I know she has Spanish heritage, but other than that, she is of impeccable breeding. The daughter of a duke, the cousin to another."

"No."

"And . . . ?" she said, raising one supercilious brow.

Because I already care for her, and we both know what happens when a man from our family cares for a lady. I can't risk that. I can't risk her.

Not that he could share any of that with this woman, the one who was determined to see the proper thing done rather than the right thing. What the right thing was he wasn't entirely certain, but he suspected it would be to eradicate all the possible rotten men in his family by any means necessary.

Was that why he was so quick with his fists? Wanting to eradicate evil?

Hm. Far too much deep thinking for teatime.

"Lady Ana Maria is like a sister to me." *A lie.*

"At least you know her, unlike any of these other ladies. And she is not actually a sister."

Excellent logic, if one weren't determined to stay away from the lady in question to protect her. In which case, it was probably not the smartest thing to have insisted he teach her how to defend herself.

Why couldn't he have kept quiet then? He had no problem being sullenly silent most of the time.

Oh of course. Because otherwise she would be manhandled and worse. He had to say something. He had to do something.

But he couldn't think of her in that way.

"I'll consider the ladies on the list," he said, snatching it up and stuffing it in his pocket. Anything to keep her from pursuing that line of questioning.

"Good." She leaned back in her chair. "Now please ring for more tea. This has gotten cold."

Nash had never been more grateful for the British aristocrat's obsession with the perfect cup of tea as he was at that moment.

Chapter Eight

"You're going to the Duke of Malvern's home. For—?"

Jane sounded as skeptical as Ana Maria felt. Though it was likely Jane wasn't also feeling a frisson of excitement at the prospect of punching said duke.

Not that Ana Maria felt that way, of course. It was purely her anticipation of a new and unusual experience, not the thought of seeing Nash in his shirtsleeves, or less, for God's sake, as he demonstrated how best to fell an opponent.

Was it possible to swoon over just a thought?

She should not be discovering the answer to that question. Not in front of Jane, doubtful expression and all.

"The duke has said he would show me some things that will be necessary if I am to—" But she hadn't said anything to anybody about traipsing about London. Not now, not that she was a lady.

"If you are to—?" Jane prompted.

They were in Ana Maria's bedroom, the two of them discussing just what, precisely, one wore to a gentleman's home when said gentleman would be wearing the aforementioned shirtsleeves.

But that wasn't a response.

The problem with people who'd known you since you were young is that they *knew* you. Ana Maria had never said anything about her conflicted—one might say "oxymoronic"—feelings about Nash, but that was probably because she hadn't had to. Jane had likely figured it out long before Ana Maria had begun to catalogue his kindness, his fierce protectiveness, and those strong arms.

Swooning is not allowed, she reminded herself sternly.

"If I am to visit the fabric places I wish to go to." She spoke as though it were entirely reasonable that a young lady, a daughter of one duke, the cousin to another, would want to frequent fabric merchants. Some, shockingly, even from countries other than England.

Not for the first time, Ana Maria wished that she could have stayed in her previous role as servant. It was a ludicrous wish, and she did not miss a bit of the actual work—she wasn't a self-sacrificing idiot—but she did miss the freedom associated with being someone nobody thought much of.

Why couldn't she have been the daughter of a country squire, the cousin of another country squire?

Though those ladies were likely even more

constrained, given that they knew far fewer people and didn't have the luxury of a bustling city like London to travel around in.

Fine. She would begrudgingly accept who she was, but that didn't mean she had to accept its limitations.

Which made her think about just those limitations—things like not spending time alone with a gentleman when one was an unmarried lady. Not acting on one's impulses either. Impulses such as kissing said gentleman when one had the . . . *impulse* to do so.

He was the perfect candidate for kissing, even if one discounted the fact that he was extraordinarily handsome. He would never speak about it, since he didn't speak in general, and he was exceedingly loyal, and would never do anything to damage her reputation.

Not that she was necessarily going to kiss him. But if the impulse occurred to her—which, of course it was going to occur to her given how swoony she was about his entire form—she might indeed act on it.

"Why haven't you hired a chaperone? That would solve the problem and you wouldn't need to bother the duke," Jane asked in a reasonable tone. "And why do you need to go to those places, anyway?"

A chaperone was the obvious solution. But even without the allure of Nash, she did not want to hire someone to be her shadow, not when she was so determined to be who she wanted to be on her own. She was twenty-eight, not eighteen. Other women her age, less fortunate women, were deemed spinsters, and therefore not required to answer to anybody.

Ana Maria had been expecting both of Jane's questions, though she had thought it might be Thaddeus who asked first. But Thaddeus was in over his head with being the duke, and he'd spoken only a few words to her since reminding her—as though she needed reminding, she reminded herself of it all the time—that Nash was not to be thought of in that way.

"I've been thinking about what I would like to do." She held her hand up as Jane's mouth opened to ask the inevitable questions. "I would like to help people such as Miss Octavia in their decorating needs."

When she said it aloud like that, it sounded ridiculous. And small. And meaningless.

But she knew for herself how crucial it was to surround oneself with things and colors and items that brought pleasure. Her mood had improved dramatically as soon as she'd redecorated the small salon, and she was already itching to tear everything apart in her bedroom.

So she couldn't let her own, or anybody else's doubts, subsume her.

If she couldn't do something as ridiculous and small and meaningless as control her surroundings, what was the point of being a lady of privilege in the first place? If she couldn't then share her abilities with others who just needed a respite from the drab browns and grays of their world, then she might as well just give up and accept Lord "I Won't Do Anything for Myself" Brunley.

"That's an excellent idea," Jane said, entirely surprising Ana Maria. Thankfully forgetting about the chaperone issue as well.

"You really think so?"

Jane nodded. "I don't know if you recall, but there was that time a few years back when the head gardener miscalculated something for the duchess"—the last two words said in a growl—"and the house was overrun with lilies. Her Grace was livid about it, since she thought lilies were vulgar"—at which she rolled her eyes—"but we put them everywhere. They made even polishing the silver more pleasurable."

Like Ana Maria, Jane had begun her life in the house as a scullery maid, working her way up to lady's maid after the duchess had died.

"I do remember," Ana Maria said with a smile. "Fletchfield tried to keep himself from reacting, but even he was a trifle more joyful during that time."

"So it stands to reason that a person's surroundings would alter their mood."

One thing Ana Maria had always appreciated about Jane was her ability to cut right through to the heart of the matter.

"I'll start with Miss Octavia's club, and perhaps—if I can manage it—I'll try to find some funds to help beautify the local schools and orphanages."

"Those children aren't going to want flowers and pretty wallpaper, my lady," Jane said drily. "They want food, and a solid future."

Ana Maria's resolve faltered at the accuracy of her friend's words. But it returned as she considered the ramifications of what she might be able to do. "They do, and I'll see what I can do there. But I know myself that presenting a situation in a certain way makes it more amenable to the viewer."

"What do you mean by that?" Jane asked. She gestured for Ana Maria to turn around so she could remove her gown.

"I mean," Ana Maria said, her voice muffled by the fabric as Jane slid it up and over her head, "that if we want to get these children a promising future we have to show there is promise within them. There are very few aristocratic people, unfortunately, who will see a grubby urchin and think they should be welcomed into their home, even as the lowest employee. If we clean up their surroundings and make it appear as though they fit within those people's homes, they'll be far more likely to take a chance on them."

She herself was proof of that—prior to six months ago, nobody paid attention to her. But give her some nice gowns and even people who did not want her dowry wanted to know her.

"This one?" Jane asked, holding a gown up for

Ana Maria's perusal. It was one of the ones she'd worn back when she was the duchess's maid of all work, a castoff from the duchess that Ana Maria still had a fondness for, likely because it was one of the gowns she'd worn to sneak away and spend time with Sebastian, her younger half brother.

"That one is perfect," Ana Maria beamed.

"Huh, I've finally been able to choose something you want to wear," Jane replied in a wry tone. "And it looks like something you'd clean the grates in. Since you used to do just that."

"Oh, hush, and help me get ready," Ana Maria said, rolling her eyes.

"In here."

Ana Maria swallowed as Nash pushed the door open to his fighting room. He wasn't yet in shirtsleeves, but he also wasn't wearing a cravat, which meant she could see his bare throat.

She hadn't realized a gentleman's bare throat could be at all alluring, and yet here she was, staring at it as though it were a scrumptious sweet that she'd been forbidden to taste.

She'd like to taste it. Did people even do that? Tasting someone else's throat had not been covered in the belowstairs discussion of general intercourse. And now she certainly couldn't ask, what with her supposed to be a lady and all.

But she was still standing at the door, gawking at his strong, powerful throat.

"Yes, thank you," she said nonsensically, walking into the room.

It was mostly empty save for a few items of furniture at the edges. The walls were covered with some odd material, chosen for something other than decoration, while the floors were dull, making Ana Maria itch to polish them.

Those days are over, she reminded herself.

"Do you want anything to drink before we begin?" Nash said. He sounded so awkward it made her feel slightly less so.

"I don't think I should." Alcohol would make her even less sharp, and she might accidentally say something that she should not.

"I mean water," he replied with a chuckle. He strode over to a bureau against the opposite wall, upon which a pitcher and glasses sat. He poured two glasses, then returned to her, giving her one of them.

Her cheeks were flushed with embarrassment. Or perhaps it was that throat.

She took a swig from the glass, drinking so quickly she started to choke. He immediately began to pound her back, which made her whole body shake, so the remaining water in the glass sloshed out and spilled on her gown and the floor.

He stopped pounding her back as they both stared down at the widening puddle.

"Well," Ana Maria said in a sprightly voice, "this is getting off to an excellent start."

His expression froze, and then the most startling thing happened—he began to laugh.

Not only that, he was laughing so hard he'd flung his head back, showing even more of that damnably handsome throat. He had his hand to his chest, as though it hurt to laugh so much, his other hand still holding his own glass. Which had not spilled, despite all of his movement.

So she stepped over to him, snatched the glass from his hand, and poured all the water out onto the floor.

His eyes widened, and then he laughed harder. This time, she joined in, not quite sure what they were laughing at, but pleased to see him so joyful, for once.

She didn't remember ever seeing him laugh. She'd seen him smile on a few rare occasions, but not outright laughter.

"Anything amiss?"

Nash's manservant Finan popped his head into the room, his perplexed expression revealing that, yes, Nash's laughter was a rare occurrence.

"You all right, my lady?" Finan continued, addressing Ana Maria.

"I am fine. But perhaps a mop would be of use?" And some cloths to dry the wood adequately so that no one would slip later on, but she bit back the words because she wasn't the maid in charge of cleaning this room. Or any room.

"Right away," Finan said, his face disappearing as the door shut again.

"Stay there," Nash ordered as she began to move. "I don't want you to fall."

"I'll be fine," she replied, lifting her now-damp shoes from the worst of the spill.

"Why do you always tell me you'll be fine? When I am just trying to help?"

Her chest tightened at the sincerity of his tone.

That is why he demanded he teach her self-defense. He is a protector, he knows no other way. It had nothing to do with her, the person, Ana Maria; it was because she was in his orbit, and he cared about people in his orbit.

Just like he had hired so many of the bastards his father had scattered around the country. Not that he'd ever told her that, but she'd heard him and Sebastian speaking about it.

It should be a relief it had nothing to do personally with her. It was his need, nothing more or less. So she couldn't deny him his basic need to protect.

"Thank you. I know I should be more grateful—"

"That's not what I'm saying," he interrupted. "I just want you to agree that there are certain things that I am more knowledgeable about than you."

She raised her eyebrow. "Such as—?"

Such as. For a moment, Nash couldn't think of anything. Well, besides not talking. But he'd gotten better at talking, which must mean he'd gotten worse at not talking. Not that he was good at talking; just take a look at, for example, now.

He couldn't think of a thing to say.

"I suppose you'll say self-defense and fighting," she said, obviating the need for him to think of a response. "And that is true. But I believe that once you teach me the essential elements I will be as good as you are, albeit starting from a different place. What with being a female and all."

And that was why he found himself in the confounding position of not being able to speak.

She was a female. A female he'd realized was far too attractive for him to spend any amount of time with, and yet here he was, alone in a room in his house. With only his assorted family members who were also servants. And Finan.

So. She was a female, and he was an idiot.

"Fine," he said instead of saying anything that might reveal the extent of his idiocy. And his awareness of her as a female instead of just as the sibling of his best friend. "I don't want to talk. Let's spar."

"You are better than I am at changing the subject when you know you are wrong," she muttered.

He chose to ignore her.

He went to the bureau with the linens, drawing two lengths of linen from the drawer. "We'll need to wrap your hands."

She glanced at the linens, then held her hands out in front of her. As though she were submitting to him.

Holy hell, the thoughts that went through his mind—and to his cock—at the sight of it.

Her, holding her hands out as he slowly unwrapped her, taking his time to reveal each inch of perfect golden skin. Her, holding her hands out for him to guide her to where he wanted her. His bed? His desk? The carpet?

Her, holding her hands out, reaching for his body, sliding her palms over his skin.

That was the one he craved the most.

Though he would gladly take any of them.

"Nash?"

He jerked his thoughts away from all of that, clamping his jaw as he began to wrap the linen around her hands.

Once again, he was touching her ungloved hands. Her skin was smooth, not marked by scars and calluses like his.

"I won't be wearing linen like this if somebody accosts me on the street," she pointed out.

"No, but I don't want you to hurt yourself."

"You are very sweet," she replied.

Well, thanks to her words his concern that he would embarrass himself because of a poorly timed erection was no longer a concern, at least.

"I am not sweet."

Her mouth curled into a wicked smile. Concern back on board, given what thoughts that smile conjured in his mind.

"Oh, but you are. You insist on rescuing damsels in distress—even though I was not in distress, mind you—and you've hired people who most men in your position would prefer to ignore."

He scowled in reply.

"And you are taking time from whatever it is you're supposed to be doing—"

At which he grunted.

"—to train me in self-defense. Although, presumably, once you train me you won't have to spend time rushing to my aid. You can stay home, safe in the knowledge I can take care of myself."

That's not going to happen.

"I am not sweet," he repeated.

She rolled her eyes. "Fine. Not sweet. Can we get to the training portion now?"

The training portion. Where he'd be touching her. Not just her hands, which had already inspired images that he would be revisiting in the privacy of his bedroom. But elsewhere, adjusting her stance, demonstrating what a straight and true punch looked like. Making certain her shoulders were relaxed as she moved so the tension wouldn't make her lose momentum. Pretending to be an assailant who might want to get her into a prone position.

Goddamn it.

Was that why he seemed to be procrastinating in doing the one thing he had insisted they do together?

"Nash."

"Yes."

He nodded, then stalked behind her.

"All right. The first thing will be to gauge

your reaction time." He took a deep breath, then placed a hand on either side of her waist. Holding her still.

She shrieked and leaped away, spinning to face him, her expression one of astonishment.

"Well. Reaction time is good."

"Why didn't you warn me?"

He frowned. "If I'd warned you, you'd have had time to prepare your reaction. That wouldn't make sense."

She rolled her eyes again. "You are the most irritatingly pragmatic man I've ever met."

"I don't even know what that means." He held his hand up when she opened her mouth. "Nor do I care to. We need to work now. We can spend time tossing barbs at one another later."

Her eyebrows rose, and that wicked smile returned. Damn it. "Tossing barbs? As though that is a thing you actually do?" She shook her head, that smile still in place. "I believe you would rather *do* a thing than *say* a thing."

Well, yes. If that meant he'd rather punch a scoundrel than reason with him. Or drink a whiskey rather than talking about how it tasted.

Or kiss a woman who was just beginning to come into her own gloriousness.

The door swung open, and Finan returned along with Bertha, a young woman he'd found when making what he called his Bastard Tour of the villages near his father's estate. Now his estate.

Bertha carried a mop and pail, while Finan held cloths in his hand.

"Oh good. I was hoping there would be a mop," Ana Maria said in satisfaction.

The two stepped between them, Finan getting on his knees to wipe up the water as Bertha mopped.

"How's it going?" Finan asked, his expression and tone almost offensively banal.

Nash grunted.

"Good. As I'd expected," Finan replied, grinning.

"The duke has wrapped my hands and has tested my reaction time," Ana Maria said. "Thus far, he has not shown me how to do anything that would possibly help me in a difficult situation."

Finan raised his eyebrows as he looked pointedly toward Nash.

"It's preparation."

Finan nodded. "Of course. *Preparation*."

Why did that sound like such a loaded word?

"We'll leave you to it, then," Finan said as Bertha put the mop back into the bucket, nodding in satisfaction. "Don't forget the dowager duchess requires you at tea. Dressed appropriately," he added with a wink.

"Thank you." Ana Maria spoke before he had the chance to. Not that *that* was unusual, of course.

"Thank you," he echoed as the two left the room.

"Well. Shall we get back to it?"

"If you're actually going to show me something, then yes." That wicked smile.

He liked it when she smiled like that. Too much. He also liked it when she needled him, which was something he should ponder later, but likely wouldn't.

"Let me show you several things."

Chapter Nine

"Let me show you several things?"

When she repeated his words, she lifted her voice at the end as though it were a question. And she accompanied that question with a raised eyebrow as well as a slight tilt to her mouth. As though she were in on a secret joke.

He swallowed. The Ana Maria with the question and the wicked smile was not the Ana Maria he knew. Had known for most of his life.

This Ana Maria was more like a siren, an alluring maiden whose very expression made it impossible to resist.

He froze in place, not quite sure what to say. What did one say to the sister of one's best friend when one wished that she were anything but a best friend's relative? When one wished she were, in fact, a woman with no personal ties to him that he could fuck with abandon?

Far better to stay frozen. Though one part of him, at least, had not heeded the warning. His cock was stiffening in his trousers, an aching reminder of what he was beginning to believe would end up a full-blown never-realized desire. He couldn't give in to what he was feeling because that would be to betray both his best friend, his next closest best friend, and his own determination not to care for any person of the female persuasion. Her especially.

But he had not counted on what she might want.

"I do want you to show me things," she continued, sounding both hesitant and alluring. An intoxicating combination. She took a deep breath. "I've been thinking about what I want you to show me. And now, for example, I want you to show me how to kiss."

And before he could react, she was leaning up on her toes, putting her hands on his biceps to steady herself, and placing her mouth—her luscious, soft, sweet mouth—on his.

His hands went automatically to her waist, curling his fingers around her body. He felt her shudder, and he froze again, but then she slid her hands down his arms all the way to his fingers and placed her hands on top of his, squeezing them in reassurance.

And then she took her hands away, but immediately put them at his waist, giving a tiny tug so he inched toward her.

Their bodies were nearly—nearly—touching.

And still, her mouth stayed pressed on his. Just there. Not moving, not doing anything.

She wanted to know how to kiss? She was asking for his help? For his instruction?

He'd give it to her.

He pressed his lips more firmly against hers, then slid his tongue across her mouth, making her gasp. Which resulted in her opening for him, and his tongue, which slid in slowly as she shuddered some more.

He kept still for a moment, letting her grow accustomed to it.

All the while his cock was thickening, lengthening, straining against the fabric of his trousers. If their bodies were touching she would be able to feel it, too, and he fought the urge to yank her against him so she could feel what this was doing to him. And he could feel her.

She made a tiny noise in her throat, and then her tongue met his, cautiously sliding against it, the only noise in the room their breaths and the faint whisper of fabric as their fingers clenched the other's body.

Her hands were exploring his back, her palms spread wide against the thin fabric of his shirt.

Thank God he wasn't wearing a jacket.

The only thing standing between his upper body and her fingers was his shirt. A shirt he wore to box in, a shirt that didn't matter at all, he likely had hundreds more just like it in one of his numerous wardrobes.

It took seconds to remove one of his hands from her waist to reach to the neckline of his shirt, yanking it down so it shredded with a satisfying noise. She jumped, breaking the kiss, and he took advantage of that moment to shrug out of the shirt and toss it over his head. Standing absolutely still so she could decide what she wanted to do now.

"Oh," she sighed, and there was so much emotion in that one sound he nearly staggered. Curiosity and desire and passion and a certain hesitancy.

"Do you want to touch me?" he asked. He didn't move. Her lips were redder than before, and her cheeks were flushed. Her dark eyes glowed with a heady sparkle.

He didn't allow his gaze to go lower than her face.

"I do." She stepped forward so they were nearly touching again. "I want to kiss you some more, too. I liked it."

He released his breath and took her hand, placing it in the middle of his chest. Her fingers twitched, and he resisted the urge to hold her hand down. She wasn't a dog to be soothed. She was a woman who needed to know her own mind.

Her fingers tangled in his chest hair, and then began to explore, sliding across the planes of his chest slowly, her eyes tracking her hand's movement.

And then she looked up into his face, that maddeningly sensual smile on her mouth again.

"Your skin feels very different from mine."

He swallowed.

She kept her gaze locked with his, moving her hand across his chest, her palm grazing his nipple, making him gasp. She tilted her head and paused then. "You like that?"

He nodded, since he couldn't speak.

"Hm." She moved her hand to his side, clamping her hand on him and urging him forward with the pressure of her fingers. He came willingly, hoping there would be more of this, but hesitant to do anything that would make her feel obligated.

She raised herself up on tiptoes again, her lips an inch away from his. "I liked what you were doing before. When you were kissing me. Do it again."

And he exhaled in relief, clasping his hands at her waist again, pulling her body into his so he could feel every delicious curve as he placed his mouth on hers.

THIS WAS POSSIBLY the best idea she'd ever had, and that included when she'd chosen magenta silk to cover the wall in her salon.

After all, she was determined to discover things she liked and didn't like, on her own terms, and she definitely knew she wanted to find out if she liked kissing.

Asking *him* to kiss her was perfect; he would not expect anything more, nor would he expose her. He was the only one she could experiment with without consequences.

She should know how to kiss, shouldn't she? Along with being able to punch gentlemen she most definitely did *not* want to kiss. This was just more instruction, albeit completely inappropriate instruction.

She wanted more of that achy feeling that came when he'd—surprisingly—put his tongue in her mouth. She hadn't gotten very many specifics when learning what happened between men and women when she'd been a servant, because the focus then had been what to do to prevent that.

Thank goodness for that, since if she'd known it felt so glorious she might have wanted to start sooner. And then she would have missed having her first kiss with him.

His tongue was in her mouth again, and she nearly groaned at how delicious it felt. He was licking her lips, sucking her tongue gently into his mouth as his fingers tightened on her waist.

Her breasts felt heavy and full, and she gave in to the urge to press them close to his body. The body she'd thought about when she'd imagined—and then seen—him fighting, but hadn't realized was so brutally handsome. His chest was broad, with dark hair curling on the upper part, a narrow trail of hair on the lower part leading lower still, down into his trousers.

Mm. She wanted to follow that trail with her tongue.

She gripped his biceps with her fingers as their tongues sparred. It was hard and clearly strong, and she wondered what it would be like if he picked her up to kiss her.

Should she ask him?

But that would mean stopping kissing, and she didn't want to do that. She never wanted to do that.

Her fingers slid up further, up to his strong shoulders and then dipped onto his chest, her palm tickling from the hair there. Her other hand was at his waist, and she ran her hand around his side to the small of his back. His skin was warm, and smooth, covering planes of muscles she seriously doubted she had. Or if she did have those muscles, they were not nearly as well developed as his.

Just imagining everything he could do with those muscles made her shiver.

She felt a spark of rebellion curl inside her, a dangerous, wicked flame that made her want to do everything that had been previously forbidden.

Even though those things were also currently forbidden, what with her being a single lady of great fortune now. Even *more* forbidden. Because a forgotten servant could do all sorts of things, have all kinds of freedoms, not that Ana Maria had ever taken advantage of that.

Perhaps she should take advantage. Or more advantage. Perhaps this should be the moment when Ana Maria, suddenly thrust into the spotlight, didn't shy away from it, but took it. Did what she wanted to, when she wanted to.

So she did what she wanted to. She moved the hand at the small of his back down onto his arse, which was hard, like the rest of him, curving into the palm of her hand.

And he groaned into her mouth, holding her arms to steady her as she was still up on her tiptoes, their mouths fused together, their bodies pressed together, her whole self feeling lit up by touch.

Touching him, his touching her, their bodies touching.

It was almost too much.

And then, as she was losing herself in his kiss and her roiling emotions, he pulled away suddenly, harshly, his expression aghast.

Making her doubt the wisdom of starting all this in the first place.

She swallowed as he stared at her, his dark eyes seemingly filled with despair and confusion and horror.

No, please, she wanted to say. *Don't look at me that way. Don't ruin this moment by regretting what I've done.*

"I started it," she said. Her voice didn't sound like her voice; it was lower, breathier, and made it sound much more damning than she meant.

"I started it," she said again, lifting her chin and meeting his gaze head-on. Her voice sounded more normal now. "I apologize I took advantage of you—"

At which he snorted, but didn't say anything.

"But I thought I should learn some things, and I have always wondered what it would be like." *With you,* she didn't add. She shrugged. "And I wanted someone I could trust to teach me, someone it wouldn't mean anything with." She paused, trying to slow her beating heart. "And now I know."

She took a deep breath and dragged her gaze away from his, focusing on looking just past his shoulder. Much easier. "I will have a glass of water, and then perhaps we can work on some of my defensive maneuvers? Now that I know what I am in danger of having happen to me."

"It's not—" he began, then shook his head.

She waited, but he didn't continue; instead, he looked grim, raking a hand through his hair. He was still bare to the waist, and she allowed herself a quick peek at all that glorious expanse of male chest.

He really should pose for a statue. But his body wasn't godlike. It was entirely man-made, formed by his own strength. She could see him as Hercules, or Hephaestus, a powerful brute of a man vaunted for his power and perseverance.

"Stop looking at me like that." His voice was ragged.

She started guiltily. "Like—?" she asked.

"Like you want to finish what we started." He shook his head again. "We can't, Ana Maria. There are so many reasons why we can't." He sounded desperate, nearly forlorn, and she felt even worse for luring him into the kiss in the first place.

"It didn't mean anything," she said firmly. "It doesn't have to mean anything, and we won't tell anybody, and we can make certain it doesn't happen again." She spoke in her "well now that's decided" tone, and she hoped it would convince him, even though she knew full well *she* wasn't convinced—it meant something, it meant everything, and it was already breaking her heart that she couldn't let it happen again.

Not because she didn't want it to, of course, but because she cared about him too much to allow him to have that look on his face ever again. To hear that pained tone in his voice.

He still looked pained. "This was my choice, Nash. *Mine.* It might be a poor one, but let me own it." His expression didn't change.

So this wasn't the best idea she'd ever had. It wasn't necessarily the worst—following Lord Brunley into that room might be, or perhaps the time, soon after Sebastian gave her funds for clothing, that she wore a butter-yellow gown that made her look like a wilted sunflower.

But it was among those unfortunate decisions. Even though it was also now going to feature as one of the best memories of her life. *Contradictory oxymoron.*

Drat.

"I THINK WE'VE had enough instruction," Nash said at last. He didn't add anything, didn't move, just stood and waited.

Even though that was the last thing he wanted to do. Which meant it was the only thing he could do.

Kissing her had been—well, he shouldn't think about it. Not now, not when she was still here, alone in the room with him.

His cock throbbed, and he wished he could just give in to what he and his cock wanted, which was to strip her bare and have her on the floor of his training room.

But he could not.

She was the last person in the world he could get involved with. He already knew he liked and cared for her, and now he was realizing he desired her as well. That meant involvement, and involvement meant emotion, and emotion meant passion, which resulted in violence.

You take after me. In every way.

He would not and could not care for anyone with whom he was intimate. It was the quickest way to following in his father's fiststeps, and he would not do that.

She opened her mouth as if to reply, but didn't. He ached to hear what she might have said, even as he dreaded it. But she'd already said the most damning thing aloud, hadn't she? *It didn't mean anything.*

To him, it meant everything. It meant he knew he would never be entirely happy with his life, that his world would continue to be colored in muted shades because he didn't trust he could handle the full, glorious color of things. Like her, whose skin was soft gold, and whose hair was dark chestnut, and whose eyes were like melted chocolate.

"I'll go. Your grandmother requires your presence, after all." She swung her head up, looking defiant. "Does this mean you no longer wish to instruct me at all?"

"No. We'll just—I'll ask Finan in next time."

She narrowed her gaze. "Because I am not to be trusted." It was not a question.

"No, I—" And then he stopped, because of course he couldn't think of what to say. Everything else had changed, but at least that hadn't. He never knew what to say.

She shrugged. "Fine. You can let me know when you can find time in your very busy schedule to teach me what you insist on teaching me." Her tone was derisive, and he flinched in response. She was hurting, clearly, but there was nothing he could do about it.

Or nothing he could do about it that didn't involve resuming their previous activity.

"Oh, and you might want to put a shirt on. It could get cold."

She wasn't just hurting, she was *furious*.

And glorious in her anger—he wanted to bathe in it, to have her unleash all of her emotions onto him so he could feel their intensity, allow himself to feel all of it instead of locking it down or channeling it for a fight.

He couldn't. He couldn't even let her know how he felt, not even a minuscule amount of it, because then she would push at him, forcing him to reveal more and more, to talk, for God's sake, and he could not allow himself to do that.

He was afraid that if he started talking to her, he would never stop.

So he had to ensure their relationship was limited to what he would show her, guiding her to live her life without his protection. Because he knew, as much as he knew he could not be with her, that seeing her with some other man would break him.

So she had to be rendered safe before then.

"I'll send Finan with a note."

He leaned over to pick up his shredded shirt, then walked to the door, only turning back to her when he had his hand on the doorknob. "I'll ask Richardson"—his butler and also his half brother who was at least a decade older than he—"to escort you to your carriage."

She didn't say a word in reply, just kept her narrowed gaze on him as he left the room, closing the door gently behind him.

And then he heard it. A crash, as though something made of glass had been smashed on the floor.

Chapter Ten

Ana Maria stared at the broken shards of glass on the floor, unnerved by her own violence.

Although there was something exhilarating about acting on impulse. Though acting on impulse had gotten her to kiss him, which was both the best and the worst idea ever, so perhaps it was not only exhilarating but also incredibly foolish.

And she did not want Bertha to have to clean it up.

That was the problem with impulsive acts: one always had to clean them up after, whether it was broken glass or a spontaneous kiss.

She stepped carefully over the mess, going to the side of the room where the bellpull was. Before she could ring it, however, the door swung open and Nash's butler—Richardson?—appeared, glancing between her and the floor, his expression remaining completely neutral.

"I will send someone to clean that up, my lady," he said. "If you will follow me, I will take you to your carriage."

"I don't want anyone else to clean—" she began, but stopped as Richardson raised a dark eyebrow. She was skilled in the vernacular of upper servant, so his raised eyebrow was as close to dismissal as she could possibly get.

"Never mind," she conceded, reaching into her pocket for a coin. "Please give this to Bertha. I presume she'll be the one cleaning. It is entirely my fault."

He nodded, tucking the coin into his waistcoat. "This way, my lady."

Once ensconced in the carriage, Ana Maria leaned back against the seat cushions, blowing out an exasperated breath. Why did he have to be such a horrified lummox about it? It was just a kiss, after all.

She'd assumed he was like Sebastian, at least before Sebastian had met and married Ivy; cavalierly dashing about being charming to all sorts of ladies, all of whom knew he wasn't serious about any of them.

But Nash was as far from a dashing cavalier as she was from being a hardened flirt, so it likely made sense.

More drat.

She had been angry with him, but now she was just . . . deflated. Her glorious act of independence had actually hurt someone. *Him.* The last person she wished to hurt.

He'd been hurt in his life so much. Not recently, of course; he seemed to be the one hurting others now, others who (in Nash's view) deserved the hurting.

But back then, when he'd first started coming to the house, he'd been a thin, awkward boy with too dark eyes and a haunted expression. She'd only seen the late duke once, but he had appeared to be a cruel man, one who reveled in castigating servants and his son alike.

And from what Sebastian had let slip, the duke had actually and literally hurt Nash. That explained why he was so quick to hit people himself, although she had to wonder if that made him feel worse because that made him similar to his father, or if he was preventing himself from being treated like his father in the first place.

Just thinking about that sad, lonely boy made her heart hurt.

And she had kissed the adult version of that sad, lonely boy. Was he still sad? She couldn't tell. He seemed relatively pleased with his life, although it was clear he didn't precisely enjoy being an aristocrat, what with his dislike of social events and conventional neckwear.

Was he lonely?

He had Sebastian and Thaddeus as friends, but the former was busy with his new life as a nobody, while the latter was busy with his new life as a duke.

He had Finan, of course. And all of his servants who were also his half siblings. But did he confide in any of those people?

It had felt, that night on the terrace, as though he were confiding in her. She could be his friend. And not a friend whom he also kissed, since clearly that concerned him.

She'd have to ensure she kept her distance while also being close enough to him to invite confidences.

Walking that oxymoronic line, as usual, she thought to herself with a wry chuckle.

HE'D STALKED UP to his bedroom, intent on finding a shirt, and startled one of his younger half sisters who was also a maid into a shriek, causing another one to laugh uncontrollably.

He wasn't certain which reaction he preferred.

Finan was waiting for him, his expression far from the smug one Nash expected. Instead, his friend's face looked pained. He handed a note to Nash, who opened it and immediately scowled.

I am waiting.

It wasn't signed, but of course it could only be from his grandmother. Apparently he was already late. For what, he didn't know. Except that it would be unpleasant. He groaned and got himself not only shirted, but jacketed and cravated as well.

"Damn proper lady," he muttered as he ran his fingers through his hair. He took one last look at himself, grimacing as he saw the nearly proper gentleman looking back at him.

He went downstairs to the salon she'd been

taking tea in, flinging the door open and stepping inside.

"Good afternoon." His grandmother sounded pleased, and he had a trickle of trepidation slide down his spine. His hellcloth felt even tighter.

It became a flood of trepidation when he saw who was in the salon with his grandmother: no fewer than three young ladies. The blonde from the other evening, and two more, all perched on his sofa, three in a row, as if for his inspection.

"I have invited these ladies to take tea with us," his grandmother said. Definitely for his inspection. She narrowed her gaze at him. "Please, Duke, do sit down." It wasn't a request.

He took the chair on the side of the tea table, which meant that his grandmother was on the other side, and the three young ladies were facing him.

All of them looking at him. Just . . . looking.

"This is Lady Felicity Townshend, I believe you two have met before." Lady Felicity's expression was smug. Preening because they had met already?

"It is a pleasure to see you again, Your Grace. I did so enjoy our dance together." She accompanied her words with a shift of her shoulders, a little wriggle that looked rehearsed.

"And this is Miss Victoria Statham, she is the daughter of Mr. James Statham of the Derbyshire Stathams." As though that meant anything to him.

Miss Victoria was a slight brunette with enormous green eyes, making her look a bit like a sprite. He couldn't marry a sprite, for God's sake.

"Lady Beatrice Colm. Lady Beatrice is the granddaughter of a lady I met while making my own debut."

Lady Beatrice looked anxious, her brown eyes darting around the room like she was tracking a housefly's progress. She barely made eye contact with him during the introduction, immediately glancing around, her hands twisting into fists in her lap. Her lips were a thin line, her throat visibly moving as she swallowed.

Was he that terrifying?

Or was she that nervous?

He took a deep breath. He owed it to Lady Beatrice, at least, to try to be gentle during this unexpected visit. "I am pleased you could all come to tea."

His voice was a flat monotone. If he were listening to himself, he would assume that he was most definitely not pleased.

Which would be true, but it also would not be kind.

He needed to make certain he was kind.

He glanced again at Lady Beatrice, who appeared entranced by the drapes.

"I find tea to be a most refreshing beverage."

His grandmother made some sort of inarticulate noise. Proof, then, that they were actually related?

"Can I pour?" she asked.

Lady Felicity bounced in her seat, keeping her gaze fixed on Nash's face. "I would very much like that. I believe, Your Grace, you are also fond of whiskey?"

Was this proper teatime conversation? Was he now supposed to reveal his opinions on all the beverages ranging from milk—nasty, thick beverage that he loathed—to whiskey—his daily reward for not punching anyone who didn't deserve it?

He shrugged. He could do that. Perhaps this polite Society thing wouldn't be too difficult, after all.

"My mother says that any alcohol is the devil's poison," Miss Statham announced.

Nash frowned as he considered her words. "So does that mean it will poison the devil, and is therefore a good thing? Or that the devil makes the poison and people drink it?"

He directed his question at Miss Statham, but the responses he got were from everyone. His grandmother inhaled sharply, Miss Felicity's eyes went wide, and Lady Beatrice uttered an unexpected giggle.

At least she wasn't terrified or nervous any longer.

Miss Statham didn't say a word, but she stood up suddenly, stains of color high on her cheeks. She marched out of the room and slammed the door behind her.

The wood sprite had spirit, it seemed.

"One down, two to go," he heard his grandmother murmur.

"If you will pardon me," Lady Beatrice said. "Thank you for the invitation, Your Grace. Your Grace." She rose, giving the drapes one last look, and scurried out, relief in every line of her body.

Two down, one to go.

"I would love some tea, Your Grace," Lady Felicity said. Her expression was that of a cat who had managed to snag all of the cream.

And he was the cream.

He did not want to be cream. Or to be snagged, for that matter.

This cat would be the most difficult to remove.

"As it happens, I have a meeting with my secretary to review some important things of importance."

His grandmother glared. As she should; it was clear he was making up an excuse as he went along.

"I will see you soon, Your Grace," Lady Felicity said in an overly sweet voice. *Meow.*

Nash had never been more grateful for paperwork in his life.

"WE'VE FOUND TWO more," Robert Carstairs, his secretary, said as he held a piece of paper out to Nash, who was seated at his desk.

"My father was certainly busy. And quite fertile, apparently." Nash reviewed the names and location of his recently found siblings. They were far north, likely conceived when the late duke went to visit his hunting box in Scotland.

"I've sent them the usual correspondence, asking if they need assistance or positions. One of them sent back a note asking for assurance that you are nothing like our father. The other one replied that she would be interested in a position and that she has worked as a governess."

"I hope you told her we don't have any children here."

"I thought perhaps you might speak with the ladies at the Society for Poor and Unfortunate Children? You've given them quite a bit of money in the past few years."

"Huh. I have?"

Robert nodded. "It was on the recommendation of Lady Ana Maria. I believe she takes an interest there as well."

Of course she did. Wanting to help children who were born into bad situations, like she was.

"Can you write them, then?"

"I already have, and they say they can always use more hands, but that they cannot afford to pay her salary."

Nash waved the paper. "So take care of that as well. And write that other one back and let her know I am nothing like my father." At least he hoped so, even though he knew he was wrong.

"I have already done that also. And I've done something else," he began, his expression oddly hesitant.

"What is it?"

Robert took a deep breath before speaking. "I've located your mother."

Nash inhaled sharply before advancing on Robert, his hands curled into fists. "What?"

Robert didn't move back, and the two men stood chest to chest, Nash's gaze locked on his secretary's.

Robert was one of the first of his father's bastards Nash had discovered after their father had died. He'd been working as a clerk in a London shipping office, but had leaped at the chance to work for Nash, especially since it meant he could work on finding more of the duke's offspring.

Thus far, Robert had found no fewer than a dozen—fourteen with these two new finds—and Nash had helped as many of them who wanted it, employing eight of them in his town house and sending regular funds to some of the others.

"I asked you to find our siblings," Nash said. "Not my mother." He felt the red mist of his anger rise in his vision. *Push it down, don't let it take over, never unleash it unless the person deserves it.*

Robert did not deserve it.

He hated the inexorable feeling of violence—he was usually able to deter it with a fight fueled by justice, or some whiskey, but there were other times when the anger overwhelmed him, and he could not control himself.

Like his father. No matter what he did, no matter how many siblings he found, no matter how many wrongs he righted, he always returned to his father's behavior.

You take after me. In every way.

No, he didn't. He *couldn't.*

He stared at Robert for another long moment, his half brother meeting his gaze squarely, no hint of fear in his eyes. Then Nash reached around Robert to snatch some sort of table decoration—a vase, a water pitcher, whatever it was—and raised it over his head, preparing to smash it against the wall.

Only to lower it slowly, the anger easing out of him as he recalled Robert's expression—not as though Nash were about to punch him in the jaw, but as though he knew Nash's turmoil, but also knew Nash wouldn't hurt him.

What had she said? *This was my choice, Nash.* He could choose to be himself, not his father. Couldn't he?

He placed the vase back down on the table, Robert watching his movements. For a moment, Nash allowed himself to think about what would have happened if he had smashed the vase, after all: the satisfying noise of the crash against the wall, the shards of glass falling to the carpet, the final and utter destruction of something that could never be brought back.

There was something intoxicating about that finality, about completing an action that could never be undone. But that way was a dangerous, inevitable path toward who he could not be, not without loathing himself and having everyone in his vicinity—not just people who believed his reputation—know he was as dangerous as they had heard.

What if she believed he was as dangerous as his reputation? Worse, what if she saw him engage in violence when it wasn't justified? When her safety wasn't at risk?

He didn't think he could live with himself. Which just meant he had to keep his temper tethered. He had to choose to be different.

"There you are. We must speak. Now."

His grandmother's peremptory tone matched her commanding expression. She stood at the doorway to his office, her lady's maid just behind her, both ladies radiating disapproval.

Of course.

He wished he could tell her that at least he hadn't broken the vase, but then that would be admitting he shared more of his father's tendencies than she likely knew.

"Pardon me, Your Grace," Robert said, nodding as he walked toward the door, stepping aside to let the dowager duchess in.

"Thank you," Nash called, hoping Robert would know he was thanking him for all of it—for standing strong against Nash's violence, for finding Nash's mother. For seeming to trust Nash when he didn't trust himself.

His grandmother walked slowly into the room, her lady's maid at her elbow.

"Please sit down," he said, pulling a chair out for her.

He waited as she lowered herself into her chair, pointedly ignoring his outstretched hand. Her lady's maid positioned herself in her usual place behind the dowager duchess.

"Those three were the top three on the list." His grandmother sniffed as she straightened herself even more in her chair. "And now only Lady Felicity is a possible candidate."

"Isn't it saving time to know right away?" It seemed only practical to Nash; besides which, now he wouldn't have to dance with two of the three.

"That is not the point. I know your mother left when you were young, but I would have thought your father"—never saying "my son," which showed the depths of her antipathy toward him—"would have obtained proper training for you."

Nash shook his head slowly, as though regretful. Which he most definitely was not. Being ignored by his father was a blessing. "The late duke was intent on only a few things, and obtaining proper training for me was not one of them." Instead, he'd been free to roam around the country, tagging along with Sebastian and Thaddeus on their adventures. Occasionally Ana Maria would join, when she could escape unnoticed by Sebastian's mother.

"I will have to instruct you on proper behavior,"

the dowager duchess announced. Her lady's maid nodded her agreement.

Nash gripped the arms of his chair, willing himself not to shout at both of them. "There is no need."

"There certainly is a need. Unless you can think of someone else you can ask?" She raised an accusing finger at him. "And don't think you can say you're going to learn and then just not. I will be able to tell."

Thoughts of asking Ana Maria for this instruction—in exchange for self-defense lessons—crossed his mind, but he couldn't risk spending even more time with her. The self-defense lessons were of crucial importance, whereas his learning how to navigate polite Society without alienating everyone was most definitely not.

"Fine. You can do it," he said shortly.

She looked surprised—at his capitulation? But she didn't say anything, just nodded in satisfaction.

"We will begin tomorrow," she said as she rose from the chair. He darted around his desk to help her, and this time, she accepted his assistance, not waiting for her lady's maid. "Right now, I am going to have a nap. I will need to be well rested." She gave him one last assessing look, then she and her lady's maid walked out the door, leaving him to collapse in his chair, shaking his head in bewilderment.

This getting married and siring an heir was

a lot harder than just asking someone to marry and then having sex.

If he had known it would be this difficult—but no, he would still do it. Anyone who depended on the duke's estate was in jeopardy if he didn't.

It was a burden, but it was his burden, and he needed to shoulder it.

SHE HAD KISSED him. And he had kissed her back. They had kissed.

There was so much kissing.

And then—nothing.

Did she regret it? No, not the kiss itself, but she did regret that he felt so torn about it, even though during it he had certainly seemed to feel nothing but pleasure.

But then again, how would she know? Perhaps the pleasure he'd seemed to exhibit was just a tiny portion of what was possible, kiss-wise.

How would she ever know, though, if she never got the chance to kiss him again?

Because she did not want to kiss anybody else.

The carriage pulled up to the house as her mind was whirling, and Ana Maria leaned forward to glance out the window, noting with surprise that Miss Octavia appeared to be on the doorstep.

A welcome distraction, but also a prying friend who might see that Something had Happened. And that Thoughts were being Thought.

She quickly tried to smooth her expression so Octavia wouldn't suspect anything.

"Good afternoon!" Ana Maria called as the footman assisted her friend out of the carriage.

Octavia waved in response, walking up the stone steps to the front door.

"It is lovely and unexpected to see—" she began.

"What have you been up to?" Octavia interrupted, her eyes wide. "Don't waste time being a polite hostess, we have to talk."

Well. Perhaps she should make certain never to game in Octavia's club, since it was clear her emotions were writ large on her face. Or perhaps Octavia just had a keen sense for when her friends were doing things that were not expected.

"I saw that same look on Ivy's face when your brother came to live with us," Octavia said in a whisper as Fletchfield opened the door for them.

"Tea in my salon, please," Ana Maria said in a commanding tone. She hoped nobody had overheard Octavia's words—she wouldn't want her former fellow servants to ask her about it, much less tell Thaddeus about it.

She took Octavia's arm, guiding the younger woman down the hall, shutting the door firmly behind them as they entered.

As always, Ana Maria couldn't suppress a sigh of satisfaction at how gorgeous the room was. She couldn't wait for her fabrics to arrive so she could begin redoing her bedroom. That reminded her—they should arrive today, she would have to check with Fletchfield if they had already come.

"Please have a seat, tea should be here soon."

Miss Octavia sat, pulling her chair closer to Ana Maria's. "I came over here to discuss the fabrics we bought, and if you could assist me some more, but that can wait. Where were you? Why is your face on fire?"

Ana Maria put her hand to her cheek. "Is it?" It didn't feel warm.

"Your cheeks are flushed, plus you look—how do I put this?—more disheveled than usual."

"Oh that! I was taking self-defense lessons from the Duke of Malvern." She tried to keep her voice neutral.

But of course Octavia wouldn't be put off.

"Aha! The Dangerous Duke! And he is teaching you self-defense? That is certainly intriguing."

Ana Maria decided to concede. "And I kissed him." It would be far easier to just tell her friend now rather than have her question her until Ana Maria was forced to reveal the truth.

Plus she didn't like to lie. And with the exception of Jane, who was older and nearly settled with one of the grooms, she'd never had a female confidante before. It felt . . . fun to be able to discuss just what had happened with a lively friend.

Octavia's wide eyes got even wider. "You did not!"

Ana Maria laughed at her friend's astonishment. "I assure you, I did. And it was quite pleasant," she said, "until it was not."

Octavia placed both hands on Ana Maria's

hands, which were clasped in her lap. "You have to tell me everything. From the start."

"What the hell has gotten into you?" Finan asked as Nash paced his bedroom.

Ana Maria, that kiss, Robert's finding my mother, my grandmother, Lady Felicity. Not to mention the devil's poison and fascinating drapes.

Nash shook his head, continuing to pace. He'd tossed his jacket and cravat off as soon as he'd come in the room, and now even his shirt felt constraining. *Oh, and you might want to put a shirt on. It could get cold.*

He growled.

"Nash." Finan put his hand on Nash's arm as he spoke. Nash shrugged it off, whirling on his friend.

Finan held his hands up in surrender. "You can hit me, if you want, but you'll have to explain to your staff why there's blood on this fancy carpet."

Nash froze. "I'm sorry," he said, shaking his head. "I'm not myself today."

"Seems to me you're more yourself than you've been in a while." Finan sat in the large chair at the side of the bed, the one that Nash supposed was for dukes who wanted to read before bed.

Not that he was one of those dukes. He only sat in that chair to put on his boots.

"What do you mean, 'more myself'?" Nash said, his tone suspicious.

Finan made himself more comfortable, sprawling against the back of the chair and stretching his legs out. Nash resisted the urge to upend the chair and spill Finan onto the floor.

Mostly because the chair was heavy, and Finan was small, but packed with muscle.

Finan pointed a finger at Nash. "You seem as though you're waking up from some sort of dream."

"To a nightmare," Nash shot back. Finan raised his eyebrows in question.

"I've got to get married, I've chased away all but one of the potential ladies, and I nearly smashed a vase because of something Robert said."

Finan smirked. "Is that all? At least you didn't smash the vase on Robert's head. That's progress, for you."

Nash grunted in response.

"See, that's why I say you're different," Finan continued. "You wouldn't have thought twice about any of that before. You're not just drinking and brawling anymore. Mebbe it's because the dowager duchess is here to drag you into propriety, or because you're spending time with that lady who is most definitely not your sister—"

"Speaking of which, you're going to have to attend the training sessions." Why hadn't he thought it through before he spoke? "Because, uh, I might need to demonstrate, and I don't want to hurt her."

Which was a true statement in so many ways.

"Of course it's because you need me for a demonstration." Finan's tone was skeptical. "Not because you're so busy reminding yourself she's nearly a sister."

"Shut up."

Finan raised an eyebrow, giving Nash a belligerent stare, but didn't say anything.

Perhaps he should have just punched him. It would have taken less time, and fewer words. But he had chosen not to. That was progress—wasn't it?

"AND HE SAID he doesn't want it to happen again. Do you believe him?" Octavia's tone indicated she was entirely doubtful.

"It doesn't matter if I do or I don't—he seemed so distraught after, I felt terrible. I wonder how rakes do it. Tamper with people's feelings like that."

"Most rakes aren't sensitive young ladies kissing inarticulate large dukes," Octavia replied drily.

"But even if I wanted to"—*which I absolutely do, of course, and we both know that*—"he would get all fussed up about it."

"I think you'd enjoy seeing him all fussed up—" Octavia began, only to be interrupted by the sound of the door opening. Both ladies turned to look.

"My lady?"

Fletchfield appeared in the doorway, a gleeful-looking Jane right behind him.

"Your delivery is here," Jane said in an excited voice. Fletchfield gave her a quelling look.

"And more flowers have arrived," Fletchfield said. "There is no more room in the salon." He sounded disapproving. Well, so was she—she did love flowers, but there was more to courtship than posies. Thus far, only Lord Brunley had actually made an offer, and his had been entirely wrong.

"Should I put them in—?" Fletchfield began.

"Wherever you want, it doesn't matter." Ana Maria waved her hand in dismissal as she spoke. "But my fabrics are here! Excellent!"

Not only would she be able to make plans for her purchases, she would also be able to get out of this difficult conversation. "Let's go look," Ana Maria said to Octavia.

"We'll talk about all this later," Octavia warned.

Ana Maria ignored her.

But she knew it would only be for so long.

And she would indeed like to see him all fussed up. But she would die before revealing that to anyone but herself.

Chapter Eleven

"This one would be quite good for a wall," Ana Maria said, unspooling some of the fabric from the bolt. "It's durable and thick, but not so I think it won't drape nicely."

The two ladies and Jane were back in Ana Maria's salon, where the fabrics she'd purchased were spread on the carpet, the lush colors creating a nearly blinding assault on the eyes. Purples warred with oranges, greens with fuchsias, while the room itself added its own flavor to the mix with its vibrant reds and pinks.

In other words, Ana Maria loved it.

"If you say so," Octavia said in a bored tone. She'd initially been enthusiastic, but more recently had begun to complain of a headache caused, she said, "by all of this patterned exuberance."

Ana Maria just laughed and rang for more tea.

"Why don't you just come and make the decisions for me?" Octavia said. "It is not as though I have an opinion that would go against yours—I appreciate your aesthetic, even if it makes me faintly nauseated."

"Thank you?" Ana Maria replied as Jane smothered a snort.

"And I do think the club needs to have a dash of panache."

"This is more than just a dash," Jane opined. Ana Maria glanced sharply at her, but the other woman's expression was neutral.

"So you can do it, and I'll pay you for it, just as I would any other contract worker. I'll have to ask Henry what fees are standard."

"Henry?" Ana Maria asked. Asking a banal question to deal with the fact that her heart just leaped into her throat with Octavia's casual suggestion.

It was what she had told Jane she wanted to do. And here Octavia was just—offering it to her. Without hesitation.

"The bookkeeper. He also works to toss out unpleasant patrons—he was a boxer before working for us—but he is mostly our bookkeeper."

"Extraordinary to have two such disparate skills in one individual," Ana Maria said.

"Not so disparate—a bookkeeper is precise in calculations, and a boxer has to determine precisely where to launch a blow that will take care of his—or her," Octavia said with a grin, "opponent. Plus it's being able to add up one's strengths and weaknesses—like income in and income out—to figure out if the end result is a net gain."

Ana Maria laughed in response, but then began to think about what her friend had said. "So is it your belief that all things can be calculated so precisely? Figuring out if there is a net gain, even if there are some weaknesses along the way?"

Octavia raised a mischievous eyebrow. "Of course I do. Especially when it comes to achieving one's goals. You have to invest something before you get your return on investment, after all."

"I have no idea what you two are discussing," Jane interjected, "but if it ends up with Lady Ana Maria getting something she wants, I think it is worth further pursuit." Jane nodded firmly as she spoke, making Ana Maria keenly aware of how many champions she had that she hadn't even been aware of.

Octavia looked knowingly at Ana Maria, whose cheeks started to heat under her friend's pointed expression. *Worth further pursuit.* So instead of feeling mortified by today's events, she should review them, and calculate whether or not she wished them to happen again.

Not that she would force her decision on Nash, of course; that would be wrong. But she could talk it out with him. If he truly did not want to teach her those kinds of things in addition to self-defense, perhaps he would assist her in finding someone who would.

And then there was the net gain Octavia herself had just offered.

"Do you really mean it?" Ana Maria asked. Octavia looked confused. "About the decorating of the club, would you trust me to handle it entirely by myself?"

Octavia's expression cleared. "Yes, absolutely. Don't tell me you hadn't thought of it yourself."

"She had." Jane interrupted before Ana Maria could find the words. "She said she'd like to have a hand in decorating things, that she wants to be useful. Not like before, mind, she's too much of a grand lady for that." She accompanied her words with a quelling look toward Ana Maria, as though reminding her that yes, she was a grand lady, and Ana Maria had to be fine with that. "So your suggestion isn't one she hasn't thought of herself."

Octavia looked bemused, which made Ana Maria want to laugh again, even though she also wanted to shake Jane. Two warring impulses, as suited her contrariness.

Wanting to kiss him while also wanting to punch him.

Though since the "him" in question was Nash, she wasn't certain those were contradictions; she thought that Sebastian and Thaddeus might think the same, albeit replacing the kissing part with a "drink alcoholic beverages and get ribald with one another" part.

Nash was, as she well knew, worthy of both extreme loyalty and utter frustration.

But Octavia was speaking. It wasn't the time to be thinking of Nash and his kisses and his fists.

Even though that seemed like all she could think about lately.

"And we'll draw up a contract, and your fees, and your expenses," Octavia was saying. "Henry will keep an accounting of what purchases you make, and we'll need to agree on that amount, since it won't do the club any good if we spend too much on its decoration. People really only want to gamble in a pleasant place that looks nothing like their own surroundings. At least in my experience." She glanced around Ana Maria's salon. "Well, that is, most people's surroundings don't look like this." She accompanied her words with a delighted smile, turning what could have been understood as an insult into something quite the opposite.

Making Ana Maria feel valued for her differences as opposed to being vilified for them. Or her inability to hide the difference of her birth, being made to atone for her audacity in being born at all, since she wasn't the result of the second duchess's marriage.

That constant awareness of not being wanted had stayed with her, despite her attempts to fit in. To belong.

Because, ultimately, she didn't belong. Not belowstairs as a scullery maid, and definitely not above, dreaming only of one's future husband and how many gowns one could own.

Though she did admit to enjoying the gowns.

If she hadn't known what it was like on the other side, however, she wouldn't have gained the valuable perspective of what life was like for all sorts of people.

That oxymoron thing again—both belonging and not. Of two worlds while not being anchored in either one.

"Ana Maria?"

"My lady?"

Octavia's and Jane's voices came to her through the fog of her thoughts, and she shook herself free, of her own warring emotions when it came to herself and to him.

She did know one thing for certain. She was going to take Octavia's commission and make herself—if nobody else—proud.

"What is it?" she asked, summoning the bland smile that had served her so well for all the years spent dealing with the duchess.

Only Octavia and Jane both frowned in response, and her smile faded, replaced by her own frown.

"You looked odd," Octavia said bluntly. "But you're fine now. Will you do it? Starting soon?"

Now Ana Maria's smile was warm and genuine. "Yes. If you want me—and even if you didn't—I will do it."

"Excellent," Octavia replied, her own mouth curling up into a pleased smile. "And then we will tackle your other project."

Ana Maria swept her hand out to knock her teacup over before Jane could follow up her curious look with a question.

"What is the occasion?" Sebastian asked, drawing his watch from his pocket.

Nash put his palm over the watch face. "No occasion. And no consulting your watch. I know you are in love, but you have to ignore all that just for one evening."

The two, along with Thaddeus, were in Nash's library making preparations to go out. The library was Nash's refuge, a room he'd kept determinedly closed to anyone who wanted him to make a decision. Or not drink and then punch someone.

It had been too long, what with Sebastian getting married, Thaddeus getting the dukedom, and Nash having to go be social. Nash had woken up with an urgent desire to return to the time when he could be out all night drinking and possibly brawling without any consequences.

Of course there would be consequences, he knew that, but he would ignore them until tomorrow.

"Miss Ivy's?" Thaddeus said, taking a sip of his whiskey. Thaddeus sat on Nash's sofa, the one specially tailored to fit Nash's frame. Thaddeus was nearly as tall as Nash, but he didn't take advantage of the sofa's specifications to lounge; of course not, he was a former military man who would be horrified to find himself *lounging*.

Nash wondered what it would take to make Thaddeus lose his reserve.

Nash shook his head. "No, Sebastian would spend all the time mooning about his wife."

"I would not!" Sebastian exclaimed.

Nash and Thaddeus both gave him pointed looks, at which point he held his hands up in surrender.

"We could just stay here," Nash said, glancing around the room.

"Less chance for you to get into a fight. Unless you take umbrage with something Seb says," Thaddeus remarked. "And it has been too long, I feel the need to forget about any kind of responsibility tonight." He downed his whiskey, pouring himself another draft.

Nash and Sebastian both stared at him. Thaddeus was the most moderate of them, usually.

"Being a duke is a vast amount of responsibility," Nash said. "All that having to make decisions, and provide for people—"

"Not every duke feels the need to provide for people as you do," Sebastian said. He raised his glass toward Nash. "I salute your good deeds, even though you try to hide them."

Nash felt an unaccustomed blush reach his cheeks. "I don't know what you're talking about." He dashed some more whiskey into his glass, tipping it up and drinking most of it down in one big gulp.

Thaddeus made a noise of disbelief. "You

cannot think we haven't seen. Not only do you employ all of your half siblings, but you have an open hand for anyone who needs it." Sebastian nodded in agreement.

"Shut up," Nash growled. "This is supposed to be a night of ruckus and carousing, not of recounting things I've done." He finished his glass. "A night where we spend time together as we used to, unencumbered—" *By responsibility, by grandmothers, by emotion.*

Sebastian made a motion to withdraw his pocket watch again, only to pause at Nash's accusing stare. "Fine. Is it hard to believe I want to spend time with my wife?"

Nash felt an unaccustomed pang of envy at Sebastian's fond tone. What would it be like to want to spend time with a wife?

The future he was planning for himself—that he knew was the only future he could allow—was the opposite of that. He wanted to find someone not to care for.

Damn it. There wasn't enough whiskey in the house, let alone the world, to drown out the ache in his chest when he thought about it. But as his friends had noticed, he owned his responsibilities, and he would have to ensure the title didn't fall into the wrong hands.

"Let's go to one of those clubs you insisted I join," Nash said abruptly, addressing Sebastian.

"They won't let me in any longer, now that I'm not one of you lot."

"But you are with us," Thaddeus replied, unconsciously assuming a military posture.

"The bastard scapegrace who works at a gambling house?" Sebastian said in a dubious tone.

"The *former* scapegrace. You're still a bastard, but at least you're settled down," Nash replied.

Sebastian shrugged. "Fine. And this way, if they argue about letting me in, you can begin to brawl, which I know you're eager to do anyway. How long has it been since you've been in a fight?" He paused as he thought. "It must be at least a month. That is longer than you've ever gone, isn't it?"

Right. They didn't know about his punching Lord Brunley. Or the would-be assailant at the docks. And he wouldn't tell them, since she'd said she could handle both situations on her own. Even though he knew she couldn't have. He especially didn't want any kind of scandal to erupt out of the Brunley incident—that would be the worst possible outcome.

"Mmph," he grunted in agreement.

"To the club, then," Thaddeus said, getting up from the sofa and placing his glass on the table.

THAT WAS WHAT he had been longing for, Nash thought fuzzily. He stood on wobbly legs in his bedroom removing his clothing, shedding them where he stood.

Usually Finan would be assisting him, but he'd told him to get some sleep, since he didn't know what time he'd be home.

His knuckles were satisfyingly bruised, thanks to some earl's heir taking offense at Sebastian being at the club. The gentleman hadn't put up much of a fight, and had apologized, but at least there had been *some* punching. Justified punching.

And he hadn't thought about what he had to do, or her, or about his duties for nearly three hours.

But now he was home, rapidly getting naked, and it would all return tomorrow.

And, he had to admit, it wasn't as satisfying as it was just a few months ago. Perhaps he was changing, as Finan had said. Making the choice to be a different person, as she was choosing who she would be.

But that was a thought for tomorrow also.

Right now he was just going to crawl into his bed and sleep, knowing he had done all he could that evening to return to who he used to be. Even though he knew, and was nearly grateful, that that person no longer existed.

"Nash is over there," Thaddeus said as they entered the ballroom. As though she hadn't immediately searched for him and knew precisely where he was.

Damn it.

Nash stood at the edge of the room, his grandmother seated beside him, her mouth pressed into a disapproving line. At least Ana Maria supposed it was disapproval; the Carlyles, who were giving the party that evening, were renowned for their excellent hospitality, so she didn't think it had anything to do with the food and beverage.

As if on cue, a footman passed by carrying a tray of what looked to be the tiniest of finger sandwiches—pinkie sandwiches, actually—with a festive topping of a few pieces of green something and an olive.

She nodded when the footman met her gaze, and he handed her one of the treats on top of a small square of fabric. Thaddeus picked two of them up, popping one into his mouth and chewing efficiently. Of course.

The sandwich was even more delicious than it appeared—the bread was warm, as though it had just come from the oven, and the filling was a pâté with a fig spread.

"Oh, that's good," she said, surreptitiously sticking her finger in her mouth to catch a drop of the spread.

She met his gaze across the room, and her eyes widened at the intensity she saw there. A hunger, as though she was a delicious sandwich herself, and he was starving.

Was he starving?

And if he was, why wouldn't he feast? It wasn't as though there was any pretense between them. She'd laid it all out for him. She'd said it wouldn't mean anything. That he'd be helping her.

Except the small fact that she had thought about him in a certain way for a very long time and she'd never admitted it to anyone, not even herself.

So maybe there was pretense. But there didn't have to be.

"I'll go say hello to Nash and his grandmother," Ana Maria said, wishing she didn't sound so out of breath. So breathless.

"Excellent. I will be in the gaming room."

Ana Maria looked at Thaddeus in surprise.

"Not gaming, of course. But I find the people I most wish to speak to are most often to be found in the gaming room. It makes logical sense. They are good at calculating risk, and so they like to prove their own competency."

Ana Maria nodded, not quite understanding, but not needing to. Thaddeus did not like to dance at parties, didn't seem to like parties very much in general, so it was to be expected he'd find the least party-like atmosphere possible.

Heaven help it when—or if—he fell in love. He'd have to deal with all sorts of illogical emotions.

"Well," she said, suppressing a grin, "I will meet up with you later."

"Yes."

She turned to find the quickest way to reach him, still aware of his gaze on her, a gaze that hadn't seemed to waver when she was speaking to Thaddeus. No wonder other young ladies hadn't yet discovered his charm; he was thoroughly and entirely focused on her, which would dissuade anybody who even thought about deepening an acquaintanceship.

Perhaps that was more the problem than his general gruntiness.

She paused, wondering if she should share her insight with Thaddeus when a sharp, and not altogether altruistic, emotion bubbled up inside. If he was focused on her, then he'd be . . . focused on her.

Which was a pleasant thought. Or more than pleasant, actually. A surge of something she thought might be desire, might even be passion, coursed through her, making her feel warmer than she already was.

Oh dear.

"Good evening, my lady."

Lord Brunley stood in front of her, making her draw up abruptly. He didn't look at all as though their last encounter had included a fire poker, a large, brutish duke, and the spillage of what she presumed was excellent alcohol.

He looked—smug. As though she should be honored by his condescension.

Really. Were all men this clueless, or was it just her luck to know the especially clueless ones?

Whatever the answer was, it was not a good answer.

"Good evening, my lord. If you will excuse me—?" She hated that her voice rose up at the end, as if she were asking his permission.

"I spoke with your cousin, the Duke of Hasford, and he seemed to regard my courting you as a good thing."

Lord Brunley was clueless when dealing with people of both genders. Very egalitarian of him.

"And I would like to begin again, if I may. I realize I might have seemed overly—"

"Aggressive?" Ana Maria blurted.

He looked annoyed. Which was better than smug, so she'd take it.

"Infatuated, I was going to say." He frowned, giving her a sharp look of disapproval.

Fine. She'd take his disapproval and fling it back at him, coating him as thoroughly with it as she'd been coated with the spilled brandy.

"Might I ask for the honor of a dance?" He was already reaching for the dance card that dangled from her wrist.

She couldn't refuse, not without causing a scene. Why did polite Society have to be so . . . polite all the time?

She allowed him to scribble his name on one of the lines, hoping that particular dance wouldn't be a waltz.

Her eyes found Nash again as she recalled waltzing with him the same night as the poker incident. How he looked at her, as though he were really seeing her for the first time.

The way he moved, strong and assured, as though he knew his body well and knew what it was capable of.

And now the room seemed even hotter.

"If you will excuse me," Ana Maria said, this time not waiting for Brunley to respond.

She moved toward Nash, feeling how her breath was quickening, and how her body felt tight in her evening gown.

And how his gaze tracked her as she made her way through the crowd.

NASH TRIED TO stop looking at her.

But he wasn't very good at denying himself anything—when had he ever needed to?

He was a duke, after all. Dukes did not deny themselves. Even he, who wasn't a particularly ducal duke, wasn't told no, either by himself or anyone else.

But he'd told her no.

A decision that had him in agony. He wanted to kiss her again, do more than that, find out how responsive she'd be under his touch, share her laughter. Touch her golden skin.

But he couldn't care for her—not more than he did already—and kissing her, and more, would intensify whatever feelings he already had.

"That duke's cousin is coming toward us," his grandmother remarked.

He nearly snapped at her that he already knew, but the dowager duchess had no idea of his current obsession. Or any of his past obsessions, honestly.

She didn't know him. All she knew was that he

was hopefully less bad than his father, which he had to prove by marrying and fathering an heir.

He could do this.

"I don't understand why she isn't under consideration," the dowager duchess continued. "You are already acquainted with her, she doesn't seem to dislike you, and she has good breeding, even if her brother turned out not to be the duke, after all."

Excellent recommendation for a potential spouse: familiarity with one another, an absence of loathing, and a family that was listed in *Debrett's*.

No wonder he found most of what was supposed to be his world so unexciting, if this was how they chose their marriage partners.

But she was nearly here. He clamped his jaw, willing himself not to let one speck of his desire for her emerge. That wouldn't be fair to her, especially since she had kissed him. If it then seemed he was interested, despite his protestations from earlier in the day? And then rebuffed her again?

He'd be no better than those silly debutantes who blew hot and cold, making their potential suitors frantic with confusion.

Not that he'd experienced that himself; he hadn't gotten close enough to any of those silly debutantes to gauge their emotional weather forecast.

Which was an odd way to put it.

And that kind of thinking was likely also why

he was currently unattached, with no prospects for changing that. Except for the one woman he'd explicitly told no.

Excellent planning, Nash, he thought. If he could, he'd take himself to his boxing room and slap himself silly.

"Good evening, Na—Your Grace," she said. Her cheeks were a delicious-looking pink, and her eyes sparkled. She glanced over toward his grandmother. "And good evening to you, Your Grace."

His grandmother inclined her head very slightly. As always, subtly reminding anyone who came into her orbit that she was far better than they were. At least in her own mind.

"Good evening, my lady," Nash said. His voice sounded rough, and he cleared his throat in a likely futile attempt to sound more like the other gentlemen in the room. Gentlemen who knew what to say and when to say it, who didn't have crises of conscience when lovely young women they'd known all their lives suddenly kissed them.

It was unfortunate it was Sebastian's sister he had kissed, because otherwise he could ask his much more experienced friend just what to do in this situation. But it was his best friend's older sister, and he could not let anyone know how he truly felt.

"Lady Ana Maria is addressing you, Your Grace."

He heard his grandmother's words as though through a fog, a fog that was curvaceous and laughing, that made him want to feel things.

Which was truly dangerous. That kind of feeling fog could also make him feel far too much, which would inevitably lead to passion and desire and other darker emotions. Things like jealousy and lust and longing.

"Yes, my apologies, my lady." He tried to use the tone his secretary, Robert, employed when he was letting Nash know he disapproved of something without actually saying it.

Her sparkling gaze dimmed for a moment, and he felt the rush of another intense emotion—self-loathing. Why couldn't he do this without hurting the people he loved?

No. No, he didn't love her. He cared for her, as the sister of his best friend, as a person he had known his entire life. He didn't love her.

He couldn't.

Because if he did, he would hurt her.

"I was remarking that I have a few open spots on my dance card," Ana Maria said. She raised the card in question, and he noticed the only claimed dance was with Lord Brunley.

He heard a noise, and realized it was a growl. Coming from him.

She raised an eyebrow. "So from that, I understand that you would like to claim a dance?"

His grandmother cleared her throat in a meaningful way.

But damned if he could figure out the meaning. Did she want him to dance with Ana Maria because then he would be seen dancing, and therefore, possibly, more appealing to the ladies he would dare to court? Or did she want him to gently reject Ana Maria, because then it might be misconstrued that they were courting, and therefore he was not an eligible candidate for the ladies he would dare to court?

Yes, it was entirely ironic that he wished she had just spoken instead of making a noise. Ironic and also aggravating.

But Ana Maria was still looking up at him, a challenging expression on her face.

He took the small pencil she held in her other hand and scribbled his name next to the supper dance. It would mean spending more time with her than just the usual dance would require, but it would also mean that there was no possibility she would get stuck with some lord for all that time who was only hungry for her dowry and didn't appreciate the woman attached to all that money.

"Thank you, Nash," she murmured, taking the pencil back from him. She glanced behind him to where his grandmother sat. "Pardon me, Your Grace, I am going to find my cousin, the duke." She returned her gaze to Nash. "I am looking forward to our dance. You should ask some other ladies to dance also, I am certain they would appreciate it."

But her words didn't match her expression, and now he couldn't even figure out what words meant, not when the person speaking had such a different look on their face than what one would have expected.

"Uh, yes," he said, feeling more and more like an idiot.

An idiot who was most definitely not in love with anybody and whose only strong emotions were for fisticuffs and whiskey.

Keep telling yourself that, a voice said in his head.

He gritted his teeth as she walked away, his eyes unable to keep from following the gentle sway of her hips.

"It is unfortunate you have deemed her not suitable," his grandmother said in an acerbic tone. "Because she is the only lady I have seen you speak with that seemed to understand you."

And that's what made her so dangerous.

Chapter Twelve

Ana Maria focused on keeping her posture straight and her expression cool, as though she had not just spoken with the person whose very existence was making her feel all sorts of ways all at the same time.

Perhaps her efforts would mean that other ladies saw Nash as a viable suitor, not an enormous grunting lummox who stood in the corner at parties and glowered.

And if it then meant he asked one of those now-appreciative ladies to marry him? She'd have to be pleased at the outcome, because it would mean someone would be happy.

Just not her.

"Ana Maria!"

She turned as she heard her name called, her face breaking out into an enormous smile when she saw who it was—her sister-in-law, formerly Miss Ivy, who still owned the club named after her. Now she was Mrs. Sebastian de Silva, and she and Ana Maria's brother lived in a house down the street from the club, while Ivy's sister

Octavia had taken over all the rooms in the back of the club.

"I didn't know you would be here," Ana Maria said, clasping both Ivy's hands in hers. "Is Sebastian here, too?"

Ivy shook her head. "No, he is managing the club this evening. Octavia is off doing something highly secretive," she said, casting her gaze upward in aggravation, "and I came because Lady Carlyle is a very good customer, and she invited me. I did not want to refuse, especially since I was certain I would see you."

"Let's go sit on the terrace for a moment. It has been far too long since we've seen one another." Because she and Ana Maria's brother were spending most of their time alone together lately, leaving Octavia to manage the club and Sebastian's dogs.

Ivy nodded, taking Ana Maria's arm in hers. The two ladies made their way through the crowd to the double doors that were flung open to let in a modicum of a breeze.

"Over there," Ana Maria said, nodding toward a bench at the far end of the terrace.

The night air was refreshing, and Ana Maria took a few great gulps of it, already feeling more relaxed.

Would she ever feel entirely comfortable in a room filled with Society's finest people?

She doubted it. Especially since she didn't particularly *want* to be in a room with Society's finest people—she'd far rather go to a club such as Miss Ivy's, which admitted anybody, as long as they had money to gamble with. Or to fabric shops where she could meet people who were equally passionate about warp and weft.

"I understand you and Octavia have been spending time together," Ivy said as she sat down, smoothing her skirts over her lap. "I don't think she would admit it, but I believe Octavia has been lonely since Sebastian and I set up our own household."

Ana Maria chuckled. "Your sister is keeping me from being lonely as well. Now that Sebastian has gone, and everything has changed." And she did still have friends from her former life, but she and her friends were both acutely aware that they now inhabited different worlds. She couldn't seriously complain to Jane or any of the other household workers about her discomfort at attending parties; they would think she was being spoiled. Which she supposed she would be. But it wasn't as though she could just decide to return to her old life, so this new life had to be improved somehow.

Which brought her to her plan.

"Your sister and I have spent some time together visiting fabric houses. I believe she plans to redecorate the club?"

Ivy nodded. "I think it's a good thing—it will

keep her from mischief. Hopefully," she added, with a sigh that indicated an older sister's long-suffering. "She said you were excellent at it, that she could rely entirely on your taste."

Ana Maria felt a warmth spread through her at the compliment. "That is good to hear. Because I wish to do the same for other places. Institutions like the Society for Poor and Unfortunate Children. I know it might seem frivolous to focus on redecorating those places, when they want food and shelter, but it is my belief that people will respond more to a place that appears to be well kept, and will want to donate more than if the house they lived in was shabby and poorly maintained." She'd also ensure that Thaddeus donate some of his vast ducal wealth to those places, but she didn't need to share that with Ivy at this moment. Since Thaddeus didn't know yet.

"You are correct," Ivy said in an enthusiastic tone. "When I opened the club, not only did I have to provide an excellent gaming experience, I had to make sure my customers got a certain feeling from being there. It wasn't enough just to have tables and dealers and good play. I took pains with the interior design, since Miss Ivy's was a different experience than other clubs. And you wish me to let Sebastian know?"

Ana Maria blinked in surprise. "Oh, I can tell him myself. I wanted to tell you first, as a businesswoman, to see if you thought it made sense."

"Will you charge the institutions for your services, then?" Ivy asked with a confused expression.

"No, but I will present those places as proof that I can do the work. And, eventually, I hope that some people who can actually afford it will hire me."

Ivy grinned. "You'd better be careful, that sounds perilously close to being a lady who works. I thought you fancy aristocrats weren't supposed to do anything so demeaning."

Ana Maria nudged Ivy in the shoulder. "You're a fancy aristocrat, aren't you?"

Ivy shook her head vigorously. "Not anymore, not since I had the audacity to open a gambling house and marry an illegitimate man. I far prefer this life, to be honest."

Ana Maria rolled her eyes. "I can tell that, anybody can tell that. I thought that since you seemed to take to it so well, and it doesn't seem as though Octavia has suffered, I should try. I don't think the life of a traditional aristocratic lady is for me."

"Marriage, children, good works?" Ivy asked in a gentle tone. "Do you not wish for any of those?"

Ana Maria's chest felt tight. "I do want those things." She thought of all the flowers in her salon, flowers from gentlemen who didn't know her. Didn't want to know her. But they did want to know her dowry. "But I can't see how, not in my current situation. I don't want a gentleman who wouldn't be proud of who I was before, and none of the gentlemen I have met, or will meet, would be anything but horrified at what I used to do." Except Nash, of course. Because he'd seen it all, and she knew he wouldn't judge her. If anything, he'd likely respect her more because she'd been more than a decorative object.

Ivy arched her brow. "I think you're not meeting the right kind of gentlemen. Perhaps you should spend more time at Miss Ivy's?"

Ana Maria laughed. "Is this your not-so-subtle way to get me to come lose money at your establishment? You know I would do that anyway."

Ivy shrugged. "But if you come with the purpose of losing money and meeting someone who might pique your interest, it's two goals you would accomplish instead of one."

"Very efficient of you," Ana Maria remarked.

Ivy rose, gesturing for Ana Maria to stay seated. "I have to go, your brother is at home with just the dogs for company." She winked. "And I find I miss him."

Ana Maria rolled her eyes. "People in love are so dull. Always talking about their love, thinking about their love, being with their love—"

"Just wait," Ivy warned. "It will happen to you. And you'll wonder how you ever breathed without the other person."

She waved goodbye, as though she hadn't just sent Ana Maria into a flurry of confused thoughts, then set off through the doors and back onto the dance floor, making her way toward the front of the house.

Ana Maria watched her go, longing warring with worry as she pondered Ivy's words. *You'll wonder how you ever breathed without the other person.*

She already spent far more time than she should thinking about Nash. If he weren't in her life—when he was married to some Society lady who wanted to be a Society lady—would she miss him?

The sharp ache in her heart answered her question.

SHE WASN'T IN the ballroom. The candles were just as bright, the music just as lively, the refreshments just as delicious.

But everything seemed dimmed.

He took one more thorough look, meeting a few people's gazes, their smiles changing as they saw his glower. Good. Fewer people to talk to.

Though that was the direct opposite of what he should be doing here.

"Duke!" His grandmother rapped on the floor with her cane, as though making certain he heard her.

He not only heard her, he felt her. Every time he thought about what his blackguard cousin might do to his half siblings. Every time he walked through the mansion—*his* mansion, even though it still felt odd to claim it—he felt as though there was a second duke there, one who was cruel and unforgiving and violent. The past of his father and the future of his cousin, if he didn't do anything to stop it. Him, if he allowed himself to feel.

"Yes, Your Grace?" he said, turning to look at her. Forcing himself not to fold his arms over his chest. He knew that position was deliberately aggressive, he'd used it for that very effect many times in the past, and he did not want to appear that way in front of his grandmother. Not that she would be intimidated if he did—the only thing that seemed to rattle her was when he appeared without a shirt.

Good information to have, should his goal ever be to thoroughly befuddle his grandmother.

"You should be dancing." She gestured toward the dance floor with her cane. "You're just standing there, not talking to anyone, not asking anyone to dance."

"I asked Lady Ana Maria to dance!" he retorted.

She gave a derisive snort. "The one lady you refuse to even consider marrying. You'll forgive me if I don't think that should be taken into consideration." She rose from her chair, stepping close to him. "Do you *want* your cousin to inherit?" She thumped her cane on the floor. "You need to take this seriously, Duke."

"I'm not that old," he grumbled.

"Old enough to father a child," she retorted. "The

sooner you do that, the sooner all of us who know what could happen can breathe comfortably."

His own breath felt tight, as though his chest—his responsibilities—were squeezing in on him.

He wished, not for the first time, not for the hundredth time, that someone else, anyone else, had been in line to inherit the title.

If he had just been plain Nash. Not even a "Mr." starting his name. He could live his life as he chose. He wouldn't have to funnel his anger into street fights. He could be with the people whom he most enjoyed—people who worked hard, drank hard, lived hard.

Of course, a voice reminded him, those people also don't have a choice about how they live. Many of them are poor and have to work even if they are in ill health.

He scowled.

"It's not the worst thing that could happen to you," his grandmother said, reacting to his expression. "The worst thing would be to die knowing you are allowing people you care about to suffer. I will be gone by then, but what about the other people in the family?"

"I don't suppose we could persuade my cousin not to be violent?" he said.

She clamped her lips together and glared at him.

"Right. If you will excuse me, I need to—" He walked off without finishing his sentence, desperate to get out of the crowded room filled with people he knew he wouldn't like. And who wouldn't like him.

Not that he'd give them a chance.

He was able to take a deep breath as soon as he saw her. She was seated on a terrace bench, the farthest one from the door, looking as though her thoughts were entirely elsewhere.

Was she thinking of him?

She shouldn't be. She should be thinking of anybody else, not surly men who kissed her passionately in one moment, told her it was an enormous mistake the next.

God, but she looked beautiful. Her dark hair was swept up into some complicated style, with some sort of spangly ribbon intertwined throughout. She wore a gold-and-white gown with enormous skirts that spilled out onto the stone of the terrace. Her gloves were white, while a small pendant hung at her throat.

Her skin gleamed in the moonlight. Her dark eyes were luminous in her face, those perfect lips tilting into a slight smile.

He hoped she was thinking of him. Even though he didn't.

She turned her head toward him, as though she was as aware of his presence as he was of hers. Her smile broadened, and she patted the bench beside her. "Come," she said.

He strode toward her, remembering the last time they were on a terrace together. "Terrace shenanigans," he murmured.

A terrace would be awfully uncomfortable for an intimate moment, and yet it was staged perfectly for one: darkness surrounding them, the light from the ballroom spilling out in golden beams, the faint whisper of the trees as the wind stirred them.

Her, on her knees on the bench, holding on to the wall of the terrace. Him behind her, her skirts flipped up to reveal her shapely arse. Him grasping her around the waist as he thrust slowly into her soft warmth.

Damn.

He should not be thinking about that. This was Ana Maria, the one woman he could never desire in that way.

Although he was coming to realize that there might not be another woman he would ever desire that way.

"Nash?" she said in a questioning tone as he sat down at the edge of the bench. Nearly falling off, since it was a narrow bench, and he didn't want to risk his body touching hers.

"Why are you out here hiding?" He spoke abruptly, but he knew she wouldn't take offense. One of the few women who wouldn't.

Scratch that. The only woman who wouldn't.

"I'm not hiding, I'm—" she began, then nodded her head. "I'm hiding," she admitted. "I came out for a chat with Ivy, but she had to leave. I only have two dances claimed thus far—yours and Lord Brunley's—and honestly I don't feel like dancing at all, so I guess I am staying out here to avoid any more dances."

She paused. "What are you doing out here?"

Looking for you.

"Shouldn't you be inside charming all the ladies who might marry you?" Did he imagine her aggrieved tone?

"I don't think any of them want to. Except for perhaps Lady Felicity, and I'm fairly certain she's thinking how she can successfully avoid me after we're married." Which would suit him, of course, but it did not appeal at all.

"Oh," she said in a faint tone. "So it's to be Lady Felicity?" She picked her dance card up and rubbed where he had written his name. "I don't want to make things more complicated—you don't have to dance with me."

He reached out to grasp her wrist, stilling her hand. "Stop. I want to dance with you." He was speaking the absolute truth, wasn't he?

Or not. The absolute truth would be that there was so much more he wanted to do with her. Things that involved her mouth, his body, her hands, his tongue.

And now his cock was stiffening in his trousers, and he didn't want to stand up, but sitting next to her only meant the problem would grow. So to speak.

She nodded in agreement, but her mouth was pressed together as if she was unhappy.

He wanted to make her happy.

No, Goddamn it, he didn't. He *couldn't*.

"Well," he said after a moment. "I—my grandmother demands, and I agree with her. I will see you for our dance."

He rose, nodded briefly, then made his way back to the ballroom, intent on doing anything but the one thing he wanted to most, which was stay with her.

Chapter Thirteen

My lady, I hope you received my bouquet?

My lady, do you prefer roses or lilies?

My lady, what kind of flowers will it take to get you to agree to marry me? So that I might also marry your dowry?

Fine. So the last conversation was entirely imagined, but she knew full well what these gentlemen wished they could say.

She'd returned to the ballroom with only two dances asked for, but now she'd been astonished to discover her dance card was entirely full. Gentlemen—with anxious-looking mamas at their backs—had approached her over the course of just a few minutes, each one asking if he might have the honor, etc., etc.

Her, not truly caring one way or the other.

Not because she was going to settle for one of them, of course. She wasn't a complete ninny. But because she would not settle for any of them. Not if it meant being in a loveless marriage where the most important relationship was with her money.

Nash had a reason to get married, she knew

that. But fortunately for her own situation, there was no reason she had to, beyond wanting all of that happily ever after nonsense.

Which she did. But given the current flowers-equals-romantic-interest code currently being tossed at her, she didn't see herself achieving that anytime soon.

Especially since the one person she'd like to explore that with was so determinedly against it.

If she could just persuade him to be open to it—there was no guarantee they'd suit. But shouldn't they at least try to see if it would at all work out?

According to him, no.

She sighed, glancing at her dance card for the hundredth time. The supper dance was only in a few more dances. She just had to get through a dance with Lord Brunley of the Will Not Accept a Rejection Brunleys, and then another dance with some gentleman who'd looked terrified she might refuse his request.

She had felt bad for that fellow, even though she also knew that pity was no basis for a relationship.

"My lady."

Lord Brunley arrived right as she was pondering what it would take for a non-Nash gentleman to win her heart.

Nothing less than a perfect dedication to her happiness, a wish to see her fulfilled in some sort of creative work, and a face that could launch a thousand ships, if the ships were crewed by sailors who were motivated by such things.

In other words, no one.

She shrugged as Lord Brunley led her out to the dance floor.

At least she knew she looked good enough to waste flowers on—her gown this evening was white shot through with gold thread, making her look as though she literally shimmered.

Jane had done her hair up in a simple, classic style, winding a gold ribbon through her curls. She wore topaz earrings and a matching topaz necklace, a gift Sebastian had given her when she'd turned eighteen. He had been sixteen then, and had carefully saved his allowance to purchase her a gift, since he'd known she wouldn't get anything from anybody else.

Sebastian. She smiled just thinking about him and Ivy.

"Can I hope your smile is for me?" Lord Brunley said in what she could only categorize as a smug tone. Because she was not above being judgmental, especially when the gentleman of judgment had attempted to trap her in a room alone.

Thank goodness for fireplace tools, she thought to herself.

She didn't answer, merely allowed her smile to dim a fraction. While he would weather the whole room-entrapment scandal handily, especially if they were to become engaged as a result, she could not even dare to seem as though she was not having the time of her life with him. She would be seen as snobbish, or condescending, or not knowing her place.

Any of which were just phrases designed to keep ladies from expressing their true emotions.

"I have a new pair of chestnuts," Lord Brunley said, spinning her around. At least he was an excellent dancer, even if he was a not-so-excellent life partner. "I would very much like to show them to you. Perhaps tomorrow?"

Not "Would you like to see them?" or even "I wonder if you like horses as much as I believe you like flowers?"

No, it was all about *him* showing *her* his new possession.

Like he'd show her to everyone if she said yes.

She probably should just go toss her head in the punch bowl to cool herself off. At this rate, she'd end up making some sort of fractious scene because nobody cared to ask what she wanted.

I want to kiss you.

Which it seemed he'd wanted as well, but then he'd decided, himself, what was best for both of them.

Humph.

"My lady?" Lord Brunley now sounded . . . hesitant. Not a tone she was accustomed to from him.

She must've let some of her aggravation onto her face. That was one aspect of being a lady she didn't think she would ever master—it seemed ladies who were bred for their parts since they were born were far more adept at masking what they thought.

Whereas she was likely always making a face.

Maybe she shouldn't go gambling at Miss Ivy's—the other players would be able to spot right away when she was bluffing.

But she never bluffed. And that was the problem, wasn't it? She never tried to persuade anyone of something that might not actually occur because that was too close to lying, and she also did not lie.

It was on the tip of her tongue to tell him she had an engagement tomorrow, but then she remembered she did not lie. Drat.

"Please?" he added, sounding nearly humble. "I would like to prove to you that I can be the gentleman you deserve."

The gentleman she deserved.

Not the gentleman she wanted.

She would not settle if she couldn't have the latter. But she could go drive with Lord Brunley—after all, it wasn't as though *he* would ever ask her to go out for a drive. And Lord Brunley seemed to want to make amends for his behavior.

Besides which, she wouldn't mind seeing his face when or if she told him she would continue to keep Lord Brunley's acquaintance. Even though that was entirely petty, and she should not think that way.

But she did.

"Thank you, my lord, that would be . . . fine," she said. "Yes," she added, as he looked entirely confused.

"Splendid," he replied in a relieved tone.

There would be time to take herself on her own adventure, no men required, one where she could be free to explore all of her creativity.

Except in love.

In that arena, she was destined to be thwarted.

But it was better than settling.

"YOUR GRACE." LADY Felicity was an adequate dancer, and Nash had to admit she looked pleasing this evening. Her blond hair was atop her head in a riot of curls, and her appropriately white debutante's gown managed to convey sensual innocence, even though he knew those two were opposites. Weren't they?

He grunted in reply.

"Your grandmother, the dowager duchess, is a charming woman."

He bit back the urge to stare at her in shock. His grandmother was many things—some of which he even admired—but he did not think she was charming.

"She mentioned that she is here to assist you in certain matters." The lady's coy tone made it clear she knew perfectly well what matters the dowager duchess referred to.

He grunted again. What was he to say, anyway?

Yes? And then that agreement would lead her to speak more on his terrible situation, and he would have to figure out just what to say to dissuade her while also making certain she was not entirely dissuaded?

Not that he wanted to marry her, but that was the point, wasn't it?

That he find someone he didn't especially want to marry?

And since he didn't especially want to marry her, perhaps he should.

His head was spinning worse than when Finan managed to deliver a powerful punch to his jaw. But he'd rather take the punch.

"Your Grace?" Apparently the lady required more than a grunt.

A scowl? He could manage that. A frown? That might be possible, too.

He took a deep breath, trying to figure out what would be both appropriate and noncommittal. His father had skipped that part of ducal training when he'd raised Nash.

Skipped most all the training, in fact. Only demonstrating how not to be a duke, which wasn't helpful when one was trying to be a duke. For the first time ever.

"Yes, my grandmother is in town."

Which wasn't a response. Or, rather, it was a response. It just wasn't the correct one.

But judging by how Lady Felicity graciously inclined her head, it would do.

Was that all it took? A few words that meant nothing and said less?

Perhaps he should have been speaking all this time, after all.

Or perhaps it was that Lady Felicity was so desperate to become the current duchess that she was willing to overlook his inability to form complete, cogent sentences.

Ana Maria wasn't willing to overlook anything. She would challenge him, but she also was able to understand him.

He felt his chest tighten as he thought about it. She understood him. Not entirely, obviously; if she understood him entirely, she'd run in the other direction rather than toward him.

Whereas he did not understand her at all. But he wanted to.

If that made a difference.

Which it could not.

Because if he did understand her, and she him, she would know who he was. And who he could be.

For a man who did so little talking, he was doing far too much *thinking*. He should just focus on solving his immediate problem, not wondering if a certain lady could ever know him.

"Lady Felicity," he began, noting the look of relief on her face. Because he'd spoken? "I am wondering if you would care to"—Goddamn it, what would she possibly care to do?—"allow me to take you for a drive in the park?"

"It would be a pleasure, Your Grace," she replied immediately. He didn't miss the note of triumph in her tone.

He might as well succumb to his not-caring-for-anyone-at-all fate. The alternative was far too terrifying to contemplate.

Not caring wasn't an option when he saw her dancing with that blackguard Brunley. Hadn't she learned her lesson? But no, she was smiling and dancing as though he hadn't had her trapped in a room determined to make her say yes.

If it hadn't been for his timely arrival—well, she would be betrothed to the lout by now.

Even though she'd said she had it handled. But she hadn't. That cur would have yanked her sad excuse for a weapon from her hand and had her compromised before the fire needed tending if he hadn't arrived.

"Duke. I see you danced with Lady Felicity." His grandmother sounded complacent. Which made him want to rebel, to tell her in no uncertain terms how little he cared about the lady.

But the dowager duchess herself wouldn't care about that either. All she cared about was that he marry, and soon.

"Yes."

"And—?" She sounded impatient.

"And I'm taking her for a drive tomorrow."

"Ah. So soon?"

What the hell? he wanted to say. First she was

urging him to waste no time, and now he was moving too quickly?

"We will meet tomorrow morning to review appropriate behavior."

Nash felt his hands twitch. Appropriate behavior? As though Lady Felicity would balk at anything short of his howling at the moon while wearing nothing but a sailor's hat. And even then he thought she might find some accommodation for his behavior if he made her a duchess.

"Appropriate behavior?" he said in a low, deadly tone. "Appropriate for a duke, you mean to say?" He took a deep breath, knowing he should stop, but unable to keep himself contained. "Appropriate behavior is beating your wife and child. I will not do that."

"I know," she interrupted, sounding far more fragile than usual. "I want you to be proud of who you are, of the man you can become."

He felt his throat tighten. Was she choosing now of all times to show empathy toward his situation? Now, when they were in the middle of a ball filled with people he didn't know? When he couldn't react?

Although to be fair, it wasn't as though he would be able to react even if they were the only two people in the room. He didn't do emotion very well. That was where his fists came in handy.

So to speak.

"Thank you," he said at last. "I hope I can live

up to your expectations." *Even if I can't live up to mine because I won't allow myself to.*

What would it look like if he did allow himself to?

He didn't dare. That thought was too tantalizing, too close to what he was starting to dream of.

She patted his arm, for once not using her cane for emphasis. "You will, Duke. You will."

LORD BRUNLEY REMAINED remarkably humble for the remainder of their dance together. Perhaps she should enlist Nash to punch all her suitors into submission—it would make her own interactions with them far less combative.

He had just escorted her off the dance floor to where they'd last seen Thaddeus when Nash appeared at her elbow, startling her into a shriek that she managed to tamp down to a mere yelp.

Lord Brunley tilted his head back in open appraisal. Which made Nash rise up to his full height. And made Ana Maria roll her eyes.

So much for behaving more humbly. She glanced between them; neither spared a glance at her, both of them too engrossed in staring at one another.

Honestly. It was as though she wasn't here, as though the two of them were going to masculine one another into submission.

"It is time for our dance, my lady," Nash said, sounding almost like a regular lord, and not an inarticulate duke.

Probably because he was desperately trying to best Lord Brunley in whatever this particular contest was.

She sighed, placing her hand in his outstretched one. She had been looking forward to this dance all night, but not if he was going to be all fussy about it. Besides which, it wasn't any of his business who she danced with or spoke with. He'd made that clear enough.

"I will see you tomorrow, my lady," Lord Brunley said, addressing his remark to Nash.

Nash snarled in reply.

Wonderful. Why didn't they just go and mark their territory while they were at it? It would be far more direct, and she wouldn't have to be involved at all.

And why hadn't she told Lord Brunley no? She was too kind. She knew full well he would likely try to press his suit if given the opportunity. She'd said yes because it was easier than saying no, and she wanted to see Nash's face when he found out.

But it would mean she'd have to go driving with Lord Brunley.

She was an idiot.

"That cur. He is taking you out tomorrow?"

Nash swung her onto the dance floor, and she allowed herself a moment to revel in his brute strength. But only a moment—he was being an ass, after all. Even though his reaction was all she could have hoped for. *Idiot, idiot, idiot.*

"And how is Lady Felicity?" She didn't like

how sharp her tone was. Then again, she didn't like how bossy and manlike he was being.

"Fine," he replied shortly. "Where is that oaf taking you?"

Never let it be said the Duke of Malvern could be deterred from his line of questioning.

"To see his horses."

He made a noise that managed to convey disgust, annoyance, and dismissal all at once. Impressive.

"And Lady Felicity?" she said again. Two could play that "won't be deterred" game.

"I'm taking her . . . driving."

The pause before he said the final word made her head spin with all the possibilities. Taking her . . . to his boxing room to show her his moves? Taking her . . . to the church to declare his intentions? Taking her . . . in his arms?

"Ah. Driving. Where she will see your horses. Sounds pleasant." She spoke in a stiff tone of voice. His grip on her tightened, as though he had a reaction he couldn't quite suppress.

"Look, it's—" he began, then shook his head.

She stopped dancing, making a few of the other couples bump into them and glare.

"Let's talk," she said, taking his arm and beginning to drag him through the ballroom. She spotted a few scandalized glances, but she would deal with scandal rather than have all this whatever it was built up between them.

He was *supposed* to be her friend. Her brother's

best friend, someone she could count on. Not someone to whom she had to edit her conversation. The whole point of being friends with a taciturn gentleman was that one got to say whatever one meant.

But now, now that there was all of this, started by the kiss, or even earlier, when they'd first danced the night she'd appeared in her silver gown, when it seemed as though he'd finally noticed her, and not as the best friend's sibling.

Now there was discomfort, and awkwardness, and she'd be damned if she let it continue.

"Onto the terrace," she said, edging her way through the crowd. There were far too many people, however, and after a few moments he took the lead, barreling through anybody who dared to stand in their way.

Showing his arrogant brutish self in all its glory.

Something she should not admire, given how arrogant and brutish he was behaving now, but she absolutely did.

Darn her, and darn her contradictory ways.

As soon as they were on the terrace, she took the lead again, moving past the couples in conversation to a nook with a large tree whose hanging branches afforded more privacy. She headed for the bench on which they had sat before, although as she saw it again, it didn't look large enough to accommodate—

"Oof," she said as he sat down beside her. He had his legs spread out, as though to keep himself from falling off the edge of the bench, and she suppressed a laugh. She did not think he would want her to laugh at him.

"What is it?" he grumbled. "Why did you drag me off the dance floor? I just want to know what the rotter plans to do with you."

"And that is the problem," Ana Maria replied, nudging him sharply with her elbow. He made a surprised noise, then fell onto the stone terrace.

That couldn't have been comfortable.

He didn't get up, just sat there glowering at her. Far less effective when he was on his arse on a terrace looking up rather than scowling down. She should remember that for the next time they argued.

"You don't have a say in what I do. Or if you do, then you need to tell me precisely why you have a say in what I do. If I choose to go look at Lord Brunley's wretched horses, I will and can choose to do it." She lifted her chin. "I told you before"—*when we kissed*—"that what I do is my decision alone. I have decided that I will be in charge of what I do. Even if I make mistakes," and she froze as she realized how he might take that, "and I will, but they will be my mistakes. It's just what you do, isn't it? Make your own decisions all the time? It's the privilege of being a duke, after all."

It felt good, to unleash her frustration on him. He didn't deserve all of her ire. That would only be deserved if all the gentlemen who'd sent her flowers while craving her dowry were in attendance as well.

"I admire that about you," he said slowly. "Sometimes it feels as though my choices aren't made by me, but by who I am—a duke, my fath—" He stopped speaking abruptly, and she wished more than anything that he had kept talking.

And then he started talking again, only now his tone had changed.

"So you want to do precisely what you want to do? With nobody telling you otherwise?"

His lips were twisted into a faint smile, as though he was aware of what he was saying—and what he might actually be saying.

She took a deep breath. "You said we shouldn't—"

He cut her off before she could finish. "I don't want that. Not unless you do. It's your choice, Ana Maria." He was still on the ground, his hands flat on the terrace behind him, leaning back as though it was a perfectly comfortable place to sit.

It made it look as though he was a supplicant asking her for something. For that.

It was a heady power, making it feel as though she had drunk a strong alcoholic beverage, one that slid through her with an insidious speed, making her light-headed and fearless and wanting all at once.

Her body felt tingly, as though he were touching her.

It's your choice, Ana Maria.

He'd touched her breast before. She craved that again. And more.

She stood suddenly, holding her hand out to him. "Come," she ordered.

He took her hand and rose, standing still as though awaiting further instruction.

Heady power.

She turned and led him further down the terrace, toward where she assumed there were stairs leading out to the gardens. It was dark here, and she felt along the wall, the cold stone a welcome relief to her heated fingers.

Her other hand was in his strong one as she led him down the stairs, turning abruptly so that they were against the wall but on the other side, effectively hidden from the other guests.

She could hear the sounds of the party, but overhead all she could see were the tree branches and the distant smattering of stars.

"What now?" he asked. He was so very close to her, his hand still in hers.

"Now," she said, tugging at his hand. "Now I want to kiss you."

It was deliberate, not asking him to kiss her but telling him she wanted to kiss him. It was powerful to put it that way, to make it her choice rather than something he had put upon her, no matter how much she wanted it herself.

He planted his hand on the wall over her head, his large body looming over hers. The large body she, deliciously enough, seemed to be in charge of at the moment. Doing her bidding even though he could take what he wanted.

She placed her fingers on his lapel, sliding them along the fabric down to his waist. Drawing him closer as she lifted her face to his.

And then his mouth was on hers and her hand had found its way to the small of his back and his big body was pressed against hers, and she opened her mouth as she'd done before, her tongue exploring and meeting his, the contact making her feel as though her body was melting against his.

The hand that wasn't propping him up against the wall was at her waist, gripping her tight. As though she was precious and he had to hold on to her.

And then his fingers slid up, slowly, so slowly she could stop him if she wanted, but she didn't want, she wanted his big hand on her, on her breast, on all the parts of her that ached.

There.

And there.

And there.

His fingers curled around the curve of her, sliding under the neckline of her gown, making her gasp.

His kiss was intense, his tongue questing inside her mouth, the faint noise of the music from the ballroom the only sound.

It was as though they were in their own private world, one where only they belonged, where none of this mattered, where they could do what they wanted.

She wanted this. She wanted *him*.

She wanted to kiss him. Even though both of them knew nothing could happen between them. Nothing more than this, at least.

She knew. And he knew. And here they were. Knowing.

Her mouth was so soft and warm, her kisses already more confident than before. She had her palm pressed against the small of his back, pulling him against her body, which all of him liked. Especially his cock.

He was hard, his whole body screaming at him to yank her skirts up and take her against the wall, the possibility of discovery adding a soupçon of danger to it all.

But then that would mean he would miss caressing her breast, as he was doing now. Sliding his fingers into the bodice of her gown and finding her nipple, which was stiff against his skin. He put his whole hand inside, covering her breast, rubbing the erect nipple against his palm. She made a soft noise in her throat, and he caressed her breast, awkward though it was to plunge his hand down her gown.

She was moving against him, almost as though she didn't know what she was doing. She must be aching. He wished he could assuage her ache.

Her hand had slid down to his arse, and she was

rubbing her palm over it, cupping the lower part where his buttock met his leg. That movement only pushed their bodies closer together, and now his cock was wedged between them, thrust up against her lower belly. She had to know what was happening.

And still she kissed him, and touched him, and moaned as he stroked her soft skin and licked the warmth of her mouth.

They heard a burst of laughter, as though someone was standing just above them on the terrace, and they broke apart, both breathing rapidly.

He put his hand over her mouth and leaned in to whisper in her ear. "Be still, they won't know we're here if we're quiet."

She made a huff of annoyance, as if to say she knew that, but of course she couldn't say it aloud for fear of discovery.

He chuckled against her skin. Lowering his mouth, he placed his lips on her shoulder and kissed it softly. He carefully withdrew his hand from her gown, smoothing the fabric, then placed his palm—still tingling from where he had touched her—onto the back of her neck, trailing kisses from her shoulder to her neck to her ear.

Her head was thrown back, and she was arching her back, thrusting her breasts into his chest.

"I think I like when we argue," he murmured, his lips brushing her ear.

She shuddered, and he felt the movement throughout his entire body.

"I like it, too," she whispered back. "And I cannot wait to get to actually fight you again. Preferably without Finan in the room." Her words were a dark promise.

He wanted her. The problem was, of course, that he *wanted* her. Which meant he could not and should not have her.

"What?" she said.

He drew back, his eyebrows narrowed into a frown. "What what?"

"You changed. Just now. You thought of something." She poked him in the chest. "You should stop thinking. Isn't all this enough?"

It's more than enough. It's everything.

But he knew it couldn't last because he wouldn't let it.

"Let me escort you back to Thaddeus," he said, stepping away from her and holding out his arm.

She exhaled an exasperated breath, but she took his arm without comment.

They didn't speak as he led her through the crowd to where Thaddeus stood.

"I'll come in a few days," she said as he bowed. It was not a question, and he felt a visceral reaction at her commanding tone.

He wanted to hear her tell him what to do some more. He wanted it very much. Because it was her choice.

Chapter Fourteen

The rest of the party passed in a whirl, mostly because Ana Maria couldn't stop thinking about it. All of it: his mouth on hers, her hand on him, how he'd sounded when he'd whispered in her ear.

How exhilarating it had felt to know that just above them were people who would be shocked, horrified, and also likely titillated if they knew what was happening in the garden below.

She woke at dawn, lying in her luxurious bed, the bed she still slept to one side of because she hadn't yet gotten used to the size of it compared to her earlier bed, staring out the window at the various chimneys, clouds, and the faintest hint of sun.

She felt completely and totally in control— able to do whatever she wanted, whenever she wanted.

The feeling might not last, but she needed to take advantage of it while it did.

Springing out of bed, she went to her wardrobe and drew out one of her new day dresses, a blue gown that looked like it had been dipped into the sea. It wasn't too difficult to button up, thank goodness, although she knew most ladies would insist on assistance for every little item they might put on.

But she wanted to be alone to savor how remarkable she felt.

It wasn't just the kissing, though the kissing helped; it was that she had stated what she wanted, both to herself and to him, and she had acted on her wants.

Today she was going to begin her new venture, whatever that might look like. She'd go to Miss Ivy's and consult with Octavia, then go to his house for more lessons in fighting.

Not a euphemism, though she hoped that there would be other non-fighting activities as well. Which she had told him straight-out.

From now on, she was going to say what she meant. If she could figure that out precisely. Because of course she was still conflicted, still oxymoronic, about what it was she actually desired.

Though she knew definitely she desired him.

"My lady!"

Jane burst through the door holding a tray, glancing quickly at the clock in the corner and then back at Ana Maria with a startled expression. "It is so early, what in goodness' name are you doing up?"

Jane set the tray down on the low table to the right of the bed, then approached Ana Maria and took hold of her shoulders, twisting her so her back was to Jane. Ana Maria shook the other woman's hands off as she felt them at her buttons.

"I did those already," she said in a terse tone as she spun back around.

"I just wanted to check," Jane replied.

Ana Maria glared at her friend, who just kept regarding her with a skeptical look.

"You have to let me do *some* things," Ana Maria continued, this time in a less peevish tone.

"I know it's hard for you, adjusting to all of this," Jane said softly as she gestured to the room. "But we all want you to succeed, and it will be more difficult for you if you can't stop thinking of yourself as a servant."

"I don't."

Ana Maria was taken aback herself by how quickly she spoke. But she didn't feel like a servant. Not anymore. She felt like an entire person, one who had the benefit of a title and wealth, but one who was also adept at making her own decisions—something she wasn't certain other more traditionally raised young ladies knew how to do.

"Good," Jane said. "So you'll be choosing your own husband and settling into your own household." She made it sound like an inevitability, and Ana Maria felt herself recoil.

"No!"

Jane's eyebrows rose. "But I thought you didn't want to be dependent on your cousin forever?"

Ana Maria felt as though she were choking from her emotion. She couldn't speak for a few moments, just shook her head. "I—those aren't the only options."

Jane folded her arms over her chest. "What else is there, then?"

"There's me! And what I want to do!"

Jane narrowed her gaze. "And what is that? Because I can't believe you want to return to doing what you used to. Even if it were possible."

"No, I don't." She paused. "But I want to do something. And that something is not get married to somebody with teeth and flowers just because there are no other opportunities."

"Not that big lummox!" Jane exclaimed.

Ana Maria's face grew hot. Jane looked smug.

"I thought so."

"No, that is not happening." Ana Maria spoke firmly, as if that would stop Jane from talking.

"I've seen how you look at him. You've always looked at him that way." Jane shrugged. "Now that you are who you are, finally, why can't it happen?"

Ana Maria plopped down on her bed, gesturing for Jane to sit beside her. "It sounds so easy when you say it."

"But it *is* easy. The duchess wouldn't have allowed it. She'd have been too jealous of your position, but now that she is gone and your cousin is in charge? Why not?"

"He doesn't want to for some reason."

"What possible reason could that be? Is he damaged in some way?"

Ana Maria blushed even more at Jane's implication, and the fact that she knew the answer, nearly firsthand, so to speak. "It's not that. He is most definitely not damaged."

At least not *that* way—but she knew he was hurting; his offhand comments and various grunts and growls told her that much.

"Oh, so it's like that, is it?"

"Can we stop having this conversation? I need to go to Miss Ivy's today. I am going to help Miss Octavia redecorate." Possibly she could match her cheeks to the red silk she imagined using on the walls.

And then she remembered it wouldn't be the perfect day, after all. "Drat! And Lord Brunley is coming to take me to see his chestnuts." Why had she agreed? *Idiot, idiot, idiot.*

"I just want you to be happy." Jane reached over to take Ana Maria's hand. Her fingers were rough with calluses.

"I will be, I promise." *With or without him,* she thought. Because she was in charge of her own happiness now, and she wouldn't wait while some confused behemoth sorted his thoughts. But she would go ahead and take what she wanted, if he was willing.

"What time is Lord Brunley arriving?"

Ana Maria shook her head. "I think this afternoon sometime."

"Miss Ivy's first, then, is it?" Jane said as she rose from the bed. "I thought you were going to redo this room first?"

"I can do both."

Ana Maria stood as well, gazing around at the understated colors of her bedroom. Her soul longed for color and vibrancy, and now that she was set on her course, she would get it.

"You can." Jane spoke with the same confidence Ana Maria felt. "Now let's get you on your way so you can accomplish everything you've ever dreamed of."

"And then I have to go see Lord Brunley's brown horses," Ana Maria said in a disgruntled tone.

"He likely won't allow you to redecorate them," Jane said in a sly tone, making Ana Maria laugh.

"DUKE!"

Nash groaned as he heard his grandmother's voice down the hall. He rose from his chair, going to the door of his study to find her—he didn't necessarily want to speak with her, but he wasn't going to make an ancient lady travel when he could use his own two legs to find her.

So that she could scold him or annoy him in some way.

"There you are," she said. Her lady's maid's expression was as disapproving as his grandmother's tone. "We spoke about the need for you to obtain some manners—"

"*You* spoke about it," Nash interrupted.

"And I have time now."

No question if he had time, he noticed. Although he did, so he had nothing to gripe about. Except the entire and complete intrusion and upending of his life.

"In here?" he said, gesturing toward his study.

The dowager duchess scowled. "Not 'in here.' You should say, 'Would you care to come inside?' or something more polite. And no, not there."

Nash rolled his eyes, but didn't respond as he normally would.

"Would you care to go to the ballroom, then?" he asked, making his tone deliberately formal.

"Better. And yes."

His grandmother turned, taking her lady's maid's arm and making her way back down the hallway to the ballroom.

Nash followed, having to keep his stride about half what it usually was because of his grandmother's pace. *Look,* he wanted to say, *I'm accommodating you now, only you aren't even registering it.*

Humph.

He waited as his grandmother was settled on one of the low sofas that hugged the edge of the room.

He rarely came here; this was where parties were held, and Nash did not hold parties beyond having Sebastian and Thaddeus over for whiskey.

This room was where his father had spent many evenings, which meant that Nash had an instinctive dislike of it. Even now he could picture his father—red-faced, loud, and frequently angry—standing in the middle of the room bellowing out orders as people scurried to obey.

Nash hadn't been old enough to actually attend the parties his father threw, but he had snuck out from his bedroom and watched the guests arrive. Mostly gentlemen like his father, with a few ladies he later realized were not of the aristocracy at all. He hadn't thought about it then, but he wondered now if his father and his friends had hurt the women. He didn't doubt it. He wished he could find them and make reparation, but he supposed it would have to do to hire as many of his father's bastards as he could find.

"What are you doing?" his grandmother said. "Standing around gawking at what?"

Nash shook his head. "Nothing." He felt his hands clench into fists, and couldn't help but start pacing, the fury inside him roaring to life.

The dowager duchess thumped her cane. "Come sit. I can tell it is not nothing."

Nash suppressed a sigh—a sigh! Him!—and sat beside her, careful not to jostle the sofa cushions too much with his weight.

She turned to him, folding her hands in her lap. "He wasn't a good man."

"What?" Nash said, startled.

"Your father."

"How did you—?"

"Because you looked like he used to. Right before—" She stopped suddenly, and he got a chill up his spine.

I look like him when I get angry.

"That is why I want to make certain that your heir does not inherit. He gets that look also, and I have heard of things he has done . . ." She trailed off, and he felt his chest tighten. This was why it was so important he not care. Because caring led to violence. His father had shown that.

"But at the moment the only lady who seems as though she might accept you is Lady Felicity, and while she would be suitable, she is not ideal."

Nash's eyebrows rose. "What makes you say that?"

His grandmother made a dismissive gesture. "She is a bit obvious."

"Because she wants to be a duchess?" Nash snorted. "Isn't that what all of them want?"

His grandmother raised her nose in the air even higher than usual. "Yes, of course. But it is not something a lady should exhibit."

I want to kiss you.

She said what she wanted. He liked that; otherwise, how would he possibly know? He was obviously terrible at figuring things out, since he'd never tried before. Certainly not with a lady. His friends told him what they wanted from him also: usually more whiskey, or for him to stop being an ass.

He could oblige them on the former but not always on the latter.

Marrying and fathering a child was his chance to right the wrongs that his father had done. That his cousin would do, if given the title.

"All right," he said, taking a deep breath. "What do I need to learn?"

Chapter Fifteen

So we're decided," Ana Maria said. "The magenta for the main wall, the dark blue for the others."

Octavia nodded as she looked down at the fabric samples laid on top of one of the green gaming tables. "You have an excellent eye, I never would have thought of putting those two colors together, but they work perfectly."

Ana Maria smiled in response. "And then we will re-cover the chairs in that purple later on."

"When we can afford it," Octavia said with a grimace. "The club is still doing well, but Ivy is so conservative with money." She gave an exasperated sigh. "I wish she would just leave everything to me—she could spend more time with Sebastian, but she just can't seem to let go."

"I suppose she enjoys having a purpose."

"Besides kissing your brother?" Octavia said with a sly grin.

Ana Maria made a face. "I do not want to think of my brother doing that, even though I know he does."

"She does like working, I know that. I believe

Sebastian presented her with some sort of option that would require her leaving the club, but she said no."

Being able to say no to something like that—that was what she wanted. That was what she was going to take.

As long as she could also say yes.

"And what now?" Octavia said, interrupting her decidedly inappropriate thoughts. "The Duke of Malvern's house?" Her eyebrows rose.

Ana Maria's cheeks flushed. "Not today, although—"

"You don't have to say anything," Octavia interrupted, holding her hand up. "You don't have to, it's all over your face."

"He is teaching me self-defense," Ana Maria said. Defensively.

"And he's still teaching you other things, judging by your blush." Octavia folded her arms over her chest and regarded her friend with a skeptical expression. "I want you to blush for all the right reasons. Just—be careful."

"Of course I will." It was an automatic response, one borne out of always agreeing with the other person. Something she needed to stop. "But why be careful?"

Octavia shrugged. "I've heard he is on the market for a bride, and I did not hear your name mentioned."

Ana Maria's stomach twisted. "Let me guess—Lady Felicity?"

Octavia nodded. "Yes—we have a betting book in the club, and right now she's at 2–1 odds to land him."

"People bet on that kind of thing?" Ana Maria said, appalled.

Octavia laughed. "People will bet on all kinds of things. Miss Ivy's just facilitates their foolishness."

"I'll be careful, I promise." Her eyes widened as she had a thought. "Is there a betting book on my marriage?"

Octavia winced. "Uh—yes, actually."

"Tell me."

Octavia shook her head. "You do not want to know. Just let me tell you that your self-defense instructor is at very long odds."

Oh. So even random gamblers thought it was a long shot.

Not that she wanted to marry him, of course, since he was so firm in his resolve not to marry her. And a host of other inarticulate annoyingly irritating reasons. But she didn't want to seem to be not wanted.

Because that was how she'd spent the first twenty-seven years of her life, except for Sebastian, Thaddeus, and—him.

"Instead of waiting until your next . . . lesson," Octavia said with a wink, clearly changing the subject, "why don't you come here this evening when we are open so you can take a risk yourself?"

Risks, lessons, and commands, Ana Maria thought in satisfaction as she left Miss Ivy's clutching her fabric samples.

She was going to do what she wanted, regardless of anyone else.

She was not doing what she wanted.

The afternoon was perfect—it was the rarest of days in London, temperate, sunny, with just a slight breeze.

The horses were, as Lord Brunley had promised, attractive in their equine way. Not that Ana Maria had the slightest idea of what made for an attractive horse, but she did smile when she saw their long faces.

She'd worn a new afternoon dress that made her especially happy—it was pale blue, the color of the sky right now, with sprigs of tiny flowers all over the skirt. She had a shawl in a complementary blue shade, and her bonnet was festooned with blue ribbons.

If she weren't seated next to Lord Brunley, she would be doing precisely what she wanted.

She made a mental reminder to ask Thaddeus about purchasing a carriage suitable for her to take out on her own.

"Did my flowers arrive?" Lord Brunley asked as he and Ana Maria nodded to the other couples currently driving in the park.

"I'm certain they did," Ana Maria replied. "I got an enormous delivery just the other day."

Fletchfield had curated the flowers so that the ones she liked best were in her bedroom, and the others were in the salon.

"An enormous delivery, hm?" Lord Brunley said, sounding displeased.

Of course. She wished she could smack herself on the head. It sounded as though she were bragging about her popularity, when really she was just reporting what had happened. Not that Lord Brunley couldn't be taken down a notch, but it felt mean to do it deliberately.

"I suppose some of the flowers came from the Duke of Malvern?"

Ana Maria repressed a snort. "No, Nash isn't the flower type." He'd be more likely to send her boxing gloves, or perhaps a poker especially made for thwarting aggressive suitors.

She would not mention that to Lord Brunley.

"Ah." Lord Brunley sounded pleased, which irked Ana Maria.

She wished she weren't so easily irked by him, but really, he was so smug it was impossible.

"Speaking of the duke, there he is. With Lady Felicity, if I'm not mistaken." Oh, now he sounded even more smug.

And there they were. Her eyes went to him first, noting his immaculate cravat, his well-fitted jacket, and how tall he appeared in the carriage seat next to the dainty Lady Felicity.

She was also perfectly garbed, wearing a pale

yellow gown and a delightfully festive bonnet strewn with flowers that made Ana Maria both admiring and envious.

Perfect for Lady Oxymoron.

"Good afternoon, Your Grace, my lady," Lord Brunley said, slowing his horses.

Nash's lips clamped into a thin line as he saw who was greeting them, and he barely met Ana Maria's gaze before glaring at Lord Brunley.

"Good afternoon," Lady Felicity called, taking the opportunity to place her hand on Nash's arm in what Ana Maria knew was a deliberate show of ownership.

Had he proposed already? Despite what had happened between the two of them so recently?

Her gut churned with jealousy and worry; jealousy for obvious reasons, worry because no matter what happened between them, they were friends, and she just didn't think he would be happy with someone like Lady Felicity.

But perhaps that was the point? Maybe he didn't want to be happy?

"The day is splendid, isn't it? I wanted to show Lady Ana Maria what my new pair could do, and I cannot imagine a better venue for it."

Lord Brunley even seemed to take credit for the pleasant weather. His former humility was apparently something he'd discarded in the bright light of day.

"It is." Nash spoke in a curt tone. He still had barely looked at her.

That was not to be tolerated.

"Your Grace," she said, making his eyes snap to hers, "I wonder if you are planning to visit Miss Ivy's soon? I understand they are making changes to the interior."

He looked entirely confused. Of course, since she was asking him about a gambling house and engaging him on the topic of interior design, for goodness' sake.

"Miss Ivy's," Lord Brunley said. "That is the place that anyone can go, is it not?"

Lady Felicity sniffed.

"Yes," Ana Maria replied. "It is owned by my sister-in-law, actually."

"Ah, I'd forgotten." Lord Brunley gave her hand a condescending pat. The snob.

"I have not been there," Lady Felicity said, turning to Nash. "Perhaps you would take me sometime? I don't always mind rubbing elbows with just anybody," she added, with a quick glance toward Ana Maria, as if Ana Maria could possibly misconstrue the barb.

Nash grunted in reply, making Lady Felicity preen as if he'd said yes.

But Ana Maria could have told the lady that that particular grunt was a noncommittal "I don't think so, but it's not worth my time to argue" type of response.

Lady Felicity clearly did not speak inarticulate Nash.

"Well, we should be going. I don't want to

make my horses stand around any longer," Lord Brunley said. He tipped his hat toward Lady Felicity. "We will see you both soon," he added, making Ana Maria want to smack him. His words made it seem as though he and Ana Maria were a "we," when they most certainly were not.

And there were no pokers at the ready in a carriage. She should have brought something in case he decided to plead his case again.

"Goodbye," Lady Felicity said, shooting one more superior look toward Ana Maria.

Ana Maria's only consolation was that Nash looked as uncomfortable and miserable as she felt.

If he married Lady Felicity, he would continue to be uncomfortable and miserable. She would have to broach that subject with him sometime, warn him about his future, since she knew neither Sebastian nor Thaddeus would think to.

Men.

"It's beautiful!"

Ana Maria stepped into Miss Ivy's, her eyes wide with wonder at the sight. The workmen Octavia had hired had done wonders, completing the task of re-covering the walls in only a few days. Spurred on, no doubt, by Octavia's charm and promise of extra payment if the work was done quickly.

Octavia beamed at Ana Maria's compliment, taking her friend's arm and leading her toward the walls. "It looks marvelous, and it is all thanks to you."

Ana Maria shook her head. "No, I wouldn't have even dreamt of suggesting it if you weren't so open to the change."

Octavia shrugged modestly. "I am always open to change. That is the mark of a good business person."

Ana Maria chuckled softly as she scrutinized the new hangings. She should adopt Octavia's attitude of being more open to change, especially given that Octavia never seemed to regret anything, and was likely the type of person to ask a gentleman to kiss her if she wanted him to.

And it meant a lot, then, that Octavia had taken her suggestions, since Ana Maria had no doubt her friend would say something if she disagreed with the decision. The magenta and dark blue made the room look even more sumptuous than before, and Octavia had unearthed some gold sconces to place on the walls, taking down some of the paintings her sister had initially chosen for decoration.

"It's early, so we can spend some time together before I have to start work. Come through here," Octavia said, tugging Ana Maria's arm and guiding her toward the other end of the room. She swept aside a curtain, opening a door that led into Octavia's personal rooms.

She led her toward the room that was the club's storage space, holding a desk for business and supplies for the club.

"Why here?" Ana Maria said in surprise. The other times she'd visited, they'd taken tea in the small salon between the bedrooms.

Octavia rolled her eyes. "Because your brother and my sister absconded with all the liquor except for the whiskey Ivy tucked into this drawer."

Ana Maria's eyes widened. "So we're having whiskey?"

Octavia grinned. "Of course, we have to toast to your success!"

Ana Maria allowed her friend to guide her to the chair in front of the desk, then waited as Octavia poured two glasses of the brown liquid.

Had she ever had whiskey before?

She took the glass from Octavia's hand, sniffing it gingerly. It smelled powerful.

Octavia held her own glass up, waiting for Ana Maria. "I want to thank you for your work, and I know this is just the beginning of your future."

Ana Maria felt a warmth kindle inside her, and she hadn't even had any alcohol yet. It felt so good, and so unusual, to be appreciated for something she'd done. She'd accomplished many things in her life—notably household chores and the occasional capture of runaway poultry—but nobody had ever noticed or thanked her.

"I didn't do much, honestly. I just chose the fabrics. Anybody could do that."

Octavia gestured with her glass toward Ana Maria. "Anybody could have done it, but only you could have done it so well." She gave Ana

Maria an assessing glance. "And speaking of only you could have done it so well, I do admire your gown."

Ana Maria glanced down in pleasure. The gown was another frothy confection that made her feel like a decadent dessert, encased in layers of pink tulle and satin and augmented with darker pink ribbons at the bottom. Jane had made that face when Ana Maria had asked her to bring it out of the closet, so she knew it must look stunning on her. Jane obviously didn't want to say so, but clearly she thought Ana Maria was too naive to negotiate Society and would be tempting danger by looking too fabulous.

She'd accessorized it with ruby earrings Sebastian had given her, one of the many gifts he'd bestowed on her as soon as he'd inherited the title. Making up for lost time, he'd said, even though Ana Maria thought it was entirely unnecessary.

Still, it was nice to have nice things. And, she'd discovered, she did like to look fabulous. If only for her own satisfaction.

"Thank you," she said at last, "and thank you for the kind words about the hangings."

"Words that are well deserved. Come on, now," Octavia commanded, "drink up! The club will start to fill up in about an hour. I want you to see its full splendor." Octavia downed her glass, wiping her mouth as she finished drinking.

The liquor burned her throat, and Ana Maria couldn't help but cough. As soon as that was over, however, she felt a delicious warmth flowing through her body, her mouth tingling from the sting of the whiskey.

"Good, isn't it?" Octavia said, pouring more into their glasses.

"I don't think I should have any more," Ana Maria said, clearing her throat.

Octavia squinted at her. "Because you don't want any more or you think you shouldn't have any more?"

Ana Maria tilted her head as she considered it. "Fine. One more, but then that's it."

The second drink went down smoother than the first, now that she knew what to expect, and that delicious warmth only increased, making her feel as though she were encased in soft cotton.

"Is this what it feels like to be drunk? All happy and floaty?" she asked, frowning at her friend.

Octavia shook her head. "It's just a little bit of whiskey. I think you're feeling proud and confident in your work."

"Perhaps," Ana Maria conceded. She did feel proud of what she'd done, of what she was planning to do. "Should we go back to the club? I want to see how your customers react to the new decorations."

"Don't expect them to say much," Octavia warned. "They're mostly interested in how much money they think they can win."

"I want to gamble, too," Ana Maria announced,

getting to her feet. She gripped the arm of the chair she'd been sitting in, steadying herself. She smiled widely at Octavia, who returned the smile. "I think I like choosing what I want to do. And pink gowns and whiskey," she added, giving her friend a wink.

Octavia laughed as they left the office and made their way back to the club.

NASH STRODE IN to Miss Ivy's with one goal: to get a drink. Certainly he could have stayed at home and accomplished the same thing, but here he was surrounded by people who were not his half siblings. He knew that most of them were grateful to have been rescued by him, but he did not want to be treated as though he had done anything beyond what should be done, even if nobody else had done it.

He blinked as he tried to figure out his own reasoning.

Stuff it, he wanted to leave the house, he could leave the house, and so here he was. Thirsty.

And she had mentioned Miss Ivy's, which had made him wonder if she would be here as well. Not that that was why he had come out. But it had reminded him that he did like it here.

"Welcome, Your Grace." The burly gentleman who'd nearly tossed Sebastian out the first time Nash brought him in greeted him with an expression of guarded respect. Likely because they were the only two men in the room who knew they could best everyone else in the room. Though that had yet to be put to the test.

Nash grunted in response, threading his way through the crowd to the small bar at the right-hand side of the room. There weren't too many customers there, and most of them quickly glanced away when they met Nash's eyes, which gratified him. He liked coming to Miss Ivy's because there were people of so many different types here, ranging from clerks and merchants to country squires in town for some fun to what appeared to be some housekeepers and governesses. The rule in Miss Ivy's was that anyone could enter as long as they could pay for their play.

And their drinks.

Nash sat down at the bar, waiting for the server to notice him.

"Good evening."

He turned slowly at the sound of her voice, startled out of his fervent desire for a drink. Something only her presence could accomplish.

"You're here," he said, sounding incredibly stupid to his own ears. "Gambling?"

"I'm here for the decorations," she replied, gesturing grandly toward the wall. He frowned in puzzlement, then glanced toward the wall, which did appear different from the last time he'd been here, not that he could figure out what had changed. Right. She'd mentioned something about redecorating, but he hadn't paid too much attention. He'd been too focused on wanting to toss Lord Brunley and his perfectly coiffed head onto the ground.

"I didn't do the work myself," she explained, speaking in what sounded like a deliberately exaggerated tone of voice, "but I chose the fabrics." She poked him in the shoulder. "From that place I was leaving when that man accosted me!" she exclaimed.

"When you tried to subdue him with some cloth?" Nash said in a skeptical tone.

"Yes! And that is when you decided I should have self-defense lessons. Not that you've taught me much yet," she added.

No, because the only time he'd tried, they'd ended up kissing. And then he had ended up regretting, and feeling horrible, and caring too much for her, and then he had gone and done it all again. Although she had been the one to want to do it again. He had just obliged her. Happily.

"Do you like them?"

Nash stared at the wall for a few moments, trying to form some sort of opinion. He usually avoided having to choose things, because choosing things would mean that he cared about something, and the only things he wanted to care about were ensuring his father's bastards were provided for, his ability to hit someone who deserved it, and his whiskey.

Not in that order.

"I like the colors," he said at last.

She rolled her eyes. Clearly he had not done a very good job of expressing an opinion.

"Let's try something easier."

The server came to stand in front of them, and Nash pointed to the whiskey in relief.

"I'll take one of those, too," she said to the server, who nodded.

"You?" he asked in surprise.

She gave a vigorous nod of her head. "I had some with Miss Octavia, and I think I like it. But I need more experience to know for certain."

Ah. That explained why she seemed so vivacious. The server placed two glasses in front of them, pouring whiskey into both and leaving the bottle on the bar.

"You might not want any more," he warned as she went to pick up her glass. "You'll have a devil of a head tomorrow if you drink to excess."

"You drink to excess, don't you?" She frowned. Which honestly made her look completely adorable. "Besides, it is my choice."

He took a deep breath. He didn't think he'd ever been in the position of being the reasonable one in a situation, and yet here he was, having to dissuade a young lady from drinking too much whiskey.

Because too much whiskey would leave her vulnerable to—well, to gentlemen like him who might see her literal high spirits as an opportunity for inappropriate behavior.

But she wanted to kiss me—twice—when she was completely sober.

Never mind that.

"Tell me about the fabrics," he said, trying to change the subject. "Speaking of choice, how did you come to choose those particular colors?"

There. That was a question that was more than a yes or no question, and if he could get her talking about something she was obviously enthusiastic about, perhaps she would forget she was asking him about alcohol. And how much she could drink and how much he did drink.

She picked up her glass and grinned at him as she tapped it against his, holding it up in front of her face, then taking a sip and setting it down.

So much for forgetting about alcohol.

At least she hadn't drunk all of it.

"Do you really want to know?" she asked, sounding suspicious. "Because I don't think you've ever thought about color choice before."

He tried not to look guilty. "I don't know that I have, but I think I should," he said. He'd never allowed himself to think about colors, about anything other than muting his world. But now he wanted to learn. From her. "And who better to teach me than you what the best choices are?" He gestured toward her gown. "It's obvious you care what you present to the world, what with your silver and pink gowns."

Her cheeks turned pink to match her gown. "You noticed that gown?"

How could I not? You looked like starlight.

"Uh, it's just that it was so different from what the other young ladies were wearing." *I couldn't help but notice. I notice everything about you nowadays, from how you blush when you're flattered, to how you challenge me when I try to rescue you, to how you can understand what I'm saying when I don't say anything.*

"Well, thank you," she said, raising her chin. "I never got the opportunity for fine clothing before, and it is such a pleasure to look as good as you know you can."

He rather thought that she might look as good as she could if she were entirely naked and in his bed, but he knew this was not the time to say that. *Never* was the time to say that, and he needed to remember that. Even though that was getting increasingly difficult every time they kissed.

"But as I was saying," she continued, oblivious to his imagination, "the magenta—that's the dark purplish red fabric there—has a certain richness I thought would suit Miss Ivy's, and the dark blue adds a certain stateliness, so the two combined are reflections of Miss Ivy's clientele."

"Rich and stately?" he said.

She beamed at him as though he were her prize pupil. "Precisely. Or that they wish to be perceived that way, and they want their surroundings to reflect that."

"Huh." He poured more whiskey into his empty glass.

Two more customers sat at the bar, and while Nash was usually determined to ignore everyone around him, it seemed she did not feel the same way.

"Mrs. Lee!" she exclaimed, then leaned over to see the other person next to the lady she'd addressed. "And Mr. Lee!"

"Good evening, my lady," the woman Ana Maria had called Mrs. Lee replied. She was a middle-aged woman with brown hair and a modest demeanor, wearing a gown in a very similar hue to the dark blue on the wall.

The man beside her was Chinese, also of middle age, wearing a dark suit and a much more intricately tied hellcloth than the one Nash had allowed Finan to put on him.

"We came to see the fabric ourselves," Mrs. Lee said, glancing nervously toward Nash.

"And isn't it lovely? Oh, allow me to introduce you. This is the Duke of Malvern," Ana Maria said, placing her hand on Nash's shoulder, "and these are the Lees. I've found their fabric shop to have the widest selection in London."

"Oh, thank you, my lady," Mrs. Lee replied. "It is a pleasure to meet you, Your Grace," she added.

Nash nodded toward both of them.

"We have a new shipment coming in next week," Mr. Lee said, his tone much less hesitant. "I would be glad to give you the first look at it, if you think there is something you might want."

Ana Maria looked at Nash with an excited expression. "Isn't that wonderful?" She turned back to the Lees. "Of course I would like to. Just send a note and I'll pop over immediately."

"Not without me," Nash growled.

The Lees jumped at his words, while Ana Maria frowned. "It's not necessary," she said, but then immediately held her hand up in defeat. "But I know not to argue with you, so I will allow you to come."

Nash was more than relieved he didn't have to argue with her about it, because he'd be damned if he'd let her traipse around London again, what with being so attractive. And insistent that she could protect herself with random items like fireplace pokers and bolts of fabric.

Not to mention he hadn't actually given her much self-defense training.

Because he'd given her training in kissing.

It seemed he was incapable of thinking straight when he was near her. And yet he couldn't stay away.

"TODAY I'LL SHOW you how to throw a punch."

He'd woken up resolved to give her some of the training he'd promised—and not *that* type of training.

So, to that end, he'd told Finan he would have to stay in the room with them, and had asked her to come by at noon, but only until he had to go meet with Robert at one o'clock. Not enough time for boxing room shenanigans. Similar to terrace shenanigans, only with more punching.

He'd wrapped her wrists for her, and she stood in the middle of the floor, her hair pulled back, wearing that same old gown she'd had on earlier.

"Finally," she replied, giving him a sly look. As though he had been the only one to delay the proceedings.

He ignored the provocation.

"First, curl the tips of your fingers into your palm. Like this," he said, demonstrating.

She imitated his action.

"Then place your thumb on top of those fingers. It's very important not to go the other way around. Your thumb could get injured that way."

She nodded.

"Now," he continued, "plant your feet so you have a steady base."

She squinted at him in confusion. "A steady base? What does that mean?"

"Uh—" he began.

"Show her," Finan urged, an amused tone in his voice.

Of course the blackguard had to try to cause trouble.

"Right, well, some of the force of the blow comes from your legs. You'll be punching with your whole body, not just your fist." He set himself in position, widening his stance as he dropped his right leg back. "Like this."

"Ah," she replied, her eyes narrowed in concentration.

He watched as she set herself as he had, feeling a tug of admiration at her determination to learn from him, even though she hadn't wanted this training in the first place.

"When you punch someone, the power all comes from the arm. Not the fist. So you want to shoot it out like an arrow. Like this," he said, demonstrating the action.

"Oh I see," she replied, sending her fist into the air.

"Now that's set, you should punch *him*," Finan urged.

She laughed in response.

"No, but you should," Nash said. "It'll give you the feel of how it would really be."

"I find punching him greatly relieves my indigestion."

Nash shot a quick glance over his shoulder at his friend. "You're not helping."

Her eyebrows arched. "My stomach has been a bit unsettled lately."

Nash grunted, then gestured toward his chin. "Come on, then."

He braced himself for it, wanting her to know how it felt to connect, not just to toss her hand into empty space. She would need the experience if she was to properly defend herself. He didn't want her to be unprepared.

Even though he had no intention of letting her go anywhere without him.

Her fist shot out, connecting with his jaw, making his head fly back as he staggered to maintain his footing.

He shook his head clear, hearing Finan howling in laughter just behind him. And her shocked face in front.

"It's fine, I told you to. How did it feel?" he asked, rubbing the spot she'd hit with his hand.

"Powerful," she replied. "Did it hurt? I am so sorry."

"It's fine." He worked his jaw back and forth to ease the pain out. It wasn't the worst hit he'd received—that had come from Finan, of course—but it was strong, and so he was proud of the hurt, knowing that he'd done something to protect her.

"I think you should try again," Finan said.

"Goodness, no," she blurted. "I didn't expect it to be so intense."

Which could describe this moment as well as any time he touched her. Placed his mouth on her full lips, ran his fingers down her curves.

And here he was back again, thinking about her in ways he should not possibly think about her. Although now she would be able to defend herself against anyone who might want to put their hands on her.

"Oh, I forgot to mention it. The Lees sent a note. It's to be tomorrow at the docks." She grinned up at him. "Although now you've taught me this, perhaps you don't need to bother coming?"

He growled.

She rolled her eyes. "Fine, I'm not certain precisely what time. I will send a note later." She bounced on her toes, an exhilarated expression on her face. "This is nearly as much fun as—" And then her eyes got wide, shifting quickly to Finan, clearly aware of what she'd nearly almost said.

He smothered a chuckle, regretting he couldn't finish this training session with a training kiss.

"YOU'RE GOING TO the docks wearing that?"

Ana Maria raised an eyebrow at Nash's startled tone.

He stood in her salon, hands behind his back, obviously pacing as he waited for her to arrive. They'd agreed he would pick her up at eleven o'clock, and it was barely forty-five minutes past ten. She was secretly delighted he was so early. Did it mean he was eagerly looking forward to being with her?

Although the same could be said of her, so they were paired in that sentiment.

"Are you an arbiter of fashion now?" she asked, reaching forward to tug on his sloppily tied cravat. "And what is wrong with what I am wearing?"

She glanced down, unable to resist smiling at her gown. It was made of spring green fabric, with little daisies embroidered all over it. The gown had no fewer than four flounces at the bottom, and the fichu she wore draped around her shoulders was a sheer green color also, giving a nod to discretion, but also revealing some of her bosom underneath.

"You're—it's—well, you look too good."

The other eyebrow rose. "I look too good? Goodness, Nash, you will overwhelm me with compliments!" She bit her lip to keep from giggling at his obvious discomfiture.

"You will be with me, and I am certain you will deter anybody who attempts anything because I 'look too good.'"

He rose up to his full height, drawing his arms from behind his back to fold them over his chest.

"You won't intimidate me, Nash. Remember, we know each other too well." Her eyes widened as she realized that what she said could be construed in a few ways, not all of them respectable.

"We do." His gaze slid over her, a nearly tangible thing that made her shiver.

Reminding her that only a week or so ago he'd had his hand on her breast, caressing her nipple. That he'd spoken delightfully naughty things in her ear as he touched her.

"Stop that," she said. "We won't ever leave if you insist on looking at me that way."

He stepped forward, unfolding his arms. "Maybe we shouldn't leave."

"Nash . . ."

"Call me by my name," he said hoarsely. "Ignatius."

She blinked. "Ignatius." It was such an odd name for Nash; it sounded as though it belonged to a wizened old man who spent his days in his study.

He grimaced. "Yes, I know it's ridiculous."

"It's not!" she exclaimed. "Just—just that I didn't know your name. Ever." She paused. "Do Sebastian and Thaddeus know?"

He shook his head slowly. "No. You're the only one I've told."

His admission made her warm inside, made her feel as though he did truly value her in his life. To share something with her he'd never told his closest friends meant something. Especially from "I don't speak when I could grunt" Nash.

She patted his lapel, looking up into his handsome face. "Thank you for trusting me with that. Ignatius."

He looked at her with an expression of such vulnerability, so different from his usual expression, that she had to swallow hard to keep herself from tearing up.

"So," he said in his usual tone, "we had better leave so you don't miss seeing the new shipment. I don't want to be responsible if you lose out on purchasing more fabric to beat potential assaulters over the head with."

She chuckled, giving his lapel one last caress. "Yes, Ignatius, we should leave."

He didn't know what had made him tell her. Not that it was a deep secret; it was a *name,* for goodness' sake. One that anybody could discover, if they cared to. But he hadn't used it, not since his mother had left. She was the only one who'd called him by it, and after she left, he became Nash.

Until Ana Maria.

He escorted her out to his carriage, nodding to the coachman and the additional footmen he'd insisted come along.

He knew he could take care of Ana Maria himself, but he wanted extra protection just because.

Because she was a precious thing that should never get hurt.

Because he cared for her far more than he should.

Because he wanted her to feel safe and protected anytime she was with him.

Except when he was kissing her—then he wanted her to feel wild and dangerous. Like he did.

He was falling, he knew that. And yet he couldn't seem to stop.

And it would only end in heartache.

"Are you all right?"

Her soft tone brought him out of his thoughts.

"Mm," he replied. He turned to meet her eyes, their warm brown depths making *him* feel safe, oddly enough.

He was safe with her. She would respect his opinions, challenge him when he needed it, and listen to him on one of the rare occasions he spoke.

"Why do you want so much fabric?" he asked.

"You've redecorated the salon, I can tell that much."

She leaned back against the seat cushion, giving him an affronted look. "You don't like how I redecorated?"

"I didn't say that. It's very—it's very colorful."

"That sounds nearly as complimentary as telling me I look too good," she said with a chuckle.

He frowned, knowing she was being lighthearted, but also keenly aware of his inability to communicate how he felt.

"It's very you," he said at last. "When I think of you, Ana Maria, I think of joy. Of color. Of being happy, even when things seem to be miserable."

"Oh!" she said in a startled tone. "That is—that is one of the nicest things anyone has ever said to me. Thank you. *Ignatius.*"

"Mm," he replied, completely embarrassed.

"When I think of you, I think of possibility," she said.

He raised his eyebrows in question.

"By possibility I mean that you have so much within you, things I don't think you recognize yourself. Things like kindness and empathy and power."

"I'm powerful enough," he retorted. The many fights he'd gotten into—and won—were testament to that.

"I don't mean power in your brute force, though that is certainly impressive."

He shouldn't feel proud of that compliment, but he did.

"I mean power in what you can do for people."

"Because I'm a duke, you mean?"

She shook her head. "Not just that, although of course you are able to do so much because of your position. I mean power in who you champion. I don't know if you realize how much you mean to Sebastian and Thaddeus. How much you mean to me."

He wished he could vault out of the carriage so he wouldn't succumb to all the emotion swamping him. And yet he still wanted to hear more.

"I wouldn't have survived without Sebastian and Thaddeus," he said in a gruff voice. "I was so hurt, and they let me just be with them, not having to talk about it."

"Do you want to talk about it now?" she interrupted.

He took a deep breath. "Yes." His answer was surprising even to himself.

"Tell me," she urged.

Ana Maria's chest tightened as she listened to Nash pouring his heart out—about his father's violence toward his mother, toward him. About his mother's eventual escape, her sobbing as she left her only son behind.

"Do you know where she is?" she asked. She squeezed his hand, which she'd somehow taken hold of during his recitation.

He nodded his head slowly. "I do. I didn't dare

before, but I think I should at least make sure she is safe."

"Always the protector," she said with a smile.

"I used to resent her, especially right after she left."

"Of course, you were so young, you couldn't understand." And Ana Maria didn't know what decision she'd make in that situation—to stay and face more brutality, but be with your only child? Or run, knowing you might never see your child again?

Her heart hurt for Nash's mother.

"So have you contacted her yet?" She held her breath for his answer.

He shook his head. "No. I should—I think about it. I just don't know what I would do if I discovered she was—she was unhappy, or worse."

She turned to look at him. His face—usually set in resolution—was so vulnerable she wanted to cry.

"You should. I'll be there no matter what you find out."

"And what if I can't help her?"

She gave him a disbelieving look. "You're a duke, Nash. You can use all that power and privilege to get anything done, if you want to. Don't you have some smart siblings lying around your house who could assist you?"

He winced. "You know about that?"

She rolled her eyes. "Of course I do. Servants

talk, remember? And until six months ago, I was a servant. They all know who your employees are. It's hardly a secret belowstairs."

"It was the least I could do, given my father's . . . proclivities."

"And I admire you for it."

He gave a slight nod, as though reluctant to accept praise. The usual Nash. "It was Robert, my secretary, who found her." He paused. "And when he told me, I wanted to hit him. I didn't. I didn't even break the vase I grabbed." He shook his head. "But it was close."

Ana Maria gasped. "That must have been frightening," she replied.

He opened his mouth to contradict her, then realized she was correct. It *was* frightening. It was a feeling he didn't want to have anymore—that loss of control, that worry he would do something like his father.

But he hadn't done anything, had he, even though his temper had risen? He'd put the vase back, which would not have happened before—just ask the chair he'd destroyed when his grandmother arrived.

"But I didn't," he continued slowly. "I've been thinking about what you've been saying. About choice. About deciding how you want to present yourself to the world."

"So you'll be wearing pink and silver gowns?" She accompanied her words with a soft smile.

He chuckled as he shook his head.

"Are you going to contact her?" she asked in a gentle tone.

He nodded. "I am." *Even though that terrifies me, too.* But he could not continue avoiding the things that might bring him joy or pain.

"I will be there to support you."

He reached over to take her other hand. "Thank you."

They sat in silence, holding both of the other's hands, until they pulled up at the docks.

"YOU NEVER DID say why you need so much fabric," he said, standing beside her in the ship's hold.

The Lees were also there, going through boxes of their shipments, pulling out bolts they thought would be of interest to Ana Maria. She liked how they worked together—neither speaking much, just working efficiently side by side. It seemed like an ideal partnership, although of course she imagined there were hiccups along the way. It couldn't have been easy for either one of them to be married to the other, much less run a business together.

And yet here they were, clearly doing well enough to order in quantity, enough so that a curious young lady with a penchant for bright colors could come and see what they had and buy it before it went into their shop.

"I expect to be redecorating more than a few of Thaddeus's rooms and Miss Ivy's. It is my hope that I can consult with other ladies who want to make their homes more reflective of them. Not of their mothers, or stepmothers, or husbands." She paused in her fabric-browsing to think more about it. "We seldom get the opportunity to express who we really are." She gestured to her gown. "In fact, the only way we are even offered the chance is in how we dress. And even then if what we're wearing doesn't suit what someone might think about us, we're disparaged for our choice." She shrugged. "If I can help a few ladies realize their own potential, even just through the choice of their wall hangings, it will make me happy."

"You're a veritable fabric Joan of Arc," he remarked.

"Don't make light of it. That's what people always do when ladies express an opinion." She was surprised to find she was angry. She so seldom was.

"I didn't mean to make light of it," he said, sounding humble. He put his hand on top of hers, which was resting on a length of blue-green silk. "I think I made a joke because your words resonated with me, and I don't always know what to do with my emotions." He paused. "Which is putting it mildly."

"Is that why you're so determined to keep yourself distant from anyone you might care for?"

And where did this angry, honest woman come from?

He reeled back, as though her words had

physically struck him. "I don't keep myself distant." He sounded defensive, and by his expression, she could tell he knew that, too.

This wasn't the place for this discussion, she knew that. And yet she couldn't seem to stop herself. "You care for people, but you present them with a wall of grunts and implacable strength. Nobody can ever be as strong as you are, or as privileged, or as alone, which is how you appear to want it. But Nash—Ignatius—nobody should be alone." She took a deep breath, knowing that she was about to speak on something that would be entirely inappropriate. "You can't marry that Lady Felicity."

"Why not?" It sounded as though he were asking an honest question, not being combative. For once.

"She won't care for you. She won't ever care for you. She is pleasant enough, and obviously beautiful, but there is something lacking in her."

"Like there is in me."

He spoke as though it was decided. As though there was no hope for him.

And her heart hurt for him all over again. "I promise you," she continued, her voice throbbing with emotion, "that you can find everything you think that is missing from yourself if you just give yourself the chance." *Give me a chance.*

"My lady," Mrs. Lee said, walking toward them with her arms full of fabric. "I've just found what I consider to be the best of the lot." She dumped them all onto a rough wooden table in front of Ana Maria, the colors a riotous jumble. "We will have to start moving the boxes out soon, so if you could—?"

"Yes, of course, I will get to work straightaway."

"MY EMOTIONS AREN'T lacking," he said through gritted teeth.

They were back in his carriage, bolts of fabric surrounding them, making them sit so closely their thighs were touching. The fabric of her skirts were tangled up with his legs, and she'd had to remove her hat since it kept hitting him in the head.

"I didn't say that."

"I can't—I have them, I just can't express them. If I do—"

"If you do—what?" she asked.

He twisted his head to look at her, his hands coming up of their own volition to cup her face. "If I do, then this happens."

He lowered his mouth to hers, branding her with his lips, feeling forceful and powerful and yet utterly at her mercy.

She met him with just as much power and force, her hands clasping his arms, reaching around to knot themselves around his back, pulling him into her.

He groaned against her mouth, losing himself in her taste. Her tongue tangled with his, her hands unclasping from around his back to reach to his chest. She placed her fingers at his cravat, undoing the casual folds and pulling the fabric away from his neck.

He put his right hand at her waist, splaying his fingers so that they were just under her glorious, full breast.

He lowered his other hand down her leg toward the floor, grasping the fabric of her gown and bringing it up slowly, letting his fingers trail against her leg encased in soft silk stocking.

He went slowly, waiting for her to call a halt to this. But she didn't; instead, she flattened her palm against his chest, sliding it down to his waist, then tentatively lower still.

And then her hand rested on top of his aching cock, separated only from her skin by his clothing. He wished they weren't in a moving carriage, or he'd shuck everything and urge himself into her hand, teaching her how to stroke him.

She made a soft, muffled noise of pleasure in her throat, her mouth open wide to let his tongue in, her fingers sliding back and forth on top of his erection.

Her skirts rested just above her knees now, and he reached below them to find the soft skin above her stocking.

His fingers were on her thigh, caressing her as his other hand moved further up to clasp around her breast. Its fullness filled his hand.

He hadn't seen her breast yet.

He wanted to suck and lick her nipple, make

it stand proudly for his attention. He wanted to kiss his way from her neck down to her toes, lavishing attention on every single delectable part of her.

He wanted to thrust inside her soft wetness, hear her moans of pleasure as he took his time to discover what pleased her the most.

She broke their kiss, and he braced himself for the inevitable refusal. After all, he'd done the same to her.

"Touch me," she said instead, wriggling the leg he was holding.

That was not what he'd expected.

"You want me to—?"

She nodded. Her face was flushed, her lips were already red and swollen. She looked so desirable he felt as though he might explode.

"Touch me there. I want to feel it." She put more pressure on his cock. "Just as I want to feel you."

He groaned at her touch. "You'll have to stop that if you want me to pay attention to what I'm doing to you."

"You're not doing anything yet," she teased. "Go ahead. I'm waiting. Do it."

He grunted, sliding his fingers further up her thigh, finding the crease where her leg met her body. Moving to the right to the soft curls, entwining his fingers and petting her, preparing both of them for what was to come next.

Which was hopefully her.

He lowered his mouth to her ear, kissing the skin

just below. "I'm going to put my fingers inside you, Ana Maria," he said in a husky voice. She shivered. "I want to feel your climax. To feel your pleasure. If you want that, too."

"Oh," she said in a breathy tone. "Oh, Nash. Yes, please."

He couldn't resist her. He slid his fingers down, already feeling how wet she was. "Have you ever touched yourself?" he asked.

She nodded.

"I'd like to see that. But first, I need to touch you myself." He rubbed her clitoris with his thumb as he slid his index finger inside her. She moaned, and he began a gentle rhythm, responding to how she moved and sighed, adjusting his movements with every little shift of her body.

His cock was throbbing inside his trousers, almost unbearably painful. In an agonizingly sensual way.

He didn't have much experience with bringing ladies pleasure—he didn't have much experience in general, if he were being honest with himself. He was better able to channel his urges through violence, although that idea paled now as he felt her riding his hand to her climax.

"Come for me, Ana Maria," he said in a low, urgent tone.

She moaned, and then leaned forward to fasten her mouth on his neck, biting his skin as she began to come.

She tightened around his fingers, and he relished the involuntary shakes she was making, her entire body caught up in the pleasure of her orgasm.

"That's it," he crooned, and she sagged against him, panting. He stilled his fingers, then withdrew them gently, kissing her neck as he gave her breast one last delicious squeeze.

"Oh, Nash," she murmured against him. "That was—that was wonderful."

"*You* are wonderful," he replied in an equally low voice.

This was the power he wanted. The power to bring her joy, the power to lure her into an intoxicating experience that would profoundly shake both of them.

Because he was shaken just as surely as she was.

He had never felt this intensely connected to anyone before. Not even when he was with his best friend, exchanging quips and reminiscences over whiskey.

This was power. This was—damn it, he couldn't name it. Even though his mind whispered it: *love.*

And with that thought, he froze, incapable of not imagining what was inevitable afterward. Which was why he could not allow himself to acknowledge it, even though he knew it to be true.

How could his heart be broken when an orgasmic-spent woman was lying in his arms?

And yet here he was.

Goddamn it.

The carriage slowed to a stop at the worst possible time.

"Thank you for escorting me home. And—" Her cheeks were fiery red. Anybody looking at her had to know something had happened. But before he could react, the carriage door swung open, and one of Sebastian's footmen was holding his hand out to assist Ana Maria out onto the sidewalk.

"Ana Maria!"

Thaddeus stepped out of the house, a bemused expression on his face as he saw all the bolts of fabric being unloaded from the coach.

"And Nash," Thaddeus added, sounding less welcoming.

"Thad."

"Thaddeus, Nash took me to the docks to see the Lees' shipment, and I was fortunate enough to purchase all of these."

Should he be irked that what had just happened in the carriage seemed to have entirely slipped her mind in her enthusiasm for fabric?

Not that he wanted her to possibly reveal any of what had happened—that would definitely raise some questions he did not want to answer—but he'd like it if she weren't as excited about her fabric bolts as she was about her carriage orgasm. It seemed as though there should be a hierarchy of excitement, with the latter ahead of the former.

But he didn't care about fabric, so what did he know?

"Took you to the docks?" Thaddeus repeated.

Sebastian stepped outside, too, his eyes narrowing as he saw Nash's carriage and Ana Maria. "So that is where you have been." His sharp gaze seemed to peer inside Nash, making him want to shift in discomfort. Him. Nash. Shifting in discomfort?

That was not who he was.

She was changing him. Because of her he was changing himself.

"Would you excuse us, Ana Maria? I need to speak with Nash."

"If you're angry with him for taking me there, you shouldn't be." Ana Maria took Nash's arm as she spoke. "I was going to go on my own, but he insisted so I would be safe. So you see, it is perfectly acceptable."

"Why don't you go sort your things out in one of the spare bedrooms upstairs?" Thaddeus said, making it sound less like a question and more like an order. "You can have a room for your projects, if you like."

"I will, but promise not to rake Nash over the coals. He was there as protection," Ana Maria said. She stooped to pick a yellow flower from one of the potted plants on either side of the steps, handing it to Nash.

"Thank you for a wonderful day," she said in a low tone, one only he could hear. "Especially for—" And she met his gaze, her eyes warm and knowing.

"You are welcome," he said, holding the flower. "Let me know when you can come over for more defense training."

Her lips curled into a sly smile. "More defense training? Yes, I certainly will."

She gave him one last look, then turned and ran up the stairs, already calling instructions for where to put her purchases.

"Inside, Nash," Thaddeus said. This was definitely an order. And Nash knew whatever the two of them had to say would be said eventually, so he might as well get it over with now. He tucked Ana Maria's flower into his pocket and strode up the stairs, knowing that whatever they were concerned about was nowhere near as scandalous as what had just happened.

"WELL?"

Nash lounged on Thaddeus's sofa, stretching his arms over its back. He'd hoped that Thad would order brandy, but apparently whatever needed to be said was best done without alcohol.

Which definitely meant Nash did not want to hear it.

Sebastian spoke first. "I've heard that you and Ana Maria are spending time together."

"And we know that your grandmother is here to ensure you marry soon," Thaddeus added.

Their suspicious expressions matched each other in intensity.

Nash narrowed his eyes. "And that is a problem?" He rose, feeling the sudden urge to pace. "Not that it is any of your business, but Ana Maria and I are friends. As we have always been."

Friends who explore one another's mouths with their tongues, but Nash would not share that.

"You have no intention of marrying her?" Sebastian said.

"Are you upset that I have no intention of marrying her, or are you upset that I might intend to marry her? You two are damned hard to read."

Sebastian snorted. "As though you aren't impossible to read. We don't know what is going on. Nash, can you explain it to us?"

"Why should I?" Nash glanced between Sebastian and Thaddeus, his ire growing by the second.

Not that he knew why he was so damned mad, except that he did not like being scolded by his friends.

"Because Ana Maria is under my protection, and she has many suitors." Thaddeus spoke in his most pedantic manner, and Nash's fists curled in automatic response. "We are concerned that she will not give herself the opportunity to know any of these suitors if she is with you all the time. I know many of them are in earnest, they send her roomfuls of flowers."

Nash gave Thaddeus a disbelieving look. "As though any of them are worth a tenth of her." He pointed an accusing finger at Thaddeus. "Do you know one of those suitors tried to compromise her? It was a good thing I was around!"

"Ana Maria can handle herself," Sebastian replied. "She always has."

"But she has not always been a young lady in Society," Nash retorted. "She knows how to clean floors and wash windows, but not how to protect herself when some fatuous lord decides she'd better become his bride."

"That's why we're here." Thaddeus leaned back in his chair and folded his arms over his chest, glaring at Nash.

Who glared back.

"I trust Thaddeus to take care of Ana Maria."

The words fell onto Nash like a pile of rocks. His anger felt as though it had just sparked to flame with the tinder of Sebastian's words.

"You don't trust me," he growled.

Sebastian held his hand up. "Look, we all know there is no one better in a fight than you. But that is not what is happening now. I don't recall the last time I've seen you at a respectable party, and yet you've been attending them this past month. Why? To find a bride? To watch over my sister? You are so damned oblique, I have no idea what you're thinking." It was a common refrain. Sebastian had been saying the same thing since they'd become friends so many years ago. And Nash couldn't say it was because Sebastian hadn't asked; he always asked, long after Nash had clamped his mouth shut and refused to say another word.

Damn it. There was an ultimate price to pay for not speaking. And now he couldn't possibly tell them how he felt about her. Not because it was wrong or inappropriate, but because he simply didn't know, and he didn't want to expose his confused state to them.

"You don't have to tell me why you're there, acting very un-Nash-like. Dancing with ladies, wearing a cravat, not getting into fights." Sebastian sounded wary as well as amused. "But one thing you don't have to do is watch over Ana Maria. Thaddeus has to take his place in Society, and part of his duties is to ensure Ana Maria gets as much opportunity as she can. If people see her with you too often"—he paused, then took a deep breath—"well, they'll be too intimidated by you to even approach her for anything." His voice softened. "Ana Maria doesn't have many friends."

She has me.

"Even if it weren't about finding the right husband for her, I'd want her to have the space to find friends, ladies in her own class."

Nash growled. "Because her friends in the servant class don't count?" He glared at Sebastian and Thad. "I'd expect that kind of snobbery from the ex-duke here, but not from the military man. Isn't that where men go who have only their mettle as wealth?"

Thaddeus shifted uncomfortably.

"Be reasonable, Nash."

As if I could.

"You are supposed to be finding a woman to marry yourself," Sebastian said. "You don't have to spend time with Ana Maria just because of your protective instincts."

"Besides which, the more you hang around her, the less her other suitors will think they have a chance."

Sebastian turned to glower at Thaddeus, who shrugged.

"What? That's the point, isn't it? That we think Ana Maria will be happiest when she is married?"

"Have you asked her?" Nash stared at both of them, seeing their sudden discomfort. "You haven't."

Not that he had asked her when he'd insisted on teaching her self-defense, but he had asked her when he kissed her. And touched her. And brought her to climax.

"I can believe Thaddeus wants to march around and dispense orders, but I cannot fathom how you can justify not asking your sister what she wants."

"Hey!" Thaddeus exclaimed in protest.

Sebastian approached slowly, too familiar with Nash's sudden temper to trust his friend wouldn't erupt. *I wouldn't do that,* Nash wanted to say. "Just think about what you're doing with her. We don't want her to get hurt."

Nash opened his mouth to speak, but snapped it shut again. They thought he might hurt her.

Just what he was terrified of.

Why was he even spending time with her in the first place? He would only cause harm, he knew that. Especially with what they were doing now.

But he wanted her to make her own choices, which meant he would have to let her decide, once he'd told her everything.

Because he couldn't keep it from her any longer.

But now was not the time—now was the time for him to sort it out through boxing with Finan, since he couldn't seem to think properly without his fists.

"If you'll excuse me," he bit out, striding from the room, leaving Sebastian and Thaddeus likely to wonder just what the hell he was going to do.

Which meant they had that in common.

"I WONDER WHAT they're all fussing about," Ana Maria murmured as she surveyed the glorious mess that was one of the spare bedrooms.

The bolts of fabric were spread out on the bed, with others leaning up perpendicular against the bed. The colors clashed with one another and with the room, which had been decorated in the late duchess's elegant, spare style.

Not Ana Maria's exuberantly loud one.

She'd ask Thaddeus if she could work on these rooms after she completed her own. Or she'd just go ahead and do it without permission. It was a tiny rebellion, eradicating the duchess's taste from the house, but it was one that brought her great satisfaction. Even though she hadn't quite realized that that's what she was doing.

"What is all this?" Jane walked into the room

holding several pairs of Ana Maria's shoes, obviously just fresh from being scrubbed.

It still made Ana Maria feel guilty that someone else was doing that now, but the servants would be appalled and annoyed if she tried to do their jobs.

"The Lees asked if I wanted to review their goods before they put them on sale to the general public." Ana Maria gestured to the room. "And I did."

"That duke brought you home in his carriage, didn't he?"

Images of what had happened in that carriage immediately came to mind, and she felt herself start to heat.

"And something happened with him." Jane shook her head as she clucked her tongue. "I don't know why you don't just marry that one. He certainly seems to like you well enough, and you him."

She did like him. She liked him a lot. But there was something preventing him from trusting her with whatever secrets he held, why he needed to punish himself for his father's behavior, and she would not compromise herself no matter how broad his shoulders or how clever his fingers.

"It's complicated," Ana Maria replied, advancing to the bed. She picked up one of the bolts, one of the most lively patterns, sighing in satisfaction.

"He hasn't sent you flowers but he likes you all the same."

Right. She'd forgotten. The earmarks of a presentable suitor were flowers, nearly all one's teeth, and looking tolerable.

Not what she wanted in her life, even if Society thought she should be entirely satisfied.

No. She wanted to explore, to see what she was capable of when there were no limits on her.

She did not want to have to return to taking orders or seeming compliant when inside she was frustrated, or angry, or passionate, or concerned.

She'd done that for the first twenty-seven years of her life. She'd smiled through it, even, and everyone thought she was remarkably good-tempered, given how much she was berated and taken advantage of.

She'd thought so, too, but that wasn't the truth, she saw that now. Underneath all the gentle smiles and murmured acquiescence was a furiously proud woman who wanted to decorate in the patterns and colors she wanted, anyone else's opinion be damned.

It might seem a silly point, but it was *her* silly point.

And that, as she considered it, was entirely the point in the first place, wasn't it?

So no, while Nash was most definitely teaching her things she was eager to learn, she did not want to be with him for the rest of her life. Not if it meant hiding parts of herself. Or him hiding himself from her.

She would not do that for anyone. Or accept it from anyone either.

"There you are!"

Ana Maria turned at the sound of Ivy's voice, her face breaking out into a smile as she rushed to gather her sister-in-law into a hug.

"You're here with Sebastian?"

Ivy nodded. She wore a dark blue color that Ana Maria thought did not quite suit her, and she wondered if she could persuade her sister-in-law to take a risk with some brighter colors.

Likely she could, since Ivy was all about taking risks, from opening her own gambling house to marrying Ana Maria's half brother.

Ivy pulled herself back from the embrace, her expression solemn. "I wanted to find you to apologize."

"For what?" Ana Maria snorted. "Unless you're sorry you married Sebastian, in which case you are not forgiven." She accompanied her words with a grin.

Ivy looked regretful. "I might have told Sebastian what Octavia told me. About you and Nash."

Ana Maria's chest squeezed. "Ah. So—what did you tell Sebastian, exactly?"

Ivy bit her lip before speaking. "That you two were spending more time together than you had before, and that there are rumors that he has to get married for some reason. I did mention the betting book, though, which has Lady Felicity running ahead of you with much slimmer odds."

"Oh." That was why Sebastian had demanded Nash speak with him and Thaddeus. But why were they even upset about it? Didn't they trust her to make her own choices?

Obviously not, since they were currently in a room alone with Nash telling him— "Do you know what Sebastian thinks about it all? I mean, is he for or against?"

"For or against?" Ivy's eyebrows rose. "You know, I'm not certain. He just kept muttering about how you were his sister, and you deserved to have everything you deserve."

"But not what I choose, apparently."

Ana Maria nodded to Ivy as she began to walk out of the room. "If you will excuse me? I have some relatives to yell at."

"Excellent!" Ivy exclaimed, patting Ana Maria on the shoulder as she strode past.

SHE FLUNG THE doors open and stepped inside, meeting her brother's and her cousin's shocked looks with her own angry one.

Nash wasn't there, and she felt a pang of regret he wouldn't see how she was defending herself, since that was the whole point of his lessons.

Though she didn't think she'd go so far as to punch anyone. *Yet.*

"What did you say?" she demanded, glancing from one to the other.

They both looked guilty.

"Say?" Sebastian said.

Ana Maria rolled her eyes. "Thaddeus, why did you need to call Nash in here? I believe it has something to do with me?" She folded her arms over her chest. "In which case, perhaps you should address whatever it is with me?"

"It's something we needed to talk to with Nash," Thaddeus sputtered. He made a vague gesture that only served to infuriate Ana Maria more. "It is our responsibility to ensure your safety, and so—"

"For or against?" Ana Maria said, tapping her toe.

They both blinked. "For or against what?" Sebastian asked.

"Do you want me to marry Nash, or were you warning him against me?"

"We'd never warn him against you," Sebastian said, approaching her with a tentative air. Good. She didn't necessarily trust herself not to pop him in the jaw.

And now she had much more sympathy toward Nash and his tendencies, since she could see why someone's actions could lead to violence.

"What did you do?"

Thaddeus rose from his chair, folding his arms behind his back as though he was standing at attention. "We merely told him we were concerned that your other suitors be given a proper chance."

"A proper chance?" Her voice squeaked, and now she was annoyed at herself as well. "It's not a question of fairness, you two. It's a question of how I choose to spend my time. And Nash is my *friend*, and I like spending time with my *friends*." She gave them each a disdainful look. "Unlike wanting to spend time with my relations."

"But Nash isn't—he's not—" Sebastian began.

"I know who he is." *Even though he hasn't trusted me with all of him.* "And more importantly, you know who I am. Don't you trust me enough to make my own decisions? Why are you discussing me without me in the room?" And just like that, her emotions erupted into full-blown anger.

Which normally would have been a cause of personal distress, but now was a moment for exultation—feeling so passionately meant she felt completely, and she wanted to glory in the fullness of her emotions, even if the emotions themselves were ones she did not want to harbor all the time.

And that's why she was so determined to see through whatever it was she was doing with Nash—she wanted to feel everything, she wanted to be in control and yet out of control all at the same time. Because she was Lady Oxymoron, she wanted to revel in all of it and make her own decisions.

"I'll thank you two to stay out of my affairs,"

she warned. "I'll make my own decisions, and I presume Nash will as well."

And she already knew he had decided that whatever they were doing together was not going to be permanent. And she knew she had already decided that it would never be permanent for as long as he kept himself hidden from her.

So all that was left was a temporary thing fueled by her passion.

That didn't seem so bad, did it?

SHE BURST INTO the training room as though she had a lightning storm propelling her through. Her cheeks were flushed, her eyes were wide and sparkling, and she wore that same dull-colored dress from before.

Glorious, from head to toe.

Nash swallowed at the sight. He certainly enjoyed it when she was dressed in her shimmering gowns and delicate slippers, but he felt more connected to her when she was wearing what he'd always seen her in—albeit now with a heightened sense of just how attractive he found her.

"Are you ready to be punched this afternoon, Your Grace?" she said in a teasing voice.

He grunted in reply.

"That's the sound that means that you doubt I will punch you, but you are willing to tolerate my impudence."

His eyes widened, because she was right.

"I have to wrap my hands first, correct?"

Another grunt.

"And will you need help with it? Last time I believe they were wrapped when I arrived, but now they're not."

She took his hands in hers, holding the palms up as she ran her fingers over his skin. "I'm surprised you don't have more injuries, given how often you seem to engage in fighting."

Nash scowled. "I always win."

She gave him a mocking look. "Of course you do. You just punch them, growl, and then stalk off."

"I do not," he retorted. "Sometimes I tell them why I punched them as well."

"A complete experience," she said with a grin. She moved over to the chest of drawers at the corner. "The linens are here, if I recall correctly?"

"Mm," he replied.

"Do we need Finan?"

He growled, at which she laughed. "I'll take that as a no, then."

She brought the linens out, the various lengths dangling over her hands. "You'll have to show me how to do it properly. I don't want you to get hurt when I punch you."

"You won't."

She tilted her head to regard him. "I won't punch you? Or I won't hurt you?"

"Both."

Her eyebrow rose. "Is that a challenge? Because if you teach me properly, I will know how to both punch and hurt you. Even if you don't want me to. So if I am unable to, that is your failing." She accompanied her words with a poke to his chest and a stern glare.

He liked it when she showed her fire. She had been smothered under her stepmother for so long he wasn't certain it was there. But it was there all right, and he wanted to see it burn.

See her burn.

She took a deep breath, then met his gaze. "I know Sebastian and Thaddeus spoke to you."

"Mm."

She frowned. "What did you say to them?" She held her hand up. "No, wait, you probably just made muttering noises and didn't tell them anything."

He stiffened. "I told them you deserved to decide for yourself."

Her eyes widened in surprise. "Oh!"

"They said that your other suitors got less of a chance with me hanging around. Not that I am one of your suitors," he corrected hastily.

She rolled her eyes. "Of course not, we've established that."

"They mentioned they all send you flowers."

Her face was curious. "They do. And?"

He swallowed. "You like flowers."

"I do." Now her face held a quiet smile, as though she were indulging him in his line of questioning.

"What is your favorite?"

Her eyes got dreamy. "Tulips." Not that he had the faintest clue what a tulip looked like.

"I don't know anything about flowers." He took a deep breath, then reached into his pocket, withdrawing the now sadly wilted flower she'd handed him a few days prior. "What kind is this?"

"It's a daisy." She paused. "You've been carrying that around this whole time?"

It was on the tip of his tongue to deny it, but what was the point? It wasn't as though she would think less of him. If anything, she would think more. "Yes."

"Oh," she exclaimed. "That is so sweet!"

He glowered. "I am not sweet."

"So you keep on saying, and yet—" She gestured toward him as she let out a tiny giggle.

"Fine, I'm sweet," he replied with an exasperated sigh. "But I was thinking . . ."

"Yes?"

"I recall my mother liking flowers, too." His throat got thick at the memory—his mother outside with him, picking flowers while he played. "I want to know more about them."

Her expression softened. "You want to know more about your mother. Why don't you contact her? It'd be easier than making a study of botany."

"I don't know if I can. I don't—"

She put her hand on his arm. "You're you, Ignatius. You can do anything."

Her brown eyes held a warmth that made him want to—well, he didn't know, since he'd never felt this way before. "Thank you."

She smiled as she leaned up to kiss him on the

cheek. "You're welcome." He felt bereft when she withdrew—when had her presence started to mean so much to him?

"But we should get to self-defense training, since except for one time all we seem to do is—" she gestured toward them, her warm smile now curving into something decidedly more wicked. "And that one time was only because Finan was here."

"You make a good point, my lady."

Her nose wrinkled. "Ana Maria, please."

He bowed. "Ana Maria, but only for while we are here. If I can't teach you how to properly disarm a man bent on hurting you, I won't have done my job. And since I am the man in the room at the moment, you likely will hurt me."

Her face softened. "Which I will feel terrible about, but it is far better to hurt a friend than to fail at hurting an enemy."

A friend. Were they friends? They were nearly family, because of how Nash felt about Sebastian, and by extension his older sister, who was about his own age. But actual, true friends?

Had he ever been friends with a woman before?

Well, he could answer that, since he had never been friends with anyone but Sebastian, Thaddeus, and Finan before.

She must have read his expression. "We are friends, are we not?" Her tone was earnest, and he felt something twist inside. "That's what I said to Sebastian and Thaddeus when I was railing at them."

He wished he had seen her ire. He loved how passionate she became.

He nodded. "Yes. Friends who have done more than what friends do, but yes, friends."

Now her smile was nearly blinding. It was so full of warmth and trust and happiness. Had he ever been that combination of things before?

No, because he had endeavored to do the opposite—keep everyone away from his heart except those he knew were strong enough to withstand him.

Mute his life into a series of grays so that he would never feel the vividness of anything, because that kind of strong emotion would inevitably lead to an outburst of violence.

That was truly a lowering thought.

He'd always assumed he was relatively content—if not happy. But seeing her joy, watching as her expressions shifted from delight to concern to anger to caring in just a matter of moments, made him envious. His moods, if he were being honest, were usually grumpy and not quite as grumpy. Others might say he was frequently grumpiest, but they had never seen him release all of his roiling emotions, so they didn't know just how grumpy, just how furious, he could be.

Did he even know?

He'd kept himself in check for so long he didn't know which emotions were actually his, and which were pale imitations of what he allowed himself.

"Nash?"

"Mm."

She looked hesitant, and he braced himself for what she might say, even though she had just said they were friends, and smiled because of it. He was an idiot.

"I want to do all this," she said, gesturing to the room, "but I'd also like to do those other things." Her cheeks turned even pinker. "If we could agree it means nothing beyond lessons. We know we cannot marry."

That last bit was said so firmly it made Nash want to ask *why not?* Which would be the stupidest thing he could say, given the current situation. And how Sebastian and Thaddeus felt.

"But I want to do those things with a friend, someone who knows me and will understand what I want."

A few weeks ago he'd felt as though he barely knew her, and now she was saying he understood her? He barely understood himself.

She shrugged. "Otherwise, it will all be left to chance depending on which of the flower senders I eventually accept." Her scowl left no doubt as to what she thought about those gentlemen, which made Nash feel a strong sense of relief. "But there will be someone eventually that I might consider, and I'd rather know things firsthand rather than rely on the talk I heard belowstairs as a servant."

He had forgotten that. She would be so much more aware of what occurred between a man and a woman than other young ladies of her class due to her upbringing. Did it scare her? Worry her?

Or perhaps pique her imagination?

Because goodness knows his imagination was surely piqued, and he hadn't spent much time thinking about it when he wasn't doing it before. Now it seemed that was all he thought about when the person he was doing it with in his thoughts was her.

"And besides," she added, not realizing he'd already agreed in his mind, "you're my friend, so I know you won't expose me to any kind of scandal."

"It seems we have a bargain," he said at last. "You'll teach me about flowers, and I will teach you how to fight and how to fu—"

"Nash!" she said, her eyes wide in shock.

He put his hand over hers, the one that still rested on his arm, and drew her into his body, locking his gaze with hers. "Fuck, Ana Maria. You need to know how to say it if you're going to do it."

She licked her lips, and her breath was coming faster. "Fuck," she said at last, emphasizing the hard *k* at the end, a sound that seemed as though it shot straight to his cock. "You'll teach me how to fight and fuck."

Chapter Sixteen

You'll teach me how to fight and fuck.

She couldn't believe she'd actually said the words, much less want them to happen.

But she had, and she did, and now she had an additional mission: show Nash the beauty and wonder of flowers as he taught her the beauty and wonder of what could happen between two friends who were more than friends.

Friends who were going to fuck.

"Ana Maria!"

Octavia snapped her fingers in front of her face, startling Ana Maria out of her reverie.

"Of course," she said with a smile. "I apologize, I was thinking of . . . something else."

Octavia grinned. "I can imagine. It is a good thing I am so busy with Miss Ivy's, or I would be insisting on all the details."

The thought of that made Ana Maria turn tomato red.

"Ha!" Octavia pointed an accusing finger at her. "I knew it!" She rose up on her tiptoes and lowered her voice. "I find you very attractive, Lady

Ana Maria. Nearly as enticing as my brandy, or not speaking when I'm spoken to."

Ana Maria collapsed into laughter at Octavia's very credible imitation.

The two ladies were taking afternoon tea in Ana Maria's salon. Octavia used to have a tradition of taking tea with her older sister, but now that Ivy was married to Sebastian, the two of them always seemed to be "busy," as Octavia reported with a waggle of her eyebrows and a gusty sigh.

Like Ana Maria, Octavia occupied an in-between place in Society; she had been born a squire's daughter, but had accompanied her sister to London to open a shockingly scandalous gambling den, so her reputation was not what it could have been.

But on the other hand, she was the primary hostess of one of London's most intriguing gambling clubs, so her reputation among certain types had soared.

Ana Maria got the impression that Octavia didn't care about things like reputations, anyway, so her working at the club suited her perfectly well.

"But since I am purportedly a lady, I will not ask you about the enormous behemoth."

"Isn't that redundant?" Ana Maria asked, reaching for a biscuit.

Octavia gave an enthusiastic nod. "It is, but it suits, doesn't it?"

It did.

But there was so much more to him than his size, though that sounded odd even in her own head. He was sweet, despite his protestations to the contrary; he was courteous, despite sometimes seeming like a giant at a miniature tea party; he was protective, as she knew from all of her interactions with him.

"You're mooning again, Ana Maria," Octavia chided. "Shouldn't we be discussing this evening?" Her eyes sparkled in anticipation.

They were planning to attend a ball given by a not-so-polite member of Society, which meant that Octavia would be completely welcome. Ana Maria wanted to go because she was tired of having to dance with her multitude of suitors, all of whom talked obliquely about their hopes for a complacent wife with a large dowry.

Ana Maria was always tempted to tell them that Thaddeus had changed his mind about her dowry to time just how long it would be before they excused themselves to find some other young unmarried lady to dance with—Lady Felicity, perhaps?

"You've got a sour look on your face now," Octavia commented.

"Could you stop being so observant?" Ana Maria asked in a rueful tone. "I was just thinking about the bet at Miss Ivy's. Lady Felicity. I wonder if she will be at the ball tonight."

Octavia arched her eyebrows. "I imagine she will be. She seldom misses an opportunity to spend time with eligible gentlemen. I wonder at her family circumstances—she usually has an older aunt with her as a chaperone, and I haven't heard anything about her family. Normally I am more aware of a family's finances than they are themselves, thanks to the club."

"Are you now going to make me feel sympathy for Lady Felicity? Hint at some sad poverty-stricken story that requires her to marry soon and well?"

Octavia's eyes brightened. "That would make a perfect novel! I threatened Ivy a long time ago that I wanted to write books about dangerous gentlemen like your behemoth—"

"He's not my behemoth," Ana Maria muttered.

"And ladies who seem to need rescuing, but can rescue themselves."

An odd thought struck Ana Maria as she listened to Octavia. "You want to write my story." She snorted. "Though I know you'd be bored writing about all the decorating parts."

Octavia rolled her eyes. "I'd far rather spend time writing about all the times the rescuing lady and her behemoth ended up alone together . . . in a carriage, on a deserted street, in a salon."

"On a terrace," Ana Maria added with a wicked smile.

"I cannot wait to hear how your story ends, my lady," Octavia said with a wide smile. She popped another biscuit in her mouth, making an appreciative sound as she chewed.

Ana Maria wondered how it would end also. If only he could let go of some of his secrets.

"What are you wearing this evening?" Octavia asked, taking another biscuit. "Have you had any of those fabrics made up into gowns?"

Ana Maria sighed in sartorial satisfaction. "I have, actually. And I think it is gorgeous, although Jane—my lady's maid and dear friend—thinks it all might be a bit much."

"Which likely means it's just perfect! Will you show me before I have to go back to get dressed myself?" She winked. "I don't want to accidentally arrive at the party wearing the exact same thing."

Ana Maria chuckled. "There is not a chance of that," she said.

"OOOH," OCTAVIA SIGHED as she gazed at the gown Jane had laid on Ana Maria's bed.

The silk was woven into an intricate pattern that must have taken so much skill and so many hours—Ana Maria felt a pang of remorse at how long the workers must have spent on it, and she hoped, but wasn't optimistic, that they had gotten properly recompensed.

One good mission at a time, she warned herself as she began to think about traveling to those places and finding out the work conditions.

The fabric shimmered in the light, and it was difficult to say with any certainty what color it was—seafoam green? Teal blue? Ocean blue?

The pattern was detailed with red, gold, and

green stitching, a multitude of flowers and other shapes on the skirt and the bodice.

The gold thread caught the light, and Ana Maria knew it was a good complement for her skin, which wasn't the pale English rose of most of the other young ladies in Society. Hers bore her Spanish ancestry in its golden hue, more like a pale yellow tulip. Her coloring was something her stepmother often railed about, but now seemed as though it made her a tulip among the roses—something special and distinctive.

"I told her that the gown was a bit too much," Jane sniffed, her tone both concerned and proud, "but she said she is up to the challenge."

Octavia petted the fabric and made inarticulate happy noises. Noises that were echoed in Ana Maria's brain.

"Can I see it on you? Though it's not time to get dressed yet, is it?" Octavia frowned at the clock in the corner.

"I am dining with Thaddeus in an hour, and I don't want to get anything on it, so you'll have to wait until I pick you up for the party."

Octavia looked startled. "Your cousin isn't coming, is he?" She gave a mock shudder. "Any time I see him I worry he is going to order me to make an attack, or hunker down on the front lines or something."

Ana Maria laughed, shaking her head. "He is not." In fact, Thaddeus did not know of tonight's party. She had decided not to tell him because of his arrogance in making decisions about her and not with her.

Perhaps it was a tiny bit of rebellion, but it was her rebellion.

"Oh good."

Octavia drew back from the gown with one last happy sigh, then embraced Ana Maria. "I will have to find something I can wear to live up to your splendor," she said with a smile. "I do love dressing up. That's one of the reasons I love the Masked Evenings at the club so much."

Ana Maria's eyebrows rose. "Masked Evenings?"

Octavia gave an enthusiastic nod. "Yes, at first it was just that—people wore masks to play. But now people come in costume, and it is so much fun! Last time I dressed as my Roman namesake." She struck a dramatic pose as she spoke, and then both women dissolved into giggles.

"We'll have one soon enough. Next time I'll let you know, and you can come yourself. In disguise," she added, waggling her eyebrows.

That idea sent shivers up Ana Maria's spine. She already had too many personas, she knew that—former scullery maid, unwanted stepdaughter, duke's wealthy relation, enterprising businesswoman—but the idea of being in a place where she could shed all of that was certainly intriguing.

Especially if she could get another person to shed all of his personalities and show who he truly was.

"But I've got to go. You'll come by at ten o'clock?" Octavia said, nodding goodbye at Jane as she made her way to the door.

"Ten o'clock. Yes."

"ENOUGH!" FINAN SAID, holding his hands up in surrender.

The two of them had been boxing for well over two hours, the two hours since Ana Maria had left the house after her remarkable request.

The image of her lips moving to say "fight and fuck" would never leave his brain.

The only thing he'd been able to fathom doing was to exorcise his mind in violent physical energy. Finan had obliged, as usual, but for once was giving up.

Nash raised his arm to wipe his forehead of sweat. His shirtsleeve was already soaked, however, so there was no relief.

"Here." Finan tossed him a dry towel, which Nash caught. He ran it over his head, then his chest, frowning down at his thoroughly soaked shirt. He shrugged, then pulled it off and tossed it on the floor, continuing to wipe his skin with the towel.

"What is it today? The dowager duchess making you mind your p's and q's too much?"

Finan squinted at him, his own face drenched with sweat.

"Take one of those towels for yourself," Nash ordered. "You're going to have to get me dressed in a few hours for another one of those parties." He spoke as though it was a hardship, but tonight's should be less so than the usual ones. Given by a somewhat scandalous widow on the edge of propriety, tonight's party wasn't one the dowager duchess would deign to attend, and he knew that Ana Maria and Miss Ivy's sister Octavia were going, so he thought he would as well.

And when had he become someone who would willingly attend a party?

As soon as she'd appeared in that ballroom a few weeks ago, all starlight and sparkle.

He knew neither Thaddeus nor Sebastian would be there either—the former was long overdue for a dinner with fellow officers at his club, while the latter was working at Miss Ivy's when his sister-in-law was out at the same party, so he wouldn't have to face their scrutiny either.

"How has your search been going, anyway?" Finan asked, going to sit on one of the chairs at the edge of the room.

"Search?" Nash winced. His search for a bride. Right. "Oh that. Fine, fine," he replied, giving a dismissive wave.

To a man who would not be dismissed. "Fine how? You know who you like or at least can moderately tolerate? Does the dowager duchess approve? You're gonna have to tell whoever it is that you've hired all your father's by-blows, you know."

Nash glowered at his friend, who grinned in an obnoxious way.

"I see it's going very well. *Fine*, you might say."

Nash's hands curled into fists, which made Finan laugh. "No, no, you've done that too much today. You should develop another hobby. Some other way to relieve your tension." He gave a knowing look. "Perhaps take your energy out in another way?"

Fight and fuck.

And then Nash felt himself start to get warm. Goddamn it, was he blushing? He did not blush!

Thankfully, he was already so sweaty that likely his reddened face would be attributed to the fighting, not the embarrassment.

Finan rose, tossing his towel into the basket to the side of the chest of drawers. "I'm going to go see what Cook has in the kitchen. Getting beaten up by you gives me one hell of an appetite."

"Back at nine o'clock," Nash called as Finan pushed the door open and walked out. His only response was a wave of Finan's hand.

It was only seven o'clock, and he wasn't hungry. What did he want to do?

Well, he knew what he wanted to do, but she wasn't here.

A bath. He'd take a bath.

He strode out of his training room and down the hall to his bedroom, yanking the bellpull as he entered.

The room still didn't feel like his. It had belonged to his mother, but his father had changed everything in it when his mother left. Nash refused to even consider using his father's room—that room would be a spare bedroom in the unlikely event he'd ever have so many guests he'd have to use it.

What would it look like if he asked Ana Maria to help change it?

He didn't think she'd insist on using those bright colors she preferred for her own rooms—she was too sensitive to what he might want for that.

He took the flower out of his pocket again, staring at it, thinking about what it meant to see something and to admire it. He had only ever felt a sense of triumph when he'd bested someone who deserved it.

He hadn't found beauty in small things.

Except her, he thought with a chuckle.

But what would it look like if she could show him how to appreciate small things like a flower, or a pleasantly decorated room?

A tulip? A joyful dance? Or a gorgeously gowned woman?

It terrified him, the thought that if he allowed himself to find beauty and appreciate some things for themselves . . . then what? What if it never stopped? What if his emotions kept building and building until they—and he—inevitably exploded?

That was the whole point of choosing a wife

who he would merely tolerate. If he could keep himself and his feelings in check, he would never run the risk of being so explosively violent he would hurt anyone.

But he was starting to feel.

He still held the flower. A few of its petals had fluttered to the ground, and he stooped to pick them up, cradling them carefully in his palm. Then he went to his dressing table and opened one of the small drawers at the top, the place where Finan kept combs and a mirror and other grooming implements Nash never needed.

He plucked one of his hellcloths from the dressing table, spreading it open and placing the flower and the petals in there, wrapping them all carefully so as not to crush them, then tucked it into the small drawer, all the way at the back.

He could not allow himself to feel. Not about her. He should be strong enough to separate out his desire for her with his feelings of friendship.

Even though a voice warned him that that was becoming impossible.

THERE WAS SOMETHING he did appreciate about being a duke, he thought, as he leaned back in the tub.

He'd ordered it especially sized, since his height wouldn't fit into a normal-sized bathtub.

It stood on a pedestal, close to one of the windows, so he could gaze out at the view while he bathed.

The water was hot, so hot he knew the servants had scurried to get it up to his bedroom. He'd have to give them some extra money on payday for their hot water diligence.

His muscles were sore from the time he'd spent with Finan—he hadn't held back, he couldn't hold back. Finan was the only person who could withstand what Nash delivered. Even the street fights Nash got into required him to hold back—most of the people he challenged were bullies, not accustomed to anyone actually calling on them to defend their indefensible positions.

An indefensible position. That was what he had agreed upon with Ana Maria this afternoon. If Sebastian or Thaddeus found out, he'd lose his friends. All of them.

But he couldn't seem to resist her. And he didn't want to.

That was what scared him the most. He could imagine being married to her, even though he knew it was the worst idea ever. But the thought of having her in his bed, every night, was so tempting.

If only he could know for certain he'd never lose his temper again.

His father exploded at everything—his tea was too hot, it was too cold, his dogs didn't come when he called.

His wife was terrified of him.

As was his son.

Nash's throat got thick as his mind flooded with

memories—the fear he'd felt on the rare occasions his father summoned him. Bracing himself for the inevitable sharp tweak of his ears, the too-forceful straightening of the shoulders.

The punch to the nose.

How was Nash any different from him?

He used his fists to demonstrate his feelings. He couldn't seem to say what he felt—yes, he'd gotten a reputation as someone who rarely spoke. But it was because he felt as though he couldn't.

What would it look like if he could open his mouth and all of his thoughts came pouring out? Would it make a difference?

The thought was terrifying.

Even as it was comforting—because if he could say what he felt instead of using his fists, maybe he wouldn't have to turn to violence every time. If he could choose who he would be—maybe, just maybe, he would deserve her.

We know we cannot marry.

Even so, there were things they could do.

Fight and fuck.

And he'd just fought.

He reached below the surface of the water to grasp his cock, which had already begun to harden.

He closed his eyes and began to stroke himself, thinking of her face when he made her come. How she said "please" as he touched her.

The sated, dreamy look on her face right after, when his fingers were soaked from her.

Damn. He could not wait to bury himself in her wetness. To bring her to the brink of a shuddering, gasping climax, then allow himself to thrust home to his own release.

He hadn't even seen her breasts yet, though he'd had his hands on them. On her stiff nipples that seemed to be aching for his touch. He wanted to kiss her there, lick those nipples as he caressed her breasts, watching her reactions to see if she liked it as much as he knew he would.

He knew Ana Maria was adventurous, even if she didn't seem to realize it. But he would encourage her to go on an adventure with his body, see what he looked like all over, touch him and learn what brought both of them pleasure.

Meanwhile, his hand stroked himself firmly, his balls tightening as he increased the pressure on his cock.

He imagined it was her hand touching him, her watching his face to see how her touch was affecting him.

Fuck, it felt good. It would feel so much better with her.

He felt the climax rolling in, building, and he tightened his grip more, blurring the lines between pleasure and pain.

And then the pleasure suffused him as he exploded, gasping at the intensity of the feeling.

He leaned his head back against the tub, the waves of sensual heat surrounding him. Images of her still floating in his mind, helpfully supplying ideas of what she might look like naked. Sprawled out in his bed, surrounded by the flowers she loved.

He grinned as he thought about it. Anticipated what it would be like to see her later that evening. Perhaps even say how he felt about her.

That would be remarkable.

Chapter Seventeen

"Your Grace."

Richardson stood at the doorway to the dining room, his usual unperturbable expression . . . perturbed.

Nash rested his fork and knife on either side of his plate. "Yes?"

"There's a lady here to see you as well as a gentleman. The lady says she is related to you."

Nash's spine felt frozen. *Related to you.* His mother? Or one of the half siblings he'd recently found?

He felt his chest tighten.

He'd asked Robert to contact her, but he hadn't expected her to appear so quickly, if at all. If anything, he'd thought maybe a letter would arrive.

He took a deep breath, pushing his plate away. "Bring her to the library."

"IGNATIUS."

It was her. His mother, standing beside a gentleman approximately her age, both of them dressed in the height of fashion, at least as far as Nash could tell. Her clothing was nearly as colorful as anything he'd seen Ana Maria in, while her head was covered by a bonnet with what seemed to be a ridiculous amount of ribbons and flowers and some other ruckus.

Nash's head felt as thick as if he'd guzzled an entire bottle of brandy. His chest was tight, his breath was short, and he could only stand there and stare at her.

She looked like him. Or more accurately, he looked like her: dark hair, though hers was sprinkled with gray. Dark eyes and a strong, straight nose. She was taller than the gentleman beside her, so perhaps his height came from her as well.

"Ignatius," she said again, her voice constrained, "allow me to present my husband, Monsieur DeCalles." The woman—his mother—gestured to the older gentleman she'd arrived with, an anxious expression on her face.

Of course she was anxious. She had no idea who he was, who he'd turned into. What if he was like his father?

You take after me. In every way.

"A pleasure," his mother's husband said, extending his hand. He spoke in a French accent, and bowed slightly as he touched Nash's hand.

Nash took it with a nod. Unable to speak.

"Could I—could I perhaps sit down?" she asked, a tiny smile tugging at her mouth.

He exhaled, gesturing toward the sofa. She met his gaze, nodding, then went and sat, removing the enormous bonnet from her head and placing it on the cushion beside her.

"Pierre, perhaps you could see to the carriage?" his mother said, addressing her husband. Her words and expression were warm, and Nash felt a flare of gratitude that it seemed that her second husband was far better than her first.

"Of course. Your servant, Your Grace," Monsieur DeCalles said, nodding.

Nash sat down in the chair opposite her as Monsieur DeCalles left the room, shutting the door softly behind him.

For a moment they just regarded one another.

"I understand if this is a shock—"

"No. I mean, yes, but no." Nash took a deep breath. "I wanted to find you. So badly. It is good to see you."

His mother's expression cleared into a relieved smile. "I was grateful to receive Mr. Carstairs's letter." She paused, meeting his gaze. "It is good to see you, too, son. I am so sorry." She took a deep breath. "I wish I could have come earlier. So much earlier."

Nash's throat got thick, and he was startled to realize his eyes were starting to tear. He did not cry, damn it.

Except it seemed he did.

He reached toward her, but the distance was too great, so he got up and moved his chair closer, then took her hand. Keeping his gaze on their fingers rather than looking directly at her—he didn't know if he would be able to speak otherwise.

No, he *knew* he wouldn't be able to speak. That was him, that was who he was. The person who couldn't say anything, who could only do things.

You take after me. In every way.

Was it true, though?

He had so much to tell her. And it didn't matter that he might not find the right words. He would get his meaning across somehow.

"Mother, I—" he began.

"OH MY GOODNESS!"

Ana Maria couldn't help but gasp as she and Octavia walked into the ballroom. The hosts had decorated the room as though it was underwater, with blue silk hanging from the walls and papier-mâché fish and other aquatic animals dangling from the ceiling. The male servants were dressed like pirates, while female servants wore mermaid garb.

"I wonder who did their decorating," Octavia said in a sly tone.

"I am envious," Ana Maria said, gazing at the splendor.

The room was halfway full, and the dancing hadn't begun, although there was music playing—Ana Maria could see the musicians at the far corner behind a fishing net. The guests were wandering about, mostly examining the various decorations or exclaiming at the servants' costumes.

"Your gown lives up to all of this," Octavia said in an admiring tone.

Ana Maria looked down at her gown, which was as beautiful on as it was off. Its colors set off her coloring, and the cut and drape augmented her curves, making her look more sensual than was usually approved of in Society.

"Thank you," she said at last. "I feel as though I've finally decorated myself in a style I am comfortable with." Even though parts of her revealed sensuality made her feel all prickly and uncomfortable, albeit in an exciting way.

The two ladies paused to look around the room, Octavia waving at a few people she recognized. Ana Maria didn't recognize anyone, which made her breathe a tiny sigh of relief.

The people looked more like the customers at Miss Ivy's than the usual Society gathering; there was a looser feeling here than Ana Maria was accustomed to. It felt comfortable, as though this was the place she could be both Ana Maria of belowstairs and Ana Maria the duke's cousin.

Lady Oxymoron, as usual.

"Good evening, Miss Octavia." A couple stood in front of them, the pair fashionably dressed, though something about their demeanor suggested they were wealthy rather than aristocratic.

"Good evening," Octavia replied. She gestured toward Ana Maria. "This is Lady Ana Maria Dutton, and these are the Marchfields. Mr. Marchfield has interests in several ventures. I believe you are finding funding for a railway at the moment?"

Mr. Marchfield's mouth eased into a twinkling smile. "Don't give away my secrets," he said, wagging his finger censoriously, but speaking in a humorous tone. "In fact, it is because of that venture we wanted most particularly to speak to you."

"Yes," Mrs. Marchfield said, "we have a presentation room where we receive potential investors, and we want to make it look as appropriate and professional as possible, and we were hoping you might help us, since Miss Ivy's looks so good?"

Octavia beamed. "The person responsible for that is actually my friend here."

"Oh!" the Marchfields exclaimed.

"Do you take commissions?" Mr. Marchfield asked.

Ana Maria gazed in shock at them for a moment before Octavia replied. "Of course she does, I will send her information round to you tomorrow. But be prepared—her work costs a pretty penny."

Mrs. Marchfield shrugged in dismissal. "If the results do what we think they will, we won't have a concern about that." She waved her hand over her head. "Dorcas! You are here!" She turned to her husband. "Come, dear, we need to speak with Dorcas immediately, her husband has expressed an interest. Do excuse us," she continued, speaking to Octavia and Ana Maria.

"Of course," they murmured.

Octavia nudged Ana Maria. "Look, didn't I tell you? You'll be able to do all the good works you want and make money. Not that you need to make money—"

"But having a purpose beyond standing in ballrooms is definitely gratifying," Ana Maria added. "Oh, goodness, that is so exciting!"

If she could truly do something with what she enjoyed she thought she might be as happy as either of the two sisters who ran Miss Ivy's, both of whom crackled with an electricity that had to have come from finding purpose in their lives.

And she could, as Octavia said, help redecorate some places to aid them in their search for funds.

"Now that you might have a purpose in life, shall we walk around and see if we can find your other purpose? Your behemoth?" Octavia asked.

"He's not my—oh never mind," Ana Maria replied, taking her friend's arm and beginning to walk.

"I don't see him. Someone that large would surely stand out?"

"It's fine if he isn't in attendance," Ana Maria said airily. As if she weren't lying through her teeth. "The evening is not for me to see him. It is to spend time with you."

"Liar," Octavia teased.

"Fine. Yes. I don't know anymore. I just know—"

"What?"

They paused at the corner of the room, turning

so they could survey the crowd. It felt so much more comfortable for Ana Maria to be here than to be in and among all of Society's best people.

Perhaps she could find some level of comfort. Maybe there would even be a gentleman who would understand her conundrum, a gentleman who wasn't terrified of being aligned with her who she was also intrigued by.

"If only you weren't looking for him. Because guess what is over there?" Octavia grinned and pointed toward where Nash stood, all toweringly tall handsomeness of him, at the entrance to the ballroom.

Ana Maria smacked her friend's hand down, feeling her face heat. "Stop that!"

"What? It's not as though he hasn't already seen you."

Ana Maria tried to casually move her gaze around the room so her focal point wouldn't be too obvious. Except that when she did look at him, he was staring right at her, so intently it felt as though he was branding her.

"Oh," she said on an exhale.

Octavia waved her hand in front of her face. "It has gotten awfully heated in here, don't you think?"

"Stop teasing me!" Ana Maria spoke in a sharp whisper.

"But it's so much fun!" Octavia exclaimed. "Your face turns all pink, and you start looking everywhere but at him. Oh, and here he is."

Ana Maria drew her gaze up from the floor, mentally preparing herself. After all, the last time they'd seen one another he'd promised to teach her how to—well, all of that. And she didn't want to not do that, but she also had to admit she was terrifyingly exhilarated by the prospect. Emphasis on the terrified part.

"Lady Ana Maria, it is a pleasure to see you." His low tone sent shivers down her spine. "Can I get you a refreshment?"

"I'm thirsty, too," Octavia interjected, a sly grin on her face.

"Uh—" he began, only to be interrupted by Octavia again.

"I am just teasing. You two go ahead, I will see what trouble I can get into here."

Ana Maria glanced at her friend, wondering just how serious Octavia was about getting into trouble. And then wondering if there was any way she could possibly stop her if trouble was what she had in mind.

"Can I take your carriage home? Later on, when it's time to go?" Octavia said with a wink.

Ana Maria rolled her eyes. "Yes, but do check the room to see if I am still here. And don't tell your sister about anything."

Octavia nodded. "Of course, I wouldn't want anybody to face the wrath of the fearsome Sebastian." Her light tone belied her words. "And if you'll excuse me, I see someone I would like to have ask me to dance." She sped off, leaving them alone.

Alone in a crowd, but essentially alone nonetheless.

"We need to talk—"

"Let's go—"

They spoke simultaneously, then stopped and stared at one another. Ana Maria's heart felt as though it were going to burst out of her chest, and his fiercely intense expression made it appear as though he were equally affected.

"Fine," she said, taking his arm. "Let's go."

Seeing her tonight felt somehow even more revelatory than usual. Not only because of what they'd discussed that afternoon, but of course because of what they'd discussed that afternoon.

And the conversation with his mother.

A tiny glimmer of hope flickered inside him.

You take after me. In every way.

No, I don't. I choose not to.

She looked even more glorious than usual, her unusual patterned gown making her look like a rare vision among all the other ladies.

"You look—" he began, then shook his head.

They were walking swiftly through the crowd, him not knowing for certain where they were headed. She seemed to be leading the way, and she wasn't walking toward the door.

"I look—what?" she prodded.

He wished he could find the words. "Like a goddess," he said at last.

"Oh," she replied, sounding startled.

"Is that an insult? I don't want to insul—"

"It's not an insult at all," she said, squeezing his arm. "Thank you."

He stopped abruptly, turning to look at her beautiful face. "My mother's back," he said in a raw tone.

"What?" Her eyes widened, and then she wrapped her arms around him in a fierce hug. "That is wonderful." She drew back, giving him an intense gaze. "Is it wonderful?"

He exhaled. "It is."

She squeezed his arm. "Oh, I am so glad. You'll have to tell me all about it."

"I will," he promised. "But I can't now." He made a vague gesture, which she seemed to understand. She always understood him. Even if he didn't always understand her. "Now just come with me."

They walked out of the wide doors onto the terrace, both walking instinctively toward the darker areas that were shadowed by the large trees whose branches hung overhead.

"Terrace shenanigans," he murmured.

"Indeed. I remember the last time we were on a terrace—" she began, her voice getting all low and breathy.

That was a good sign.

He and his cock remembered, too. Remembered how tempting it was to pull up her skirts and kneel in front of her, burying his mouth in her soft warmth.

He'd have to make certain to teach her that as well—while not technically fucking, it was definitely something she would want to know.

And he wanted to teach her.

"What do you remember, Ana Maria?" His voice was rough with passion. "How we kissed just out of sight of everyone on the other side of the wall? How my fingers slid down your gown to caress your breast? How close we came to—"

"Stop," she said in a ragged tone. "Not if you're not going to do anything about it."

His lips curled up into a slow grin. "I can do something about it," he said. "Didn't I promise?" He stretched his hand out to her, and she placed her fingers into his palm. "Come with me."

He led her down three small steps to the back garden, the sound of the party ebbing as they walked into the night.

"Where are we going?"

"Well, I'm not taking you to my boxing room, so I think we have only one option for where to go. Somewhere we can fu—"

"Nash!"

He shook his head. "You and everyone else are always urging me to speak more. And yet when I do, you tell me to be quiet."

She laughed, the sound unloosening something in his chest. He had to admit he was anxious—it wasn't as though he was suave like Sebastian or commanding like Thaddeus.

He just wanted her desperately, and he wanted to ensure her pleasure.

"You are right, I am entirely contradictory," she said, sounding amused. "You might say it is one of my defining characteristics."

He grunted in reply, leading her further into the dark. He knew there had to be a gazebo or other type of building nearby—all of the London town houses he'd been to had some sort of backyard nonsense—and he was rewarded by the sight of a small enclosed pagoda.

"In there," he said, tugging her forward.

The door swung open easily, and they found themselves in a circular room, benches against the wall, scattered cushions on top of them. There were a few lanterns placed to the right of the door, and Nash leaned over to grab one, hanging it up on a hook from the ceiling and pulling out his tinder to light it.

The candle flickered to life, the warm golden light making her look even more sun-kissed than usual, the colors of her gown shifting with her every move.

"Damn it, Ana Maria, but you are so lovely." Far too lovely for the likes of him.

He wanted to tell her how he felt, what he was starting to feel, but the words choked in his throat.

He'd have to show her.

"Can I kiss you?" he asked, his words emerging slow.

"I was hoping you would ask," she replied, stepping close to his body and tilting her face up to his. She slid her hands up his arms to link behind his neck, and she nudged him so his mouth was a breath away from hers.

"Kiss me, Nash," she said, placing her mouth on his.

THIS WASN'T THE brusque Nash she knew; this Nash was gentle, asking for her permission before doing anything.

It made her feel as though she was in control. As though she could guide what would happen between them, ensuring her comfort as she ventured into unknown territory.

Although that wasn't entirely correct; she knew what happened between people—she had just not done any of it herself. Until him.

And she wanted to do more of it. With him.

She opened her mouth to his, their tongues clashing as he growled deep in his throat. Now she could add another Nash noise to her lexicon—sexual growl that meant he was barely holding himself back.

Because she could feel his hands grasping her waist, his fingers flexing as though wishing they could move other places.

She broke the kiss, whispering softly toward him. "Touch me, Nash. Everywhere."

It was as if she had unleashed a fury with her words; his mouth captured hers again, his palm went to her breast to squeeze her, and his other hand slid down to grasp her skirts, slowly sliding the fabric up her legs.

The cool evening air made her skin prickle.

And then he stopped everything, and she had a moment of panic—did he want to stop?—but instead he was frantically removing his jacket and his cravat, tossing them onto the cushions, tugging his shirt from his trousers, raising it over his head and tossing that off, too.

His chest was made of marbled muscle, and she felt her mouth water as she regarded him in the candlelight.

He was Hephaestus. He was a god come to life, here to savage his way through her defenses.

And he'd called her a goddess. She felt like one, too, so powerful she could make this man hunger for her.

Before she realized what he'd done, he'd seated her on the cushions and was kneeling on the floor in front of her, his hands on the bottom of her gown. He kept his gaze locked with hers as his fingers raised the hem.

Up past her shins. Past her knees.

Then onto her thighs.

He licked his lips as he stared at her, and it was as though she could taste his hunger. How could he make her feel so alive just by looking at her?

Not to mention raising her gown scandalously

high as they were alone together in a secluded house.

So perhaps it wasn't so surprising.

She smothered a giggle, then gasped as his fingers touched the bare skin of her leg.

They followed the same path the fabric had taken—first shins, then knees, then thighs. And then to the place he'd touched in the carriage, when it had felt as though she'd seen stars.

His clever fingers. Telling her more than his words how he felt about her.

Her eyes widened as he lowered his mouth to her knee, kissing it softly as his fingers pushed at her inner thighs, making her spread wider. Open for him.

She resisted the urge to snap her legs closed, instead biting her lip as his mouth moved up her leg, kissing her on her thigh, then—

"Oh my God," she said as his mouth made contact with her there.

It felt like too much, and she shuddered, rivulets of pleasure sliding over her skin. He chuckled softly against her, his hands now on her hips, holding her still for his mouth.

His tongue darted out to lick her there, and she shuddered again, her hands clamped onto his shoulders.

"You like this." He murmured against her skin, and she shifted in exquisite agony against him.

"Mm," she moaned.

"Tell me," he urged, his words muffled. She

could barely form words, but if she didn't—would he stop?

"I like this," she gasped out.

"What do you like?" he asked, his words punctuated by soft licks. "You like it when I kiss your sweet pussy?"

She gasped again, both at how amazing it felt and his explicit words. She swallowed, then spoke. "Yes, I want you to kiss my pussy." She felt exhilarated by saying the word. By having him on his knees, literally, before her. Branding her with his tongue. Ruining her for anyone else.

As though she didn't know that already.

"Mm," he murmured, continuing his sensual onslaught. "Come for me, Ana Maria. Show me you like what I'm doing."

She gripped his head, her fingers threading through his hair, every feeling focused on what he was doing, and how he was making her feel.

This was heaven. And hell, because it was torture to feel all of it, but she never wanted it to stop.

He grunted as he worked her, and she moaned, her hands gripping his shoulders so tightly he would likely have bruises.

And then—and then she fell apart, crying out her pleasure. It felt as though she had summited a mountain, albeit one she'd climbed with the help of his lips and tongue.

"Mm," he said again, giving her one last tender kiss there before leaning up to press his mouth against hers.

She could taste herself.

He kissed her thoroughly, his hands cupping her face.

She slid her hands down his shoulders to his waist, pulling him into her. He was still on his knees, but shuffled forward to press against her.

And then she moved her fingers to his waist-band, and lower, feeling the hard ridge of him through his trousers.

"Oh yes," he said against her mouth. "Yes."

"Tell me what you want," Ana Maria replied, squeezing him.

SHE WAS THE most intoxicating thing he'd ever tasted. He'd feasted on her pleasure, and he'd nearly forgotten he hadn't climaxed yet, he'd been so focused on helping her find her own climax.

But now she had her fingers on his cock, and she was asking him to speak, to tell her what he wanted.

He wanted it all.

He wanted to thrust into her warmth, he wanted to bring himself to climax all over her gorgeous breasts, he wanted to have her put her mouth on him as he had done to her.

"What do you want, Ignatius?" she asked, rub-bing her fingers up and down his length. It was awkward, through his trousers, and his hand went quickly to his waistband, undoing the placket so she could touch him directly.

"I want you to touch me," he said, taking her hand and sliding it up and down his shaft, showing her what he liked.

"Like this?" she said, following his movement.

Nash buried his head in her neck as he groaned. "Yes, like that. Goddamn, Ana Maria."

She learned quickly, gripping him tightly from the base of his cock to the tip, sliding her fingers around him, keeping the pressure on as she worked him.

"Are you going to fuck me?" she asked in a low tone.

He growled in response, biting her neck softly and then drawing back to gaze in her eyes. "Do you want me to fuck you, Ana Maria?"

Her eyes fluttered closed as she replied, "God, yes. So much."

He grinned at her forceful reply, then got up onto the bench, straddling her legs on either side. She kept her hand on his cock, continuing to rub, only less urgently.

It was an uncomfortable position, and he knew his knees would pay for it later, but he didn't care. She had asked him so nicely, after all. How could he deny her?

"Spread your legs wider," he ordered as he moved her hand to his waist. "And hold on."

She followed his direction, putting her other

hand on the other side of his waist, holding him tightly as she bit her lip.

"Are you anxious?" he asked. He would stop, even if it was agony, if she was in any way unsure. "We can stop if you want."

She shook her head. "No, I want this. I want *you.*"

He growled, taking himself in hand as he nudged the tip of his cock to her entrance. She moaned, and he began to press in, bit by bit, holding his breath as he worked himself inside.

She was so tight, but she was so wet it eased the way in. And then he was fully seated, her hands holding his waist tightly, one of his hands gripping the back of the bench, the other hand at her hip, holding her.

"I'm going to move. Is that all right?" he asked.

She gave a vigorous nod.

And then he withdrew halfway, feeling the slick heat of her, his cock as hard as it had ever been, pushing back inside slowly, clenching his jaw to force himself not to push too hard.

She slid her hand around his back to clutch his arse, pressing him in tighter.

"How does it feel?" he asked, barely able to manage the words.

"Good," she said, looking down at where they were joined.

He followed her gaze, watching as the plump head of his cock moved in and out of her, the skirts of her gown draped around her waist, the only sound in the room the sound of the soft friction between their bodies.

He began to move faster and more forcefully, sliding his way back and forth, her channel gripping his length.

He put his fingers on her clitoris, rubbing gently as he thrust, rewarded by her moan as she began to shift under him.

He'd never brought a woman to climax while riding her—he would have thought it impossible, but now she was gasping, her fingers gripping his arse as if to dare him to try to stop.

"God, please, please," she said, opening her eyes to meet his gaze. She looked dazed, and he likely looked the same—he had never felt this much pleasure in his life, and he hadn't even climaxed yet.

He rode faster, thrusting in and out as he kept his rhythm on her nub, his breath growing shorter as the climax built, making his balls tighten and his entire body feel as though it were on fire.

She flung her head back and tightened even more around his cock, pulsing as she climaxed.

If he wasn't on the verge of climax himself, he would take a moment to be exceedingly proud of his efforts.

He withdrew just as he came, spilling onto the bench, giving a hoarse cry that echoed around the gazebo.

Sated, he sagged against her, his whole body

completely relaxed, every nerve ending awash in a wave of pleasure.

They remained there for a minute or two. Nash didn't think he would ever want to move again.

She patted him on the arse. "Uh—I'm getting a cramp. Do you mind—?"

He shifted quickly off her, standing up and putting himself back in his trousers.

She looked up at him, a wryly satisfied look on her face. "Well. You've certainly taught me a lesson."

He barked in surprised laughter. Of all the things to say directly afterward, he had not expected that.

"There's so much more I want to teach you," he said, leaning forward to kiss her softly on the lips.

Because if there were more lessons, then there would be more time for them to spend together.

Perhaps enough time for him to figure out the words he needed to say to persuade her to be with him always.

Because—because goddamn it, he loved her. Even though it terrified him. Even though all those good reasons not to get too attached to her were still good reasons.

But he had no idea how to say it.

He'd have to show her.

Chapter Eighteen

Ana Maria wriggled in her seat, trying to get sensation back into her legs.

Wondering if her legs would buckle under her if she tried to stand up.

That was incredible. She wanted to do it all immediately again, only she wasn't certain she could remain upright.

"Let me take care of that," Nash said, gesturing to the bench. He picked his cravat up from the floor, then began to wipe up, stroking her thighs to clean them of his spill.

She knew what he had done, of course, and why he had done it; she hadn't even thought to ask about preventing childbirth, idiot that she was, and she was grateful he had. Because there was no way she wanted to bear his child, not in their current circumstances.

"Thank you," she said quietly, glancing up at him.

He arched an eyebrow. "For—?"

She felt her cheeks heat and was grateful for

the relative dark. "For all of it. For this, and for making sure we don't—"

"Of course," he said. Did he sound disappointed?

But he was the one who was insisting there be nothing permanent between them.

Even though they'd just done all of this.

It was all very confusing. She was very confused.

She wanted him, more than ever, but she also knew that to take him now would be a compromise, and she was done with compromises.

"What are you thinking about? Don't think it was a mistake," he said, his tone urgent.

"No, no, of course not," she replied, reaching for him.

But he was out of reach, since he was standing, and she was still on the bench, the skirts of her gown hiked up nearly around her ears, entirely exposed to him.

The distance felt as though it meant something, even though he had only moved away because she had asked him to.

Wasn't she supposed to feel exhilarated after such an experience?

She still felt the remnants of the pleasure he'd brought her, but she also felt mournful, as though this was the start of their inevitable end.

"If you don't think it was a mistake, is there something you want to tell me?"

She snorted in response. "Oh, that's rich, coming from you. The one who never says how he feels."

Instead of returning to his usual nonverbal arrogant stance—standing proudly inarticulate, arms folded over his chest—he stood in a very un-Nash-like stance, his hands hanging at his sides, his expression concerned, his gaze on hers.

"I don't choose not to speak."

His words were halting.

"I—I don't always know how."

She ached for him, for his closing himself off so thoroughly. This felt even more momentous than the time only a few minutes before, when she'd engaged in the most passionate experience of her life. Was he about to finally open up to her? Tell her everything that was in his heart?

"Tell me," she said, patting the bench beside her.

He nodded, then came to sit on the bench, his hands loosely clasped between his knees.

She adjusted her skirts so they fell back toward the gown and shifted a bit to the side so she could see him.

"It's hard to explain. Obviously," he added ruefully.

"What would you say if you could say it?"

He gazed forward, clearly lost in thought. A few long moments of silence passed between them.

She was conscious of the noises from the party wafting toward them—people chattering, music playing, the occasional clink of glassware.

People living their lives a short distance away, completely unaware of what had happened here.

Thank goodness, of course. Because if they

knew, there would be no choice but for them to marry. Or risk her disgrace forever.

Would she remain true enough to her own values to choose the latter?

"I tried to talk at first."

She waited.

"But there were no words for how I felt."

More silence.

"How you felt about what?" she prompted.

"My mother. The duke." She noticed he didn't say his father. "I was about ten years old when she left, and she didn't say why. She didn't even say goodbye. She couldn't, I know that now, but I didn't know that back then."

Her chest felt tight with the ache for him. To be that young, to have your mother leave you—of course her mother had died when she had been just months old, but she wasn't aware of any of that at the time.

"I knew not to ask him"—*him* clearly meaning his father—"but I asked anybody else. They all just gave me this frightened look, a look I'd seen on her face." He shrugged. "Then it just became easier to demonstrate how I felt by showing people, not telling them."

Had he just shown her how he felt about her?

But no. She had asked him for this; he was merely acceding to her wishes.

"And after a while it felt odd to say anything at all. I was a duke's heir, I could do whatever I wanted. As long as my father didn't notice."

"What—what happened if he noticed?" she asked, dreading the answer.

"You have to know. You must have seen the bruises."

Her throat got thick. Of course she'd seen the bruises, but back then she hadn't realized what they meant.

"He was a monster."

He took a deep breath. "He was—and so am—"

"Perhaps they are in that building there," a voice said loudly. Octavia. "If only we could find the duke and Lady Ana Maria, I am certain they just came out here to take the air."

Octavia warning them.

Ana Maria scrambled to stand, shaking her skirts out and trying to smooth her hair, even though she had no idea if it had gotten disheveled in the course of their—activities.

"We're here," Nash called, sounding casual even while he was frantically tossing his shirt back over his head, tucking it into his trousers. He eyed the cravat lying on the bench, met her gaze, and shook his head.

She grabbed it as she turned to face the door, clasping it behind her back.

The door swung open, and Octavia entered, her expression one of warning even though her words sounded entirely relaxed.

"Of course they are here, I told you that Lady Ana Maria felt a bit faint, and since the duke here is practically a relation, it only makes sense that he would escort her for some air."

"Ana Maria!" Sebastian's tone was unusually stern.

Not only was Sebastian there, but Thaddeus stood beside him, both of them radiating disapproval.

"You two," she said, glancing from one to the other.

"Octavia, you should return to the party," Sebastian said.

Octavia glanced toward Ana Maria, who nodded.

"Fine," she said. She advanced toward Sebastian, poking her finger in his chest. "But don't you dare hurt my friend."

"She's my sister!" Sebastian retorted.

"Humph," Octavia replied. She gave Ana Maria a quick kiss on the cheek, then scampered back toward the ballroom.

"If you want to avoid a scandal," Thaddeus said in a grim tone, "you will come with us, Ana Maria." At least *he* sounded the way he usually did, since he always seemed to be issuing commands, even when asking someone something as innocuous as to pass the sugar. "Or you can tell us that you want to get married, given what you two have obviously been up to."

Did she want to avoid a scandal? Did she want to marry him?

She'd just had the most incredible experience of her life—not just *that*, but also his confiding in her. Sharing some of the secrets that seemed as though they might throttle his soul.

If he could just speak to his emotions. Just say he wanted her completely, not as an interlude or a training lesson.

Just speak, Ignatius.

"You two," she began, glancing between Sebastian and Thaddeus, "have spent a lot of time trying to decide what is best for me. And telling me what to do."

Sebastian's mouth opened as though to object, but she shook her head. "No. Not now. It is my turn."

She straightened her shoulders and looked straight at Nash, whose face was unreadable.

Though his fists were not—they hung by his side, and she could see how tightly he was gripping them. So tightly that there were white marks around his knuckles.

Obviously he was agitated, but she had no clue what about—possibly being forced into a marriage he'd said repeatedly he did not want? Being chastised by his best friends? Regretting opening up to her as much as he had?

She wished she could read him better.

Or perhaps not, since maybe he didn't want her, after all.

"Nash is my friend." She saw a muscle tic in his jaw. "He should not be forced to save my reputation because somebody decides to gossip about us." She flung her hands up in frustration. "Until six months ago, I didn't have a reputation to worry about! Except for if I smudged the silver."

She shook her head in frustration. "What is important to me is that the person I marry—whomever that person is—is able to say why he wishes to marry me. Not that he should, or that others think he should. Or that it just seems to make sense." She planted her hands on her hips and spoke directly to Nash. "I want to know why."

I want you to tell me you want me in your world.

She kept her gaze locked on his face. She still couldn't read it.

"Well?" Sebastian said, turning to Nash.

Who kept his mouth closed. And his fists clenched.

"Sebastian and Thaddeus are right," he said at last, the words sounding as though they were being extracted from him by force. "I'm not worthy of you. But if you think I am, and we want to—" He stopped speaking, shaking his head as though the words were gone.

That was an even worse proposal than the one Lord Brunley had given her. At least Lord Brunley had pretended he wanted to get married. Nash's words made it sound as though he were being pressured, and the one thing she absolutely did not want was someone to take her reluctantly.

She'd had that already when Sebastian's mother had been forced to accommodate her in the household. She refused to be resented every day simply because of who she was, and what she had done. What *they* had done together.

The one thing she knew for certain was that she would not compromise—she would own her contradictions. She could want to be with him even though she would never agree to it, not with the kind of weak offer he was making now.

"You are right in one thing," she said. "You don't deserve me."

Even though she loved him. And that he likely loved her, but there was something so wrong, so damaged, that was blocking him from telling her.

This was the worst possible time to realize it. Not that she hadn't suspected for some time—her acute fascination with him, her intense desire to kiss him, her need to make certain he was at least relatively happy might have been clues.

"Tell me why I'm wrong." She kept her gaze locked on his face, feeling her heart hurt at his shuttered expression. *Tell me.*

What was worth keeping so hidden? Was it worth making himself miserable for the rest of his life? Making them miserable?

Because it wasn't arrogance to know that he would be miserable without her. Everything he'd shown her—even if he had yet to tell her—told her that.

And still he stayed silent.

She was good enough to fight and fuck, but not good enough to love.

"Tell her!" Sebastian demanded, poking Nash in the arm.

Nash looked grim.

"If you can't tell her whatever it is she needs to know," Thaddeus said, "perhaps you can tell her you will leave her be so she can find her own happiness. She deserves better."

Nash growled in response.

"You want to hit me, don't you?" Thaddeus said, glancing to Nash's fists. Which unclenched as Ana Maria watched. "You won't talk, so you hit."

"I'm not going to hit you," Nash replied, each word emerging as though it was being dragged from his lips. "I choose not to." He glanced over at Ana Maria, just for a moment, and then he stalked past them, all of them, through the gardens and out of sight.

Ana Maria watched his retreating form as she felt her heart crumble into pieces.

HE DIDN'T DESERVE her.

That was the only thought that kept screaming through his head. He felt raw and bruised, aching from wanting to tell her how he felt, thwarted in his attempts because of his own failure.

He raised his fist to punch the wall of the carriage, but froze before impact. It wouldn't do any good. He knew that now.

Ironic that the most incredible time of his life—being with her in that building, watching as she broke apart—was followed by the worst time in his life.

Although perhaps he was wrong. Perhaps there would be even worse times still. Times when he had to watch as she married someone else, someone who gave her flowers and warmth and words.

While he existed.

He didn't want to just exist anymore.

Rich, coming from him, the person who'd decided years ago to only think of things in shades of gray. Never allowing himself to enjoy, or even feel, the colorful world she inhabited for fear he would lose control.

But now he did want to live in her world. Even though it terrified him. Even though the thought of saying any of it out loud struck him silent as the agony of his love tore through him.

What if those colors overwhelmed his emotions so much he lashed out?

What if he wasn't able to tolerate such extremes, and lost himself in a world of color and furiously intense behavior, a place where reason wasn't welcome?

But he'd be with her. She would keep him on a measured course. She knew how to navigate this world that terrified him.

Did he just want her because he didn't trust himself?

No. He loved her. He thought he might have

always loved her, back from when he'd first clung to Sebastian's friendship right after his mother had left.

He'd not known it himself, of course. His love had been shielded for what it was by his natural protective instincts.

But it was love. And it was more frightening to face than being in the ring with a massive boxer whose arms were the size and strength of railroad pistons.

"IGNATIUS?"

His mother peered into the library, her expression one of concern.

He waved her in, and she entered, shutting the door behind her. She took a seat beside him on the sofa, picking his hand up and holding it in hers.

"What is wrong?" she asked in a soft voice.

And he told her.

Speaking as he never had before.

At the end of his recitation, she leaped up from the sofa, her eyes wet from crying. "You cannot think you are anything like him." She spoke fiercely. "He was cruel, and you are nothing like him." Her hand shot out in an accusing gesture. "Is it the actions of a monster to find and protect the people whose births were no fault of their own?"

Nash began to speak, but couldn't say anything before she continued. As usual.

"I wanted to come earlier, I told you that." She

was pacing in her agitation now, proof indeed that she was his mother. "But I didn't until I knew for certain who you were. You found me, but of course I knew where you were. I'd gotten news of his death, and I nearly came then, but I—" She shook her head as she bit her lip. "I wasn't sure who you were. If you were like him. But I made inquiries, and everything I heard—everything anyone has said about you—is that you are a generous person who wants to right all the wrongs in the world." She gave a soft chuckle. "Not that you could have accomplished that, of course, but you have done what you could. I made certain to ask the people who were most affected by you, your father's children, what they thought."

"You spoke to them?" Nash said, surprised.

"No, but I hired people who got them to share their experiences of you. I didn't want to return to your life until I knew for certain that you would be worthy of it. And you are, Ignatius, you are." She sat back down, taking his face in her hands. "Your father was a monster. You want to right wrongs, and sometimes you use your fists. But that does not mean you are him." She shook her head. "You were so young when I left, it is no wonder you have the wrong idea about who you are. But you have to believe that you are the best possible person you can be."

A pause as she took a deep breath. "You cannot allow the boy you were at ten to define your life now."

He gazed at her, feeling her words settle into his brain. Was she right? Was he the best possible person he could be? Was that the person he was choosing to become?

They both turned at the sound of the door opening, and then the dowager duchess made her way inside, using her cane for support.

Nash got up to draw his chair closer to her, and she sat, resting both her hands on top of the cane.

"I heard you arrived, Helen," the dowager duchess said, looking at his mother. "I was hoping you would come."

"It is good to see you, Your Grace," his mother replied. She glanced at Nash, who had positioned himself near the fireplace, leaning on the mantel. "Ignatius has been speaking to me about his father."

The dowager duchess's expression tightened. "I regret everything I didn't do to help you."

Nash's mother leaned forward to pat the dowager duchess's knee. "I know that. You helped me as much as you could."

The dowager duchess nodded.

"And now it appears that Ignatius has fallen in love."

The dowager duchess's eyebrows rose in surprise. "Lady Felicity?"

"No," Nash said. "Definitely not Lady Felicity."

"Oh good," the dowager duchess replied. "When any idiot can see it is that Lady Ana Maria you are in love with."

Nash snorted. "I gather I am the idiot?"

The dowager duchess waved vaguely. "If the description fits," she began, sounding her most supercilious. "But I was hoping for this, even though you insisted she was not being considered. Likely you had some idiotic reason—"

"Such as worrying I would end up like my father?" Nash interrupted.

The dowager duchess gave a vigorous shake of her head. "I have been here only for a short time, but I know that you are nothing like him."

"That is what I have been telling him," his mother exclaimed.

"If you were, you would have tossed me out on my ear when I demanded you marry. But you knew it was for the greater good, even though I could see how much it chafed at you. And there's the little matter of you taking in all of my son's . . . mistakes."

Did everybody know?

"This lady, this Ana Maria," Nash's mother said, looking intently at him. "Do you think you can convince her that you are worthy?"

He glanced between his mother and grandmother, both of whose eyes glimmered with compassion, and spoke honestly. "I don't know. But I have to try."

THE CARRIAGE RIDE home—or more accurately, to Thaddeus's house—was a silent one.

Because it wasn't home, even though it was the only home she'd ever known.

She had never felt as though she belonged, and right now, she felt that not belonging even more acutely. It was as though she were suspended on a wire between a dirty kitchen grate and an elegant ballroom, and she didn't want to be in either one.

She wanted to be where she belonged.

"Ana Maria?" Thaddeus spoke tentatively, not at all in his usual way. "Is there—do you want to talk?" He gestured toward his study as he spoke.

"Yes."

She led the way to his study, the images of the day—now long into evening—flooding her memory.

His care in her pleasure. His attention on her as he taught her the things she'd asked for. How he'd looked when they'd been discovered.

His clenched fists. But he hadn't used them. He'd chosen not to.

"Look," Thaddeus began, sitting at his desk, "you have every reason to be angry with me. With us."

Ana Maria nodded. "I do."

Thaddeus blinked in surprise. "Yes. Well. The thing is, we only want what is best for you."

She tilted her head. "How is Nash not best for me?" She spread her hands out in question. "Isn't he your friend?"

Sebastian strode into the room, glancing between the two of them as he heard her question. His expression tightened.

Ana Maria turned to face him. "I was just asking Thaddeus why he believes Nash isn't the best for me. Perhaps you have something to share on the topic?"

It felt exhilarating to challenge them, even though it also felt enervating.

Lady Oxymoron.

"But you don't want him, you just said so!" Sebastian exclaimed, flinging his hands up in the air.

"I am entirely contrary," she replied. "But on second thought, never mind. Don't answer the question. It doesn't matter anymore."

Sebastian took a deep breath, then stepped forward to wrap her in his arms. She allowed it, curling her face into his chest, feeling herself beginning to sob.

"We love you so much," he said. She felt another hand on her back, and knew that Thaddeus had joined the circle.

"Yes, we do," he said, sounding stiff. "We likely wouldn't think anybody would be good enough for you. Even our closest friend."

She sobbed harder, and Sebastian held her tightly as Thaddeus patted her back.

"Do you love him?" Sebastian asked after a few minutes.

She nodded, lifting her head to speak. "It doesn't matter, though. It doesn't."

"We could hit him," Sebastian suggested in a hopeful tone. She chuckled slightly in response.

"That wouldn't solve anything." Nash himself could attest to that.

"But it would make us feel better," Sebastian said.

She took a deep breath, stepping out of his arms, turning to face both of them. "Thank you both." She wiped her eyes and straightened her shoulders. "I am not going to rely on you two to solve my problems," she said. "I am going to solve them myself."

"IF YOU WILL pardon me, sir, I have work to do."

Nash put his hand on the merchant's arm. "I just want to tell you what I like about your range of fish."

The merchant rolled his eyes. "I have to work, sir."

Nash dug into his pocket, withdrawing some coins, handing half of them to the merchant, whose face lit up. "If you'll just give me a bit more time," he said.

"Of course," the man replied, his tone changing at the sight of the coins.

"Tell me, are sprats always this small?" He reached into the pile of fish and withdrew one, holding it up to his nose. It had a fishy smell, naturally. "Of course they are, I can see that." He reached over to another pile. "Whelks are odd little creatures, aren't they? I wonder who was the first individual to think to eat them. That person had quite a lot of imagination, wouldn't you think?" He raised the shell to eye level, rotating it to view from all sides. It was beautiful, truly, when you truly looked at it. That he could see the beauty was something new—he'd kept himself shrouded from emotions for so long that recognizing beauty was a terrifying and incredible experience.

Was this how she walked through life every day? Looking at things and noting their size, or their fishy smell, or their beauty?

"Thank you for letting me discuss your fish," Nash said, putting the whelk back onto the pile.

The merchant gestured to his wares. "Don't you want any of it? You paid me plenty."

Nash waved his hand. "No, thank you, I paid for the privilege of speaking with you today."

He nodded, then made his way determinedly down the street, walking toward the flower sellers.

It had taken three days for him to venture out of his house after that evening. Not because he didn't want to see her, because of course he did, but he needed to ensure he was prepared for what he was going to do. And he also had to make everything right in his own house before going to hers.

First he'd spoken to all of his staff members, both individually and as a group. He'd never told them about his experiences with his father, nor had he bothered to ask them about the same thing.

But he'd spoken with his mother, sifted through his memories, and discovered he and his half siblings had a lot more in common than just a parent. The people he'd gathered in his house weren't just people he owed because of someone else's callous cruelty; they were family.

He'd never truly had family beyond Sebastian and Thaddeus.

It felt terrifying and amazing.

He and his mother were forging a relationship as well. He was grateful to find that her husband worshipped the ground she walked on, and she was actually happy.

His grandmother asked him every time she saw him what he was going to do about Lady Ana Maria.

He'd told her he needed to make sure he was good enough for her. That seemed to satisfy her until the next time she saw him.

And now he was walking the streets of London, practicing telling people what he thought. Speaking to them instead of passing them by or ignoring them.

There were three separate flower sellers side by side in the market. Each had an assortment of roses and—and a bunch of other types of flowers that he did not recognize.

"Tell me," he said, walking up to the first seller and picking up a posy, "what is this flower?"

The flower seller was an older lady, likely around his mother's age, with gray hair pulled into a tight bun at the back of her head, a white apron tied around her waist. She was very fair-skinned, with bright patches of red on her cheeks.

"That is a gloriosa, my lord," she said. The flower was striking, sharp purple tendrils emerging from a pale green base. The flower looked like it could double as a weapon, and Nash imagined Ana Maria would appreciate its dual use, given her own duality: Cinderella, both before and after. The scullery maid transformed into a lady, but not because of some fairy, but because of her. And still clearly conflicted about the transformation.

"And this one?" He picked up another flower, this one a meek yellow-and-orange flower that was not at all weapon-like.

"Marigold," she replied.

"Come and see what I have, my lord," the second seller said. Nash nodded, searching in his pockets for more coins. He dropped an equal amount into each of their hands.

"Do you have any tulips?"

All three sellers nodded, then each began to pluck flowers from their buckets. "It is a pleasure to find a gentleman who is interested in flowers," the first seller said. She selected a few flowers from each of her sections, handing him a small bouquet. Then the other two did the same, and the first seller took all the flowers from his grasp, fashioning them into an enormous bunch.

"That looks splendid, don't you agree?" the first seller said, turning to the other two, who nodded their assent. "Take this to your lady with our thanks," she added, handing him the bouquet.

Nash stared at it—roses, gloriosas, marigolds, and a few other blooms that must have been tulips, a glorious tumult of color in his hand. The sheer beauty of it resonated through his entire body, and he couldn't wait to see what she thought of it.

What she thought of him.

"HE STILL HASN'T come?" Jane asked, as if she didn't already know the answer.

Ana Maria didn't bother to reply.

The two women sat in Ana Maria's exuberant salon, Jane mending some of Ana Maria's garments, and Ana Maria choosing fabrics for her bedroom and the Marchfields' project.

She refused to be despondent about him—she could have had him, if she'd compromised. She would not compromise.

But she couldn't help feeling mournful about what they were both missing: the opportunity to be with someone who could understand what it was like to be them. People with family they'd chosen, people whose experiences marked them out for isolation. People who coped as they had to, whether it was to constantly stay sunny, or to shut themselves off from feeling.

She and Jane looked at each other as they heard a ferocious knocking on the door. So loud it penetrated the salon's thick walls.

Her heart leaped. It felt as though it could only be one person—after all, who else would try to punch a door?

"That's him," Jane said, nodding. She rose, gathering up her mending. "I'll take this upstairs, you can receive him here."

"How do you kn—?" Ana Maria said as there was a much quieter knock on the door.

"My lady?" Fletchfield began, opening the door, only to be shoved aside.

"I need to speak with you," Nash said, sounding determined.

"Pardon me, Your Grace." Jane walked quickly out of the room, yanking Fletchfield out of the way as she left.

And then there he was. Standing at the doorway, as tall and handsome as she'd remembered. Carrying a—bouquet of flowers?

The contrast between his usual dark clothing and the bright burst of flowers made her want to laugh, but perhaps she was just hysterical.

God, but she'd missed him. Even though it had only been a few days, which was ridiculous.

But she also loved him.

"I brought these for you." He thrust the bouquet toward her, and she noticed that half of it was made up of tulips. "I don't know which ones are the ones you like." He took a deep breath. "I went to the market to speak with people."

His words came out awkward and stilted, as usual, but what he was saying was so different it took her by surprise.

"You went to the market to speak with people?"

He nodded, then exhaled in exasperation. "Sorry. Yes, I did. I went to the market to speak with people." He sounded as though he was reciting a lesson.

This was so clearly difficult for him, and yet, she would not accept anything less.

"Look, could I come in?"

Of course. He was still standing at the doorway, vast amounts of servants and possibly Sebastian and Thaddeus likely lurking around out of sight but in earshot.

"Yes, please."

He stepped inside, shutting the door behind him. And then stood there, staring at her, a hungry desperate look in his eyes.

"Do you want to sit?"

He shook his head, then gave another one of those sighs. "No, thank you. I think I need to say what I need to say while standing."

"Do you mind if I sit?" She gestured toward the chair.

"No, please. Here," he said, reaching to hold the back of the chair as if to assist her, even though the chair was already in the ideal position for her to settle into.

She sat, folding her hands in her lap, regarding him with an expectant expression. "Well?"

She was not going to make this easy for him. Even though every iota of her being screamed at her to do just that—no. It was no longer her place to make anyone comfortable about anything, particularly not the man she loved whom she suspected loved her back.

If he couldn't say or do what was necessary . . .

But she wouldn't think about that.

He began to pace, his long legs only taking a few steps toward the edge of the room before having to turn around.

"I have so much to tell you." A pause. "First I think I need to tell you why I am such an ass."

She couldn't help but chuckle.

"I told you about my father. But not everything. I will tell all of it to you now." That was remarkable for him to say. She was so proud of him.

"He ignored me, for the most part. But there were times when he would notice my presence and insist I learn what it was to be a duke." His face set into a grim expression. "He forced me to treat people as he did." She didn't need to hear him say it to know what he meant, but he said it nonetheless. "He told me I had to use violence if I wanted to make my point. He took me to boxing matches, ones that were fought to the death, and made me watch all the way through. He told me I would always be like him."

She inhaled sharply, feeling all the terror a child would at seeing that violence.

"I didn't want to learn that lesson, but I did—the only way I could express myself was with my fists." He met her gaze, an anguished expression in his eyes. "I couldn't trust that I would be able to hold myself back."

He kept his gaze locked on hers. "I couldn't help but believe him, that I would be just like him. Inevitably. Eventually. That I would end up hurting you."

Her eyes widened. "That you'd hit me? You would never do that!"

He shook his head. "You don't know that, Ana Maria." He took more steps before speaking again. "That is, you *didn't* know that. Nor did I. But now I do." He turned to look at her, then went and knelt by her chair, putting his hand on the arm. "Once you showed me what it was like to feel, once you gave me the joy of your joy, I knew I couldn't keep myself shut down any longer. You told me I had a choice. It terrified me, but I knew I had to express everything I was feeling. To choose to be the man I wished to be."

She nodded slowly. "But why didn't you say anything after—?" After he'd shown her how it felt to be loved. After he'd loved her with his body, though not his words. After she had begged him to.

"I don't know." His words were desolate. "That is why I am an ass—I knew what I had to do, and I didn't do it. That's what I've been doing since that night, however; talking to everyone and anyone I can find, telling them how I feel and asking them how they feel."

He reached to take her hand.

"And now I have to tell you, the most important person in my life, how I feel."

Oh.

He took a deep breath. "Ana Maria, I want to spend my life trying to see things through your eyes. Every remarkable color, every flower, every gorgeous gown you put on your beautiful body. I want to live, not just survive. I want you to be by my side as I discover what it means to say how I feel. I want to tell you everything, including how much I love you."

She bit back tears as she regarded his handsome, earnest face.

"I want you to help me find the good parts of being who I am, of using who I am to do better for everyone. Joyfully. You and I, we're both of two worlds—me, who never wanted to be a duke, and you, who didn't have a choice about who you were, whether you were scrubbing kitchen grates or dancing in ballrooms. I want us to be together to create one world—one world in which two people love one another."

She saw him swallow. "And I want to know if you would—if you could possibly feel the same wa—?"

"I love you, too. Now shut up and kiss me," she replied, placing her fingers on the back of his head to draw his mouth closer to hers.

He laughed softly before complying.

NASH FELT AS though he was going to explode from all the emotion. Just seeing her had made his heart actually hurt, and now he was kissing her, and that was all he ever wanted to do for the rest of his life.

Her lips were so soft, and he tried to kiss her tenderly, but then she opened her mouth, sliding her tongue into his mouth, her fingers gripping the back of his head tighter.

He deepened the kiss with a groan, putting his hands at her waist, twisting so he was kneeling directly in front of her. She spread her legs to accommodate his body, and he pressed against her, his torso against her mound, his chest against hers.

He felt her hands at his jacket, pushing it off his shoulders, and he quickly removed his arms from the sleeves, then tore at his cravat to take that off, too. All without breaking the kiss.

He would not take the time to point out how remarkably talented he was.

Because he was kissing her. And she was kissing him back. Fiercely.

She slid her hands over his shoulders, down his chest, tugging at his shirttails to pull the cloth out from where it was tucked into his trousers.

And then she drew back as she yanked the shirt up over his head, a satisfied expression on her face as she regarded his bare chest.

"Do you suppose we should lock the door?" he said in a ragged tone.

Her lips curled into a wicked smile. "I am tempted not to, but I don't want us to be interrupted."

He nearly grunted in response, then spoke. "I will see to it," he said.

She trailed her fingers over where his erection tented his trousers, and he stifled a groan as he rose, making quick work of the lock and returning to her.

She had risen from her chair, and she smiled at him, then turned and presented her back. "Undo me, please."

His fingers fumbled at the buttons, and she shot him a few impatient glances over her shoulder. Finally, however, he was able to slide her gown off, and she stepped out of it, clad only in her chemise and corset.

And then it was just her chemise.

And then he had his hands at the hem of her chemise and was drawing it up, over her luscious curves and then her head, flinging it past her shoulder to land on one of the tables that flanked the doorway.

He knelt back down, holding his hand up to assist her. She took it, sliding her naked body down to sit beside him.

"Thank God you appreciate the use of carpet," he said.

She laughed, which lit up her entire face. Then one eyebrow rose and she gestured toward him. "How is this at all fair? Get yourself unclothed, Ignatius."

He grinned, his hands going to the placket of his trousers. He undid them, then lay flat on the carpet, pulling the trousers down until they snagged at his boots.

Damn. He'd forgotten he was wearing them.

He sat up, undid them, then tossed them with an audible thunk to the edges of the room. That obstacle out of the way, he quickly removed his trousers and smallclothes, leaving them both naked.

In a locked room.

"Ana Maria," he said, feeling the emotion well up yet again, "I love you. You understand that, don't you?"

She nodded, her hand reaching toward his chest, her fingers gliding over his skin, her eyes lit up with curiosity and desire.

"Since we are in agreement, I want to know if I have your permission to entirely compromise you?"

Her eyes met his. "Please do."

An hour later, they emerged from the salon,

looking only slightly more disheveled than when they had entered it.

Only to stop in surprise as they faced Sebastian, Thaddeus, and Jane, with several interested faces peeking from around corners and abovestairs.

"Well?" Thaddeus said, folding his arms over his chest.

Ana Maria glanced at Nash. "He deserves me."

Nash took her hand, raising it to his lips to kiss. "I do."

Keep reading for
a sneak peek at

A Wicked Bargain for the Duke

The next book in
the Hazards of Dukes series
by Megan Frampton

Coming soon from Avon Books

Chapter One

Ducal Duties

(to be accomplished within a year of assuming the title)

1. *Learn the names of the upper staff.*
    a. *Learn the names of the lower staff within a year and a half.*
2. *Survey the properties and assess their efficiency.*
3. *Acquire a civilian wardrobe.*
    a. *No pastel colors.*
4. *Make connections in Society.*
    a. *Avoid any who seem to require a set strategy for dealing with them.*
5. *Secure the dukedom with the addition of a suitable wife and subsequent heir.*

Thaddeus Dutton, Duke of Hasford, leaned back in his chair and folded his arms over his chest, glaring with dissatisfaction at the list he'd written.

Not that it was the list's fault; it was his entirely. The list was proper, in correct order, and comprehensive. *Disciplined.*

Like him.

Boring, his cousin Ana Maria had once said in reaction to his respectable wardrobe—she would far prefer he wear fashionable pastels, for example—but he knew her opinion went beyond that at times. Particularly when he was managing her.

He felt his lips curl into a rueful smile and drew out another sheet of paper, plucking a pen from the surface of his built-entirely-for-efficiency desk. He'd ticked off all the proper items on the list; he had hopes that accomplishing #5 would invigorate both himself and his life. He put the pen to paper and began writing quickly.

A Suitable Woman will:

1. *Be unassuming in looks and manner.*
    a. *Be pleasant to look at.*
2. *Come from a respectable family. Her relatives must be as well-bred in blood and behavior as she.*
3. *Have a general knowledge of all topics but not be too obsessed by any one of them. Her first priority should always be her husband and, eventually, their children.*

4. *Be able to immediately handle her duties as his duchess.*
    a. *Running the household(s), appearing with him at Society events, and comporting herself with the utmost honor and respectability.*

He took a deep breath before quickly scribbling the last item on the list.

5. *Engage satisfactorily in sexual congress.*

That was a daring line item, and one he cared deeply about, although of course there was no way to verify the candidate's ability until after marriage.

The only surprising thing about him lately, he thought exasperatedly, was his becoming a duke in the first place, when it was discovered that his cousin Sebastian's mother had secured the dukedom for her son through illegal means. His cousin, the former duke, was now plain Mr. de Silva, while Thaddeus had left his command in Her Majesty's Army to take up command in Her Majesty's Aristocracy.

Being a duke was not dissimilar to being a military officer.

There was the general ordering about of things and people; the awareness that you were the most important person in the area, unless you happened to be keeping company with royals or generals; and there was the knowledge that if you made a misstep, you could cause the loss of lives or livelihoods for thousands of people.

It was the last bit that made him snap awake at night, nearly as much as he had when navigating a tricky battle strategy.

But with a wife he would have a second-in-command, someone who would assist him with the general ordering about of things and people.

Who would be his equal in the bedroom, giving as much pleasure as she got.

He felt himself stiffen, though not just in *that* way, and hastily balled the paper in his fist, stuffing it into his top desk drawer, which he locked immediately. He was sitting in the library, which he used as his office. Although there were comfortable chairs and plush carpet in the room, Thaddeus only ever sat in one of the two straight-backed wooden chairs behind a solid wooden desk.

Like him.

"Melmsford!"

Why he raised his voice to yell when he knew his secretary was likely hovering just outside the door was beyond him.

"Your Grace?"

Melmsford was, if possible, even more efficient than Thaddeus. A tall, slender man with prematurely thinning hair, Melmsford's chief attribute was his encyclopedic knowledge of anything to do with the Hasford holdings. He'd been Sebastian's secretary, whom Thaddeus had inherited along with the rest of Sebastian's staff.

It had been Melmsford who had helped Thaddeus navigate the first few perilous months of his taking the title, and Melmsford who even now guided him through the more delicate minutiae of his new role.

If he and Melmsford ever spoke even once about anything not pertaining to business, he might even say he was a friend. But they had not, so he could not.

He should add *Converse with Melmsford about something besides business* to his list.

"Yes, come here." Thaddeus gestured toward the front of his desk. "Sit down."

Melmsford folded his long frame into the chair as he regarded Thaddeus with the proper mixture of deference and awareness.

"It is time to approach item number five," Thaddeus announced. Melmsford looked confused; of course, he hadn't seen Thaddeus's latest list. "A wife." Melmsford's eyes widened, but he didn't speak. "I wish to attend events where there is the greatest opportunity to meet suitable candidates."

"Of course, Your Grace." Melmsford rose to gather a sheaf of papers from the small desk he used. "I have several invitations in hand." He sorted through them, a frown creasing his brows together. "Might I suggest the Baron Raddleston's party? It is being thrown in honor of Mr. Percy

Wittlesford, a novelist. He will be doing a reading, I believe."

"Novelist, hmm?" Thaddeus said with a snort. He gestured to the bookshelves behind him and on each of the walls in the library. Books that had yet to be touched by him. "There's no time for reading for pleasure, there's too much to be done."

"If I might, Your Grace," Melmsford interrupted gently, "Mr. Wittlesford's latest book is the current favorite of a certain group of young ladies, young ladies who would seem to fit your requirements." He cleared his throat. "I believe the books are of a certain type?"

Thaddeus frowned in confusion. "A certain—oh!" he exclaimed, realizing Melmsford's usual discretion was even more discreet. At least the reading would not be boring. Or disciplined, for that matter. "In that case, I will attend the Raddlestons' party."

"Excellent, Your Grace."

And if he was fortunate, he would meet a lady of excellent birth, a quiet demeanor, of a pleasing appearance, who was also sexually adventurous.

And while he was at it, he might try to find a black cat in a coal cellar, a needle in a haystack, and a duke who both did his job well and wasn't entirely dull.

"Vinnie, how can you possibly get away with it?" Jane's expression was horrified, her lovely eyes wide, her perfect mouth making a perfect O.

Lavinia nodded toward Percy, who sat in the corner of the drawing room, one lock of dark brown hair falling elegantly over his brow. He was the epitome of the tortured author—a pen in his hand, smudges of ink on his strong chin, papers scattered all over the table at which he sat.

It would be perfect if the papers he was working on was a novel of torrid prose and not the household's budget.

"He's the one who's going to have to get away with it." Lavinia shrugged. "I just write the books. I don't have to read them aloud."

Percy looked up, his remarkably handsome face marred by the frown creasing his brow. Although, Lavinia had to admit, that wasn't necessarily true, since Percy looked remarkably handsome no matter what. He got all of their father's looks, whereas Lavinia had inherited her mother's height (short), her figure (exceedingly curvaceous), and her ability to focus (her father had none, except when it came to his work).

"Are you trying to undermine my confidence, Jane?" Percy asked, getting to his feet.

The three siblings—or more correctly half siblings, since Percy was their father's child by his mistress—were in the drawing room before dinner, Lavinia choosing the passage of her work that Percy would read that evening, Percy reviewing the budget, and Jane observing, her expression anxious.

Jane's face fell at Percy's question, and Lavinia

immediately rushed to her sister, sitting down beside her on the sofa and wrapping her arms around her. She glared at Percy, who rolled his eyes in reply.

"I'm sorry, dear." Jane was the most sensitive of the siblings, even including five-year-old Christina, who would sulk for hours if she were denied anything, even something she did not actually want. The last enormous sulk had been because she was denied a serving of oatmeal, which she didn't even like. She'd received toast sprinkled with cinnamon sugar—one of her favorites—but since her siblings were having oatmeal, she took umbrage.

Jane, Lavinia, and Christina were their family's legitimate offspring; Percy and Caroline were the illegitimate offspring, with Percy their father's mistake, and Caroline their late aunt's child, born out of wedlock to Adelia, their father's sister, and a minor European prince, Lavinia always forgot which one. Her father had taken both Percy and Caroline in when they were mere children.

The entire family, along with their parents and a few of their parents' older distant relatives, lived in an enormous mansion in Mayfair, any potential for being shunned by virtue of their family's various scandals offset by their father's incredible wealth, and connections—his financial acumen meant he was a financial adviser to Queen Victoria, who overlooked their family scandal. Their father frequently forgot his various children's names, but he could recall to a penny what the queen had spent on bric-a-brac in a particular month. And that was usually quite a large sum.

Their mother more than made up for her husband's lassitude with her ambition for her family's status.

"I wanted to be here to support you," Jane replied, her words muffled. She raised her head and looked at Lavinia, then over her head at Percy. "Both of you. And I wanted to be sure I wouldn't reveal the secret, and I thought I would be less likely to if I wasn't surprised this evening." She returned her gaze to Lavinia. "You're not going to choose anything too scandalous, are you?" she added in a hesitant tone.

Sometimes Lavinia wondered if Jane had been switched with another child at birth. Unlike her siblings, half siblings, and cousins, she was quiet, well-mannered, and very gentle. If it weren't for the strong resemblance to their parents, Lavinia would be concerned there was a reckless girl—her true sister—somewhere out there horrifying a staid family.

"Of course not," Lavinia assured her. The passage she'd chosen was the characters' first meeting in a rose garden, entirely exemplary behavior, although there were mentions of thorns and poking and blooming, mentions that certain listeners would comprehend entirely, while others—like Jane—would entirely miss.

Lavinia had borrowed a variant of her half

brother's name to publish under because lady novelists did not sell as well as male novelists. Percy Waters had become Percy Wittlesford, and she had happily collected the royalty checks from her publisher.

But then her latest book, *Storming the Castle*, had taken the fancy of many Society ladies, and there was great interest, her publisher said, in the author. Lavinia and Percy had discussed how to proceed, and the two had settled it between them that Percy would pretend to be the author.

Once the interested ladies discovered Percy Wittlesford was actually Percy Waters, the handsome illegitimate son of one of London's sharpest minds—well, it wasn't long before Percy was being asked to give public readings.

Even though he would much rather be home working on numbers. He took after their father in that way, but his illegitimacy meant he could only work behind the scenes. That might change, now that Society believed him to be a successful author. Even the queen's propriety could bend if there was fame involved, which was why Lavinia had encouraged him to make public appearances and why he had agreed to do so. The only other person who knew that Lavinia had actually written all of Percy's four published works was Jane.

Baron Raddleston, at whose party Percy would be reading, was one of Society's most influential tastemakers. He and his wife prided themselves on launching the careers of a variety of artists, from Italian opera singers to Russian harpists to homegrown British authors such as Percy.

Lavinia would do anything for her siblings, even including oatmeal-sulking Christina. If her talent for writing meant that Percy could finally do what he truly wished to, she'd happily pretend forever, just making certain Percy was familiar with most of the plots of the books. It was a relief, honestly, not to have to write the books and be the public face of the author.

Plus there was Jane to be considered—all quiet Jane wished for was to marry the equally quiet Mr. Henry McTavish. He and his family were their neighbors, though the two families were complete opposites. The McTavishes, it had been explained many times, were entirely correct and would never allow their only son to marry any type of scandal, even though the "scandalous behavior" was from an earl's family, and adviser to the queen, no less. But there had been an incident many years past, and it didn't seem to matter to the McTavishes that the Capels were well-thought-of by many.

Recently, however, the McTavishes seemed to be weakening in their resolve against Henry and Jane since the two were so devoted to one another.

Which would be wonderful, except Jane and Lavinia's parents—or more specifically, their mother—had insisted Jane and her beauty be introduced to Society in hopes of landing a husband who was in the upper echelons of Society, not a mere neighbor's son who was respectable. Lavinia knew Jane would suffer anxiety at meeting that many people on her own, and she might end up accidentally engaged to the wrong person if Lavinia weren't there.

It was Jane and Lavinia's plan for Jane to be so quiet in Society that nobody would notice her. It wasn't working—Jane's dowry overcame her quietness—but thus far her only suitors were desperate men, and their mother would not accept a desperate man.

So, if the Season ended and Jane had not found a suitably important man to marry, their mother might be persuaded to change her mind and let Jane marry Henry, after all.

If Lavinia had made a list of all her tasks for the next few months—which she had not, since Christina had used all their paper on drawing pictures of apparently distressed goats—the list would read thusly:

Lavinia's List of Responsibilities

1. *Keep Jane unmarried until Mama is persuaded to consider Mr. McTavish.*
    a. *Keep Jane unmarried until Mr. McTavish's parents are persuaded to consider Jane.*
2. *Try to keep the family out of any current scandalous behavior.*
3. *Secure Percy's reputation as an excellent novelist who is also sharp with numbers. Have*

him announce his retirement from writing to devote himself to his father's business.

4. *Convince Papa to allow Percy to join the business.*
5. *Figure out which minor European prince is Caroline's father.*

"Jane! Lavinia!"

Their mother stood at the doorway, glaring disapprovingly at them as she simultaneously gave Percy a warm smile.

It was a remarkable talent.

"Yes, Mother?" Lavinia replied.

"You should be dressing for the evening." Lady Scudamore glanced at the clock in the corner. "You only have three hours!" She advanced into the room as Lavinia resisted rolling her eyes too obviously.

"They don't need that much time to look lovely," Percy said, so obviously exerting his charm, Lavinia nearly snorted.

Percy was not, of course, Lady Scudamore's child, but she treated him better than she did her own children. Or at least better than she did her younger daughter. Lavinia thought it was due to Percy's appearance and that he was male.

It was entirely unfair.

"*You* don't need that much time, Percy dear, but I've heard the Duke of Hasford will be attending the Raddlestons' party this evening." Lady Scudamore pursed her lips as she regarded Jane, whose anxious expression had returned. "And there is only one reason he would be going out. He has been extraordinarily reclusive. He must be searching for a bride." She stepped forward to slide her finger down Jane's cheek. "And you are lovely enough to be a duchess."

Lavinia glanced between Jane and her mother, noting the panicked look in her sister's eyes as well as her mother's determined gaze.

Oh dear.

"What gown should I wear, Mother?" Lavinia asked.

Not that she wanted her mother's opinion, but she did want her mother to stop focusing so intently on Jane. Her sister was too delicate to handle the pressure, and there wouldn't be much that Percy could do in this particular situation—the reason their mother wanted her daughters to marry well was because elevating their status would ameliorate the scandal of having Percy and Caroline living with them in the first place. There was only so much a large amount of money and the queen's favor could do, after all.

"You should choose whatever you want," her mother replied, clearly dismissing the topic as unworthy of her attention. "Jane, you should wear the white satin and I will lend you my diamond earrings." She gave a happy sigh. "A duchess! It would be all I've ever dreamt of!"

Lavinia took Jane's hand, tugging her toward the door. Jane stumbled as though frozen in place.

"The white satin then," Lavinia echoed. "We'll just go start, shall we?"

"THE DUKE OF Hasford," the butler announced.

Thaddeus paused at the entrance to the ballroom, glancing around at all the people who were currently staring at him.

If there was one thing he hated most about being a duke, it was that everyone gawked whenever he appeared in public. That would likely ease if he appeared in public more often, but that would mean appearing in public more often, and he had little tolerance for frivolity.

A small voice in his head said perhaps he would be less rigid if he had more tolerance for frivolity, but he quashed that quickly. He couldn't manufacture a tolerance he didn't have.

Another impetus for getting married—he could settle at home with his wife, tending to his business affairs and working on begetting an heir.

Literally mixing business with pleasure.

He stepped into the room, schooling his features to look blandly polite as opposed to annoyed. He was here for a *purpose*, he reminded himself. He didn't want to scare off any potential duchesses with his stern face, which his soldiers had assured him was terrifying.

"Good evening, Your Grace." A woman fluttered up to him, the feathers in her hair nodding gently as she moved her head. "I am Baroness Raddleston, and this is my husband, the baron." A gentleman appeared at her shoulder, both of them wearing exceedingly pleased expressions. Likely because they landed a duke at their party, not because they were particularly delighted to see *him*.

Although to be fair this was the first time they had met, so why would it be otherwise?

Perhaps the baron would prove to be a marvelous friend, and the two of them would discover they had common interests such as—well, damn. He didn't have any interests. Or hadn't allowed himself to have any because there was too much work to do.

He made a mental note to add "develop interests" to his list. And "frivolity."

The Raddlestons' ballroom was elegantly decorated. Chandeliers hung from the ceiling every six feet or so, and the lit candles cast golden shadows throughout the room, lending it a certain mystery. The servants, garbed in unobtrusive attire and holding silver platters, wound their way through the guests, dispersing what appeared to be tiny bites of food and the occasional glass of champagne.

There was a string quartet playing quietly in the background, obviously just something to pass the time until the evening's main event—the reading of the lurid material.

"Mr. Wittlesford will be reading in about an hour," the baron said, as though privy to Thaddeus's inner thoughts. He hoped not, actually, since in addition to wondering when the reading would be, Thaddeus was also wondering how early he could leave and still be polite to his hosts.

"Meanwhile," the baron continued, "we have refreshments and beverages and plenty of other guests. I don't suppose you have met—"

"Baron!" a lady said loudly. She was about ten feet away, with a few people in between them, but her voice was piercing enough to make Thaddeus wince. Or more specifically, to make him wish he could wince, but he couldn't, because it would be rude to do so.

"Lady Scudamore," the baron replied, turning to the lady, who was pushing her way through the crowd, dragging two ladies behind her.

Lady Scudamore was a middle-aged woman with a strong jaw and a commanding figure, even though she was short.

The ladies she had trailing after her, Thaddeus could now see, were younger, both likely in their twenties. The more beautiful of the two wore a bright gown of white satin, her golden hair glinting in the candlelight. The lady had a serene expression, her pale blue eyes looking not at Thaddeus but somewhere over his shoulder.

The other woman was short, with darker hair than the first, strands of it falling onto her face. Rather than staring fixedly in one spot, as the first woman was, her eyes were darting around the room as though she were cataloguing everyone within.

And then her gaze shifted to him, and he saw

her look at him openly and brazenly, raking her eyes up and down his body until she settled on his face. There was something so active and engaged in how she looked it was appealing, even though the judgmental part of him thought she was forward.

He didn't intend to, but he couldn't help but notice how enticing her figure was; more lush than the other woman, who was slender and perfectly formed. This woman's bosom was impossible not to notice, the curved white mounds nearly spilling out of her pale blue gown.

He felt an immediate visceral response to her, something so nearly crude he was startled at his reaction. This lady wasn't someone one would make polite conversation with; she was someone a person would hunger after, making it impossible to speak at all.

This woman was someone he would have to steadfastly avoid.

He liked things and people he could place in their appropriate boxes: soldier, servant, wife. His friends mocked his adherence to efficiency and routine, but it was what made him good at being first a captain and then a duke. Someone who didn't fit, who made him question his own reactions, was too dangerous to his state of mind.

"Good evening, Baron. Baroness." The older woman spoke, taking hold of the first lady's arm and keeping her gaze fixed on Thaddeus.

"Lady Scudamore, a pleasure." The baron gestured toward Thaddeus. "Your Grace, may I present Lady Scudamore? And her daughters, Lady Jane and Lady Lavinia?"

All three ladies curtseyed, and when they rose, the first lady—Jane, it seemed—still had that serene expression, but Lady Lavinia's lips had curled into a mischievous smile, revealing a deep dimple in her cheek. Her presence felt like a tangible thing. Probably his immediate and visceral reaction was a blend of desire and envy—he wished he could be as vibrant as she seemed to be. To engage everyone around her with enthusiasm and electricity.

Another item to add to his list, perhaps?

"Good evening, ladies," Thaddeus said, bowing. "A pleasure to meet you."

The younger ladies murmured something indistinct in reply, but their voices were drowned out by their mother. "Are you here for the reading? It is our own Percy who is the author." She leaned forward as though imparting a secret. "Naughty boy, we had no idea he was writing such books."

Lady Lavinia made a quickly smothered noise as Lady Jane's cheeks turned bright red.

"Percy Wittlesford is the author of *Storming the Castle*," the baron said. "Have you read it?"

Thaddeus shook his head. "No, I don't get the opportunity to read for pleasure." *And if I did, I wouldn't read books like those.*

"His books are quite—" And the baron paused.

"Delightful," Lady Lavinia supplied, that impish look still on her face. Lady Jane's cheeks turned even more red, if possible. "Impossible to put down," Lady Lavinia added. "One might say the books are ahead of their time."

"I look forward to the reading," Thaddeus said, knowing how stiff and awkward he sounded. And yet unable to do anything to stop it.

"Your Grace, my Jane mentioned she was very interested in your former career in the military."

Lady Jane glanced quickly at her mother, then smoothed her expression again. It was obvious she had never expressed any such interest.

Thaddeus felt himself admiring her ability to keep her emotions in control. An attribute to be greatly desired in a powerful titled lady.

"Yes, Your Grace," Lady Jane said. "I wonder what it is like in battle. If you could describe it."

Thaddeus took a deep breath, preparing to summon the stock answer he gave when anybody outside of the army asked him when Lady Lavinia spoke.

"I imagine it is something very difficult to describe," she said, a sympathetic look in her eyes.

He gave a brief nod.

"Do try," Lady Scudamore urged.

"Mother." Lady Lavinia's tone was nearly reproving. Of course. Someone who was so obviously observant would have seen his discomfort. It was unsettling to have someone see him so clearly, and so soon after meeting him.

Someone who was so determined to keep someone else from discomfort that she was willing to speak back to her mother.

Definitely someone to avoid. As well as someone to envy.

Had he ever spoken to his parents like that? He knew full well he had not—his father had also been a military man, and carried that demeanor to his child. His mother had been just as rigid, showing her maternal love in ensuring he was properly fed and clothed. He could remember just one time when she had hugged him, or allowed him to hug her, and that was when his father had died.

"Battle is, as Lady Lavinia says, difficult to describe." He kept his focus on Lady Jane. Far easier to look at, not just because she was so classically beautiful, but also because she lacked her sister's direct gaze. She was easy to put in a box: beautiful, eligible young lady. Not nearly as disconcerting as her sister. "It is filled with chaos, and loud noises, and confusion."

"Rather like a Society party," Lady Lavinia remarked dryly.

Everyone but Thaddeus chuckled.

"But you are out of that now, thank goodness," Lady Scudamore said. "And now you can leave the protection of our country to others."

"Yes." Thaddeus spoke shortly, and he caught Lady Lavinia's quick glance at him. He wanted to squirm under her sharp notice, but of course he did not squirm. And even if he had ever squirmed before, he was absolutely certain that dukes did not squirm.

"If you will excuse me, I wish to get something to drink," Lady Lavinia said. "Jane, are you thirsty?"

"Indeed," Lady Jane said.

"Perhaps the duke is thirsty as well." Lady Scudamore spoke in an arch voice that made it clear what she wanted to happen.

"Mother," Lady Lavinia warned again.

"I would be happy to escort the ladies to the refreshment table," Thaddeus found himself saying. Lady Scudamore beamed at him.

He could not resist shooting a glance toward *her*, only to find her eyebrows raised in disbelief, her expression revealing that she was already disappointed in him.

And they had just met.

If you give her this, you will find yourself accommodating her forever, her look seemed to say.

Perhaps I am fine with that, he wanted to reply. *I am looking for a bride.* And why not Lady Jane? A lady of beauty and good manners who was clearly able to control her emotions.

You are entirely predictable, her look shot back. *And therefore entirely disappointing.*

Next month, don't miss these exciting new love stories only from Avon Books

Ten Things I Hate About the Duke by Loretta Chase

Cassandra Pomfret holds strong opinions she isn't shy about voicing. But her extremely plain speaking has caused an uproar, and her exasperated father, hoping a husband will rein her in, has ruled that her beloved sister can't marry until Cassandra does. Now, thanks to a certain wild-living nobleman, the last shreds of Cassandra's reputation are about to disintegrate . . .

How to Catch a Queen by Alyssa Cole

When Shanti Mohapi weds the king of Njaza, her dream of becoming a queen finally comes true. Shanti and her husband may share an immediate and powerful attraction, but her subjects see her as an outsider. When turmoil erupts in their kingdom, Shanti goes on the run, and King Sanyu must learn whether he has what it takes both to lead his people and to catch his queen.

A Duchess a Day by Charis Michaels

Lady Helena Lark has spent years trying to escape her wedding to the vain and boring Duke of Lusk. When her family's patience runs out, they pack her off to London to walk down the aisle. Helena has another idea: find a more suitable bride to take her place. But when Helena finds herself babysat by a handsome bodyguard, her plans take a more drastic—and romantic—turn.

AVONIMPULSE